WORDSWORTH

Selected Poetry

Edited by NICHOLAS ROE

PENGUIN BOOKS

PENGUIN BOOKS

Published by the Penguin Group
Penguin Books Ltd, 27 Wrights Lane, London w8 5tz, England
Penguin Books USA Inc., 375 Hudson Street, New York, New York 10014, USA
Penguin Books Australia Ltd, Ringwood, Victoria, Australia
Penguin Books Canada Ltd, 10 Alcorn Avenue, Toronto, Ontario, Canada m4v 3b2
Penguin Books (NZ) Ltd, 182–190 Wairau Road, Auckland 10, New Zealand

Penguin Books Ltd, Registered Offices: Harmondsworth, Middlesex, England

This selection first published in Penguin Books 1992
5 7 9 10 8 6

Introduction and notes copyright © Nicholas Roe, 1992
The moral right of the editor has been asserted
All rights reserved

Filmset in 10.5/12 pt Monophoto Ehrhardt
Printed in England by Clays Ltd, St Ives plc

Contents

vii

Introduction

In a letter to the Whig statesman Charles James Fox, 14 January 1801, Wordsworth explained that his poems 'The Brothers' and 'Michael' had been 'written with a view to shew that men who do not wear fine cloaths can feel deeply'. These poems – and Wordsworth's *Lyrical Ballads* as a whole – affirm the strength of the human heart against the destructive effects of industrialization and the social dislocation forced by economic changes. As Wordsworth knew, poems could not of themselves reconstruct a more equable commonwealth in Britain. But in the resilience of kindly relationships between human beings – the 'strength of love' expressed in 'Michael' – Wordsworth (like his friend Coleridge) recognized a possible basis for social melioration. At the end of the twentieth century, when we face the alienating pressures of contemporary life and the global threat of environmental disaster, Wordsworth's vision has never been more relevant to our common needs. This new selection from Wordsworth includes poems from all stages of his career, from the experimental verse of the 1790s in which Wordsworth discovered his voice as a poet, to *The Prelude* as published after Wordsworth's death in 1850.

Some of Wordsworth's first readers detected a revolutionary 'Jacobin' design in *Lyrical Ballads*, and not without cause. Poems such as 'Goody Blake and Harry Gill', 'Simon Lee, the Old Huntsman,' 'The Last of the Flock', and 'The Old Cumberland Beggar' are sympathetic to unaccommodated humanity: the poor, the aged, the dispossessed, the disturbed. Yet these poems offer more than the circumstances of distress which might justify political protest. In 'The Last of the Flock', for example, the cycle of prosperity and decline recounted in the shepherd's tale is a prelude to understanding his humanity: his distracted state of mind and his heart-rending alienation from his family.

William Hazlitt, writing about 'Mr Wordsworth' in *The Spirit of the Age* (1825), remarked that Wordsworth characteristically takes 'a subject or a story merely as pegs or loops to hang thought and feeling on'. The poems, in Hazlitt's view, subordinate action to contemplation, thought and feeling; Wordsworth's preferred mood is the 'wise passiveness' advocated in 'Expostulation and Reply', the meditative introspection of 'Tintern Abbey', 'Ode. Intimations of Immortality', and *The Prelude*. His disinclination to treat action was, in part, a rejection of the melodramatic idiom of contemporary poetry, plays and novels. And this literary revolution in favour of a poetry that 'thinks into the human heart' (Keats's words) was in many respects continuous with the democratic spirit of an age of revolutions in America and France.

William Wordsworth was born on 7 April 1770 at Cockermouth, a prosperous town in the north of the Lake District, the son of John Wordsworth (law agent to Sir James Lowther, Earl of Lonsdale) and his wife Ann Cookson. William had an older brother Richard (1768–1816), and three younger siblings: Dorothy (1771–1855), John (1772–1805) and Christopher (1774–1846). Wordsworth's earliest memories in *The Prelude* recall the family home at Cockermouth, and its garden terrace that overlooked the River Derwent:

> Was it for this
> That one, the fairest of all rivers, loved
> To blend his murmurs with my nurse's song,
> And, from his alder shades and rocky falls,
> And from his fords and shallows, sent a voice
> That flowed along my dreams? For this, didst thou,
> O Derwent! travelling over the green plains
> Near my 'sweet Birthplace', didst thou, beauteous stream,
> Make ceaseless music through the night and day
> Which with its steady cadence, tempering
> Our human waywardness, composed my thoughts

To more than infant softness, giving me
Among the fretful dwellings of mankind
A knowledge, a dim earnest, of the calm
That Nature breathes among the hills and groves.
When, having left his mountains, to the towers
Of Cockermouth that beauteous river came,
Behind my father's house he passed, close by,
Along the margin of our terrace walk.
He was a playmate whom we dearly loved.
Oh, many a time have I, a five years' child,
A naked boy, in one delightful rill,
A little mill-race severed from his stream,
Made one long bathing of a summer's day;
Basked in the sun, and plunged and basked again
Alternate, all a summer's day, or coursed
Over the sandy fields, leaping through groves
Of yellow groundsel; or when crag and hill,
The woods, and distant Skiddaw's lofty height,
Were bronzed with a deep radiance, stood alone
Beneath the sky, as if I had been born
On Indian plains, and from my mother's hut
Had run abroad in wantonness, to sport
A naked savage, in the thunder shower.

The steady, fluvial cadences of Wordsworth's blank verse announce the theme of *The Prelude* in nature's fostering of the imagination and the spirit. The River Derwent's 'ceaseless music' *composes* the child's mind, and the poet will return to this alluvial scene of early life, recognizing it as the guardian source of his creative power.

It was a 'fair seed-time', as Wordsworth writes, but it did not last long. The Wordsworth children were orphaned when William was thirteen years old (their mother died in March 1778, their father in December 1783), and the young family was broken up. After her mother's death Dorothy was raised by cousins in Halifax. William (who did not see his sister for nine years) boarded at Hawkshead Grammar School; in October 1787 he went up to St John's College, Cambridge, where he made a promising start to his studies, and graduated from the university in January 1791.

Wordsworth's first poems date from his years at Hawkshead, where he was encouraged to write by his schoolmaster William Taylor (the first in a series of mentors that included the revolutionary soldier Michel Beaupuy, the philosopher William Godwin, Dorothy Wordsworth, and Samuel Taylor Coleridge). The earliest of his poems to attract public notice, *An Evening Walk* and *Descriptive Sketches*, were composed during his undergraduate years and published in January 1793. These poems demonstrated Wordsworth's competence in the fashionable genre of topographic verse, and his skill in handling the rhyming couplet. Elaborately literary, they also had a basis in Wordsworth's own experience: *An Evening Walk* recalled Lake District scenes, and *Descriptive Sketches* drew upon Wordsworth's walking tour to the Alps in summer 1790. This undergraduate adventure was also Wordsworth's first encounter with the French Revolution. It was recalled in his political sonnets of 1802, and in *The Prelude* Book Six: ''twas a time when Europe was rejoiced', Wordsworth wrote,

> France standing on the top of golden hours,
> And human nature seeming born again.

Wordsworth's memory here is true to the generosity of the early Revolution, although the verse modulates into a conditional mood which acknowledges subsequent disappointment. More positively, on the other hand, *The Prelude* recognizes the French Revolution as a schooling in human nature that was tributary to his imaginative power as a poet.

Wordsworth returned to France once again during 1792, a crucial year in the poet's personal and intellectual life. After visiting the sights 'of old and recent fame' at Paris, including the ruins of the Bastille, Wordsworth travelled south to the Loire valley where he stayed at Orléans and Blois. Here he met and quickly fell in love with Annette Vallon (1766–1841); by March 1792 Annette was pregnant, and their daughter Caroline (1792–1862) was born the following December.

Wordsworth's passionate relationship with Annette during this year was accompanied by his self-commitment to France as a revolutionary. It was Wordsworth's friendship with Michel Beaupuy – a soldier in the patriot army, a man of action – that encouraged his allegiance to the republican cause. Yet it was the sight of ordinary men and women transformed by zeal for humankind that convinced him the Revolution was a movement for universal good:

> Even files of strangers merely, seen but once,
> And for a moment, men from far with sound
> Of music, martial tunes, and banners spread,
> Entering the city, here and there a face,
> Or person singled out among the rest,
> Yet still a stranger and beloved as such;
> Even by these passing spectacles my heart
> Was oftentimes uplifted . . .

The militant, crusading spirit of the revolutionary armies was an inspiration for Wordsworth. Indeed, to such heartening sights and experiences we can trace the origins of Wordsworth's sense of his own missionary purpose – a poet who (in Coleridge's belief) was uniquely called to 'do great good' for humankind after the failure of the Revolution in France.

In retrospect, Wordsworth was able to vindicate the feeling of 'substantial dread' that he had felt on visiting Paris just after the massacres of September 1792: following his return to London from this trip, war broke out between Britain and France. 'I felt / The ravage of this most unnatural strife / In my own heart', he remembered. Emotionally and intellectually committed to the Revolution his own countrymen now sought to destroy, Wordsworth found himself estranged and isolated in his native land. This was a bitter reversal, although, looking back, Wordsworth believed it had precipitated the quest inwards that led to the discovery of his identity as a poet.

When the French Terror began in 1793, Wordsworth sought to disentangle his hopes for the Revolution from the violent course of events. The crucial figure at this period for

Wordsworth (and others of his generation) was William Godwin, whose *Political Justice* argued for the perfectibility of human beings through the exercise of reason. As the killing went on in the streets and squares of Paris, Godwin's 'revolution of mind' opened an alternative prospect of progress without recourse to action. Yet *Political Justice* was flawed, a partial account of human behaviour in that it denied the validity of emotional and instinctual life. Ironically, too, there was a disturbing affinity between the rationalism of *Political Justice* and the abstract principles on which Robespierre justified terrorism to safeguard the Revolution. The guillotine – that 'reasonable' killing machine – represented the final betrayal of humane idealism by revolutionary action.

Wordsworth's discontent with Godwin (which dated from mid-1795) initiated a period of self-examination, crisis and recovery that accompanied his reunion with Dorothy and his early friendship with Coleridge. At this time it is likely that Wordsworth had realized his separation from Annette and Caroline would be permanent, although he remained to the end of his life concerned for their well-being. Moving away from the political and intellectual circles he had frequented in London during 1795, Wordsworth now made his home with his sister at Racedown Lodge in the Dorsetshire countryside. That settlement – at once a recovery of his childhood family and a return to the living presences of nature – encouraged Wordsworth's growth as a poet who took the French Revolution as the 'model' for poetry uniquely appropriate to the modern world. His subjects, as Wordsworth announced in his Advertisement to the first edition of *Lyrical Ballads* (1798) were 'human passions, human characters, and human interests'.

The first poem in this selection is 'The Baker's Cart', a blank verse fragment composed during the poet's residence at Racedown Lodge. It describes a meeting with a woman and her 'five little ones', a scene of deprivation common in literature of protest in the 1790s. The poem is distinctively Wordsworth's, however, in that its democratic idiom – its matter-of-factness – attains an intensity of vision more usually associated with the 'spots of time' in *The Prelude*. In many of Wordsworth's later poems comparably mundane figures assume extraordinary significance: Margaret, for example, in 'The Ruined Cottage'; the Discharged Soldier and the Old Cumberland Beggar; Simon Lee, and the Leech Gatherer in 'Resolution and Independence',

> a Man from some far region sent;
> To give me human strength, and strong admonishment.

The Leech Gatherer's strange, monitory presence warns against despondency, and is a representative witness to the human strength that forms the subject of so much of Wordsworth's poetry.

Wordsworth's poems in *Lyrical Ballads* (1798) were written during the *annus mirabilis* that began in July 1797, when he moved with Dorothy to live at Alfoxden House, Somerset, near to Coleridge's residence in the village of Nether Stowey. Many of these poems treat 'incidents of common life', in so far as they reveal the essential terms of human relationship and behaviour; maternal and paternal love in 'The Idiot Boy' and 'Old Man Travelling'; gratitude in 'Simon Lee'; childish understanding in 'We are Seven' and 'Anecdote for Fathers'. A vital word in all of these poems is 'kindness', defining the mutual relationship of individuals as human beings. The 'hearts unkind' mentioned at the close of 'Simon Lee' are not merely ill-disposed to other persons, they are destructive to all humanity. And in 'Tintern Abbey', written in July 1798 at the close of Wordsworth's Alfoxden year, 'acts / Of kindness and of love' affirm much more than a considerate bearing towards another person. 'Kindness', here, embraces the universal cause formerly associated with the revolution in France. Written at the end of the revolutionary decade, 'Tintern Abbey' admits the realities of change, loss, disappointment – but the poem also asserts a 'cheerful faith' that nature and memory may yield 'life and food / For future years'.

In addressing this crisis, 'Tintern Abbey' fulfilled Coleridge's idea that Wordsworth should write a philosophical poem, entitled *The Recluse*, that would 'do great good' in the aftermath of the French Revolution. The plan for *The Recluse* dated from March 1798, and during that spring Wordsworth thought of 'The Ruined Cottage', 'The Old Cumberland Beggar' and 'A Night-Piece' as contributing to this greater work on 'Nature, Man, and Society'. *The Recluse* was never formally completed, although it preoccupied Wordsworth to the end of his life. During 1798, however, the idea of *The Recluse* prompted Wordsworth to take stock of his own abilities as a poet, encouraging the introspective tendency apparent in 'Tintern Abbey'. In the winter of 1798–9, when Wordsworth and Dorothy were living at Goslar, Germany, the mysterious 'Lucy' poems were written and the first verse towards *The Prelude* – the poem on the history of his own mind – began to flow.

Intended as a preliminary to *The Recluse*, the earliest version of *The Prelude* (always thought of by Wordsworth as 'the poem to Coleridge') was completed by December 1799. This 'Two–Part Prelude', included here in full, treated the formative experiences of childhood and adolescence, especially those un-forgotten moments – Wordsworth termed them 'spots of time' – which retain a power to quicken the imagination in later life. Wordsworth resumed work on his autobiographical poem in 1804, and extended it to include his life at Cambridge and London, the French Revolution, and his earliest calling as a poet at Racedown and Alfoxden. This thirteen-book poem was completed at Dove Cottage, Grasmere, in May 1805, and extracts from it are also reproduced in the selection here. After extensive reworking and revision over the remaining forty-five years of Wordsworth's life, 'the poem to Coleridge' was published in July 1850, three months after the poet's death. It was titled *The Prelude* by his widow Mary.

Wordsworth and Dorothy had settled at Dove Cottage, Gras-mere, in December 1799 – a return to the domain of their early childhood and the Lake District landscape of fells and water. Here, as at Alfoxden, the wealth of observation in Dorothy's journals proved an essential resource for Words-worth's imagination. The following ten years saw Words-worth's marriage to his childhood friend Mary Hutchinson, on

4 October 1802, the birth of four of their children, and the tragic drowning of John Wordsworth in the wreck of the *Earl of Abergavenny*, February 1805. Many of Wordsworth's greatest poems date from the Dove Cottage years, and a generous number of them are included in this book: the Lake District pastorals of 1800, 'The Brothers' and 'Michael'; the lyrics of spring 1802 including 'Resolution and Independence', and the political sonnets of August–September that year; the great 'Ode. Intimations of Immortality', completed in 1804; and Wordsworth's 1805 elegies for his brother John.

These poems define Wordsworth's great decade and, with *The Prelude*, they remain the foundation of his achievement as a poet. All of them had been composed by May 1808, when the growing Wordsworth family quitted Dove Cottage and moved across Grasmere Vale to Allan Bank, a larger but an uncomfortable house with chimneys that smoked. In 1813 (after the deaths of two of their children, Catharine and Thomas) they moved again, to Rydal Mount near Ambleside – Wordsworth's home until the end of his life. The poet's later years were saddened by Dorothy's mental illness, and by the death in 1847 of his much-loved daughter Dora. To the public's eyes, however, Wordsworth at Rydal Mount had become a figure of the literary and political establishment, a national institution. From 1813 he had served as Distributor of Stamps for Westmorland; he celebrated the defeat of Napoleon at Waterloo in a 'Thanksgiving Ode', and, in 1843, he succeeded his old friend Robert Southey as Poet Laureate.

Much of the poetry written in the latter years of Wordsworth's life shows a decline in imaginative power, although there are notable exceptions. *The Excursion* (published in 1814 and Wordsworth's major poem for the Victorians) stands as a very substantial achievement. 'Yarrow Unvisited', 'Yarrow Visited' and 'Yarrow Revisited' show how a landscape known and loved over many years could reawaken the memorial imagination of 'Tintern Abbey'. 'Extempore Effusion upon the Death of James Hogg' and the valedictory sonnet 'On the Departure of Sir Walter Scott from Abbotsford, for Naples' are evidence that Wordsworth's power as an elegiac poet survived to the last decades of his life.

The panegyric to Edmund Burke, written for *The Prelude* in 1832, is a testament to the change in Wordsworth's politics. Yet the passage also discloses Wordsworth's enduring trust – as republican, as High Tory – in the 'vital power' of human community. It was Wordsworth's imagining of essential humanity during the revolutionary decade that initiated his life as a poet; two hundred years later his work is of undiminished relevance and power. An abiding concern for nature, humankind, and society places Wordsworth with Shakespeare as the essential poet for our times.

Acknowledgements and a Note on the Text

I am grateful to the University Library at St Andrews, and the National Library of Scotland, Edinburgh, for assistance in locating texts for this volume. James Butler, Beth Darlington and Jonathan Wordsworth have generously allowed me to reprint their texts of early Wordsworth poems (noted below). Molly Lefebure has been most helpful in establishing topographical details of the Lake District for the endnotes. My wife Jane has given valuable time, criticism and advice during the preparation of this volume. The scholarship of Stephen Gill, J. C. Maxwell, Mark Reed and Jonathan Wordsworth has been an indispensable reference in preparing the selection and the endnotes. I acknowledge this indebtedness with gratitude.

The poems are arranged according to the chronology of composition, except for the extracts from the 1805 and 1850 editions of *The Prelude*. Unless otherwise indicated, I have reproduced poems from the earliest text published in a Wordsworth volume; in these poems Wordsworth's spelling and punctuation have been largely retained, with a minimum of editorial imposition.

'The Two-Part Prelude' is reprinted by permission from '*The Pedlar*', '*Tintern Abbey*' *and The Two-Part Prelude*, ed. Jonathan Wordsworth, copyright © 1985 by Cambridge University Press. Extracts from the 1805 and 1850 versions of *The Prelude* have been drawn from *The Prelude: A Parallel Text*, ed. J. C. Maxwell, in the Penguin English Poets series. 'The Baker's Cart' and 'The Ruined Cottage' are reprinted by permission from '*The Ruined Cottage*' *and* '*The Pedlar*', ed. James Butler, copyright © 1979 by Cornell University. 'A Night-Piece' and 'The Discharged Soldier' are reprinted by permission from Beth Darlington, 'Two Early Texts: "A Night-Piece" and "The Discharged Soldier"', in *Bicentenary Wordsworth Studies in Memory of John Alban Finch*, ed. J. Wordsworth, copyright © 1970 by Cornell University Press.

In this volume, square brackets within poems denote passages which are illegible or missing in the original manuscript.

The Baker's Cart

I have seen the Baker's horse
As he had been accustomed at your door
Stop with the loaded wain, when o'er his head
Smack went the whip, and you were left, as if
You were not born to live, or there had been
No bread in all the land. Five little ones,
They at the rumbling of the distant wheels
Had all come forth, and, ere the grove of birch
Concealed the wain, into their wretched hut
They all returned. While in the road I stood   10
Pursuing with involuntary look
The wain now seen no longer, to my side
[   ] came, a pitcher in her hand
Filled from the spring; she saw what way my eyes
Were turned, and in a low and fearful voice
She said, 'That waggon does not care for us.'
The words were simple, but her look and voice
Made up their meaning, and bespoke a mind
Which being long neglected and denied
The common food of hope was now become   20
Sick and extravagant – by strong access
Of momentary pangs driv'n to that state
In which all past experience melts away
And the rebellious heart to its own will
Fashions the laws of nature.

Old Man Travelling;

Animal Tranquillity and Decay,
A Sketch

           The little hedge-row birds,
That peck along the road, regard him not.
He travels on, and in his face, his step,
His gait, is one expression; every limb,
His look and bending figure, all bespeak
A man who does not move with pain, but moves
With thought – He is insensibly subdued
To settled quiet: he is one by whom
All effort seems forgotten, one to whom
Long patience has such mild composure given,
That patience now doth seem a thing, of which
He hath no need. He is by nature led
To peace so perfect, that the young behold
With envy, what the old man hardly feels.
– I asked him whither he was bound, and what
The object of his journey; he replied
'Sir! I am going many miles to take
A last leave of my son, a mariner,
Who from a sea-fight has been brought to Falmouth,
And there is dying in an hospital.'

Lines Left upon a Seat in a Yew-Tree

Which Stands Near the Lake of Esthwaite,
on a Desolate Part of the Shore,
Yet Commanding a Beautiful Prospect

– Nay, Traveller! rest. This lonely yew-tree stands
Far from all human dwelling: what if here
No sparkling rivulet spread the verdant herb;
What if these barren boughs the bee not loves;
Yet, if the wind breathe soft, the curling waves,
That break against the shore, shall lull thy mind
By one soft impulse saved from vacancy.

————————————Who he was
That piled these stones, and with the mossy sod
First covered o'er, and taught this aged tree,   10
Now wild, to bend its arms in circling shade,
I well remember. – He was one who owned
No common soul. In youth, by genius nursed,
And big with lofty views, he to the world
Went forth, pure in his heart, against the taint
Of dissolute tongues, 'gainst jealousy, and hate,
And scorn, against all enemies prepared,
All but neglect: and so, his spirit damped
At once, with rash disdain he turned away,
And with the food of pride sustained his soul   20
In solitude. – Stranger! these gloomy boughs
Had charms for him; and here he loved to sit,
His only visitants a straggling sheep,
The stone-chat, or the glancing sand-piper;
And on these barren rocks, with juniper,
And heath, and thistle, thinly sprinkled o'er,
Fixing his downward eye, he many an hour
A morbid pleasure nourished, tracing here
An emblem of his own unfruitful life:
And lifting up his head, he then would gaze   30

3

On the more distant scene; how lovely 'tis
Thou seest, and he would gaze till it became
Far lovelier, and his heart could not sustain
The beauty still more beauteous. Nor, that time,
Would he forget those beings, to whose minds,
Warm from the labours of benevolence,
The world, and man himself, appeared a scene
Of kindred loveliness: then he would sigh
With mournful joy, to think that others felt
40   What he must never feel: and so, lost man!
On visionary views would fancy feed,
Till his eye streamed with tears. In this deep vale
He died, this seat his only monument.

If thou be one whose heart the holy forms
Of young imagination have kept pure,
Stranger! henceforth be warned; and know, that pride,
Howe'er disguised in its own majesty,
Is littleness; that he, who feels contempt
For any living thing, hath faculties
50   Which he has never used; that thought with him
Is in its infancy. The man, whose eye
Is ever on himself, doth look on one,
The least of nature's works, one who might move
The wise man to that scorn which wisdom holds
Unlawful, ever. O, be wiser thou!
Instructed that true knowledge leads to love,
True dignity abides with him alone
Who, in the silent hour of inward thought,
Can still suspect, and still revere himself,
60   In lowliness of heart.

4

The Ruined Cottage

A Poem

Give me a spark of nature's fire,
Tis the best learning I desire.
. . . . .
My Muse though homely in attire
May touch the heart.

Burns.

PART I

Twas Summer; and the sun was mounted high.
Along the south the uplands feebly glared
Through a pale steam, and all the northern downs
In clearer air ascending shewed their brown
And [   ] surfaces distinct with shades
Of deep embattled clouds that lay in spots
Determined and unmoved, with steady beams
Of clear and pleasant sunshine interposed;
Pleasant to him who on the soft cool grass
Extends his careless limbs beside the root   10
Of some huge oak whose aged branches make
A twilight of their own, a dewy shade
Where the wren warbles, while the dreaming man,
Half conscious of that soothing melody,
With sidelong eye looks out upon the scene,
By those impending branches made [   ]
More soft and distant. Other lot was mine.
Across a bare wide Common I had toiled
With languid feet which by the slippery ground
Were baffled still; and when I sought repose   20
On the brown earth my limbs from very heat
Could find no rest nor my weak arm disperse
The insect host which gathered round my face
And joined their murmurs to the tedious noise
Of seeds of bursting gorse which crackled round.

I rose and turned towards a group of trees
Which midway in the level stood alone,
And thither come at length, beneath a shade
Of clustering elms that sprang from the same root
30 I found a ruined Cottage, four clay walls
That stared upon each other. – 'Twas a spot!
The wandering gypsey in a stormy night
Would pass it with his moveables to house
On the open plain beneath the imperfect arch
Of a cold lime-kiln. As I looked around
Beside the door I saw an aged Man
Stretched on a bench whose edge with short bright moss
Was green and studded o'er with fungus flowers;
An iron-pointed staff lay at his side.
40 Him had I seen the day before – alone
And in the middle of the public way
Standing to rest himself. His eyes were turned
Towards the setting sun, while with that staff
Behind him fixed he propped a long white pack
Which crossed his shoulders: wares for maids who live
In lonely villages or straggling huts.
I knew him – he was born of lowly race
On Cumbrian hills, and I have seen the tear
Stand in his luminous eye when he described
50 The house in which his early days were passed
And found I was no stranger to the spot.
I loved to hear him talk of former days
And tell how when a child ere yet of age
To be a shepherd he had learned to read
His bible in a school that stood alone,
Sole building on a mountain's dreary edge,
Far from the sight of city spire, or sound
Of Minster clock. He from his native hills
Had wandered far: much had he seen of men,
60 Their manners, their enjoyments and pursuits,
Their passions and their feelings, chiefly those
Essential and eternal in the heart,
Which 'mid the simpler forms of rural life

6

Exist more simple in their elements
And speak a plainer language. He possessed
No vulgar mind though he had passed his life
In this poor occupation, first assumed
From impulses of curious thought, and now
Continued many a year, and now pursued
From habit and necessity. His eye   70
Flashing poetic fire, he would repeat
The songs of Burns, and as we trudged along
Together did we make the hollow grove
Ring with our transports. Though he was untaught,
In the dead lore of schools undisciplined,
Why should he grieve? He was a chosen son:
To him was given an ear which deeply felt
The voice of Nature in the obscure wind,
The sounding mountain and the running stream.
To every natural form, rock, fruit, and flower,   80
Even the loose stones that cover the highway,
He gave a moral life; he saw them feel
Or linked them to some feeling. In all shapes
He found a secret and mysterious soul,
A fragrance and a spirit of strange meaning.
Though poor in outward shew, he was most rich;
He had a world about him – 'twas his own,
He made it – for it only lived to him
And to the God who looked into his mind.
Such sympathies would often bear him far   90
In outward gesture, and in visible look,
Beyond the common seeming of mankind.
Some called it madness – such it might have been,
But that he had an eye which evermore
Looked deep into the shades of difference
As they lie hid in all exterior forms,
Which from a stone, a tree, a withered leaf,
To the broad ocean and the azure heavens
Spangled with kindred multitudes of stars,
Could find no surface where its power might sleep,   100
Which spake perpetual logic to his soul,

And by an unrelenting agency
Did bind his feelings even as in a chain.
So was he framed, though humble and obscure
Had been his lot. Now on the Bench he lay
Stretched at his length, and with that weary load
Pillowed his head – I guess he had no thought
Of his way-wandering life. His eyes were shut;
The shadows of the breezy elms above
110   Dappled his face. With thirsty heat oppressed
At length I hailed him, glad to see his hat
Bedewed with water-drops, as if the brim
Had newly scooped a running stream. He rose
And, pointing to a sun-flower, bade me climb
The [   ] wall where that same gaudy flower
Looked out upon the road. It was a plot
Of garden-ground, now wild, its matted weeds
Marked with the steps of those whom as they pass[ed],
The gooseberry trees that shot in long [   ],
120   Or currants shewing on a leafless stem
Their scanty strings, had tempted to o'erleap
The broken wall. Within that cheerless spot,
Where two tall hedgerows of thick willow boughs
Joined in a damp cold nook, I found a well
Half choaked [   ].
I slaked my thirst and to the shady bench
Returned, and while I stood unbonneted
To catch the current of the breezy air
The old man said, 'I see around me [   ]
130   Things which you cannot see. We die, my Friend,
Nor we alone, but that which each man loved
And prized in his peculiar nook of earth
Dies with him or is changed, and very soon
Even of the good is no memorial left.
The waters of that spring if they could feel
Might mourn. They are not as they were; the bond
Of brotherhood is broken – time has been
When every day the touch of human hand
Disturbed their stillness, and they ministered

To human comfort. As I stooped to drink,   140
Few minutes gone, at that deserted well
What feelings came to me! A spider's web
Across its mouth hung to the water's edge,
And on the wet and slimy foot-stone lay
The useless fragment of a wooden bowl;
It moved my very heart. The time has been
When I could never pass this road but she
Who lived within these walls, when I appeared,
A daughter's welcome gave me, and I loved her
As my own child. Oh Sir! the good die first,   150
And they whose hearts are dry as summer dust
Burn to the socket. Many a passenger
Has blessed poor Margaret for her gentle looks
When she upheld the cool refreshment drawn
From that forsaken well, and no one came
But he was welcome, no one went away
But that it seemed she loved him. She is dead,
The worm is on her cheek, and this poor hut,
Stripped of its outward garb of household flowers,
Of rose and jasmine, offers to the wind   160
A cold bare wall whose earthy top is tricked
With weeds and the rank spear-grass. She is dead,
And nettles rot and adders sun themselves
Where we have sat together while she nursed
Her infant at her bosom. The wild colt,
The unstalled heifer and the Potter's ass,
Find shelter now within the chimney wall
Where I have seen her evening hearth-stone blaze
And through the window spread upon the road
Its cheerful light. – You will forgive me, Sir,   170
I feel I play the truant with my tale.
She had a husband, an industrious man,
Sober and steady; I have heard her say
That he was up and busy at his loom
In summer ere the mower's scythe had swept
The dewy grass, and in the early spring
Ere the last star had vanished. They who passed

At evening, from behind the garden fence
Might hear his busy spade, which he would ply
180 After his daily work till the day-light
Was gone and every leaf and every flower
Were lost in the dark hedges. So they lived
In peace and comfort, and two pretty babes
Were their best hope next to the God in Heaven.
– You may remember, now some ten years gone,
Two blighting seasons when the fields were left
With half a tillage. It pleased heaven to add
A worse affliction in the plague of war:
A happy land was stricken to the heart;
190 'Twas a sad time of sorrow and distress:
A wanderer among the cottages,
I with my pack of winter raiment saw
The hardships of that season: many rich
Sunk down as in [a] dream among the poor,
And of the poor did many cease to be,
And their place knew them not. Meanwhile, abridged
Of daily comforts, gladly reconciled
To numerous self denials, Margaret
Went struggling on through those calamitous years
200 With cheerful hope: but ere the second spring
A fever seized her husband. In disease
He lingered long, and when his strength returned
He found the little he had stored to meet
The hour of accident or crippling age
Was all consumed. As I have said, 'twas now
A time of trouble; shoals of artisans
Were from their daily labour turned away
To hang for bread on parish charity,
They and their wives and children – happier far
210 Could they have lived as do the little birds
That peck along the hedges, or the kite
That makes her dwelling in the mountain rocks.
Ill fared it now with Robert, he who dwelt
In this poor cottage; at his door he stood

And whistled many a snatch of merry tunes
That had no mirth in them, or with his knife
Carved uncouth figures on the heads of sticks,
Then idly sought about through every nook
Of house or garden any casual task
Of use or ornament, and with a strange,   220
Amusing but uneasy novelty
He blended where he might the various tasks
Of summer, autumn, winter, and of spring.
The passenger might see him at the door
With his small hammer on the threshold stone
Pointing lame buckle-tongues and rusty nails,
The treasured store of an old household box,
Or braiding cords or weaving bells and caps
Of rushes, play-things for his babes.
But this endured not; his good-humour soon   230
Became a weight in which no pleasure was,
And poverty brought on a petted mood
And a sore temper: day by day he drooped,
And he would leave his home, and to the town
Without an errand would he turn his steps
Or wander here and there among the fields.
One while he would speak lightly of his babes
And with a cruel tongue: at other times
He played with them wild freaks of merriment:
And 'twas a piteous thing to see the looks   240
Of the poor innocent children. "Every smile,"
Said Margaret to me here beneath these trees,
"Made my heart bleed."' At this the old Man paused
And looking up to those enormous elms
He said, ''Tis now the hour of deepest noon.
At this still season of repose and peace,
This hour when all things which are not at rest
Are cheerful, while this multitude of flies
Fills all the air with happy melody,
Why should a tear be in an old Man's eye?   250
Why should we thus with an untoward mind

And in the weakness of humanity
From natural wisdom turn our hearts away,
To natural comfort shut our eyes and ears,
And feeding on disquiet thus disturb
[   ] of Nature with our restless thoughts?'

PART 2

He spake with somewhat of a solemn tone:
But when he ended there was in his face
Such easy cheerfulness, a look so mild
260   That for a little time it stole away
All recollection, and that simple tale
Passed from my mind like a forgotten sound.
A while on trivial things we held discourse,
To me soon tasteless. In my own despite
I thought of that poor woman as of one
Whom I had known and loved. He had rehearsed
Her homely tale with such familiar power,
With such a countenance of love, an eye
So busy, that the things of which he spake
270   Seemed present, and, attention now relaxed,
There was a heartfelt chillness in my veins.
I rose, and turning from that breezy shade
Went out into the open air, and stood
To drink the comfort of the warmer sun.
Long time I had not stayed ere, looking round
Upon that tranquil ruin, and impelled
By a mild force of curious pensiveness,
I begged of the old man that for my sake
He would resume his story. He replied,
280   'It were a wantonness, and would demand
Severe reproof, if we were men whose hearts
Could hold vain dalliance with the misery
Even of the dead, contented thence to draw
A momentary pleasure never marked
By reason, barren of all future good.
But we have known that there is often found

12

In mournful thoughts, and always might be found,
A power to virtue friendly; were't not so,
I am a dreamer among men – indeed
An idle dreamer. 'Tis a common tale,   290
By moving accidents uncharactered,
A tale of silent suffering, hardly clothed
In bodily form, and to the grosser sense
But ill adapted, scarcely palpable
To him who does not think. But at your bidding
I will proceed.
              While thus it fared with those
To whom this Cottage till that hapless year
Had been a blessed home, it was my chance
To travel in a country far remote.
And glad I was when, halting by yon gate   300
Which leads from the green lane, again I saw
These lofty elm-trees. Long I did not rest:
With many pleasant thoughts I cheered my way
O'er the flat common. At the door arrived,
I knocked, and when I entered with the hope
Of usual greeting, Margaret looked at me
A little while, then turned her head away
Speechless, and sitting down upon a chair
Wept bitterly. I wist not what to do
Or how to speak to her. Poor wretch! at last   310
She rose from off her seat – and then – Oh Sir!
I cannot *tell* how she pronounced my name:
With fervent love and with a face of grief
Unutterably helpless and a look
That seemed to cling upon me, she inquired
If I had seen her husband. As she spake
A strange surprize and fear came o'er my heart
And I could make no answer – then she told
That he had disappeared, just two months gone.
He left his house; two wretched days had passed,   320
And on the third by the first break of light,
Within her casement full in view she saw
A purse of gold. "I trembled at the sight,"

Said Margaret, "for I knew it was his hand
That placed it there, and on that very day
By one, a stranger, from my husband sent,
The tidings came that he had joined a troop
Of soldiers going to a distant land.
He left me thus – Poor Man! he had not heart
330   To take a farewell of me, and he feared
That I should follow with my babes and sink
Beneath the misery of a soldier's life."
This tale did Margaret tell with many tears:
And when she ended I had little power
To give her comfort and was glad to take
Such words of hope from her own mouth as served
To cheer us both – but long we had not talked
Ere we built up a pile of better thoughts,
And with a brighter eye she looked around
340   As if she had been shedding tears of joy.
We parted. It was then the early spring;
I left her busy with her garden tools;
And well remember, o'er the fence she looked,
And while I paced along the foot-way path
Called out, and sent a blessing after me
With tender cheerfulness and with a voice
That seemed the very sound of happy thoughts.

I roved o'er many a hill and many a dale
With this my weary load, in heat and cold,
350   Through many a wood, and many an open plain,
In sunshine or in shade, in wet or fair,
Now blithe, now drooping – as it might befal –
My best companions now the driving winds
And now the music of my own sad steps,
With many short-lived thoughts that passed between
And disappeared. I measured back this road
Towards the wane of summer, when the wheat
Was yellow and the soft and bladed grass
Sprung up afresh and o'er the hay-field spread
360   Its tender green. When I had reached the door

I found that she was absent. In the shade
Where now we sit I waited her return.
Her cottage in its outward look appeared
As cheerful as before; in any shew
Of neatness little changed, but that I thought
The honeysuckle crowded round the door
And from the wall hung down in heavier tufts,
And knots of worthless stone-crop started out
Along the window's edge and grew like weeds
Against the lower panes. I turned aside   370
And strolled into her garden. It was changed:
The unprofitable bindweed spread his bells
From side to side, and with unwieldy wreaths
Had dragged the rose from its sustaining wall
And bowed it down to earth; the border tufts –
Daisy, and thrift, and lowly camomile,
And thyme – had straggled out into the paths
Which they were used to deck. Ere this an hour
Was wasted. Back I turned my restless steps,
And as I walked before the door it chanced   380
A stranger passed, and guessing whom I sought
He said that she was used to ramble far.
The sun was sinking in the west, and now
I sate with sad impatience. From within
Her solitary infant cried aloud.
The spot though fair seemed very desolate,
The longer I remained more desolate.
And looking round I saw the corner stones,
Till then unmarked, on either side the door
With dull red stains discoloured and stuck o'er   390
With tufts and hairs of wool, as if the sheep
That feed upon the commons thither came
As to a couching-place and rubbed their sides
Even at her threshold. The church-clock struck eight;
I turned and saw her distant a few steps.
Her face was pale and thin, her figure too
Was changed. As she unlocked the door she said,
"It grieves me you have waited here so long,

But in truth I've wandered much of late
400   And sometimes, to my shame I speak, have need
Of my best prayers to bring me back again."
While on the board she spread our evening meal
She told me she had lost her eldest child,
That he for months had been a serving-boy
Apprenticed by the parish. "I am changed,
And to myself," said she, "have done much wrong,
And to this helpless infant. I have slept
Weeping, and weeping I have waked; my tears
Have flowed as if my body were not such
410   As others are, and I could never die.
But I am now in mind and in my heart
More easy, and I hope," said she, "that heaven
Will give me patience to endure the things
Which I behold at home." It would have grieved
Your very soul to see her: evermore
Her eye-lids drooped, her eyes were downward cast;
And when she at her table gave me food
She did not look at me. Her voice was low,
Her body was subdued. In every act
420   Pertaining to her house affairs appeared
The careless stillness which a thinking mind
Gives to an idle matter – still she sighed,
But yet no motion of the breast was seen,
No heaving of the heart. While by the fire
We sate together, sighs came on my ear;
I knew not how and hardly whence they came.
I took my staff, and when I kissed her babe
The tears were in her eyes. I left her then
With the best hope and comfort I could give;
430   She thanked me for my will, but for my hope
It seemed she did not thank me. I returned
And took my rounds along this road again
Ere on its sunny bank the primrose flower
Had chronicled the earliest day of spring.
I found her sad and drooping; she had learned
No tidings of her husband: if he lived

She knew not that he lived; if he were dead
She knew not he was dead. She seemed not changed
In person or appearance, but her house
Bespoke a sleepy hand of negligence;   440
The floor was neither dry nor neat, the hearth
Was comfortless [   ],
The windows they were dim, and her few books,
Which one upon the other heretofore
Had been piled up against the corner panes
In seemly order, now with straggling leaves
Lay scattered here and there, open or shut
As they had chanced to fall. Her infant babe
Had from its mother caught the trick of grief
And sighed among its playthings. Once again   450
I turned towards the garden gate and saw
More plainly still that poverty and grief
Were now come nearer to her: all was hard,
With weeds defaced and knots of withered grass;
No ridges there appeared of clear black mould,
No winter greenness; of her herbs and flowers
It seemed the better part were gnawed away
Or trampled on the earth; a chain of straw
Which had been twisted round the tender stem
Of a young apple-tree lay at its root;   460
The bark was nibbled round by truant sheep.
Margaret stood near, her infant in her arms,
And seeing that my eye was on the tree
She said, "I fear it will be dead and gone
Ere Robert come again." Towards the house
Together we returned, and she enquired
If I had any hope. But for her babe
And for her little friendless Boy, she said,
She had no wish to live, that she must die
Of sorrow. – Yet I saw the idle loom   470
Still in its place. His sunday garments hung
Upon the self-same nail – his very staff
Stood undisturbed behind the door. And when
I passed this way beaten by autumn wind[s],

She told me that her little babe was dead
And she was left alone. That very time,
I yet remember, through the miry lane
She went with me a mile, when the bare trees
Trickled with foggy damps, and in such sort
480   That any heart had ached to hear her begged
That wheresoe'er I went I still would ask
For him whom she had lost. Five tedious years
She lingered in unquiet widowhood,
A wife, and widow. Needs must it have been
A sore heart-wasting. I have heard, my Friend,
That in that broken arbour she would sit
The idle length of half a sabbath day,
There – where you see the toadstool's lazy head –
And when a dog passed by she still would quit
490   The shade and look abroad. On this old Bench
For hours she sate, and evermore her eye
Was busy in the distance, shaping things
Which made her heart beat quick. Seest thou that path?
(The greensward now has broken its grey line)
There, to and fro she paced through many a day
Of the warm summer, from a belt of flax
That girt her waist spinning the long-drawn thread
With backward steps. – Yet ever as there passed
A man whose garments shewed the Soldier's red,
500   Or crippled Mendicant in Sailor's garb,
The little Child who sate to turn the wheel
Ceased from his toil, and she with faltering voice,
Expecting still to learn her husband's fate,
Made many a fond inquiry; and when they
Whose presence gave no comfort were gone by,
Her heart was still more sad. And by yon gate
Which bars the traveller's road she often stood
And when a stranger horseman came, the latch
Would lift, and in his face look wistfully,
510   Most happy if from aught discovered there
Of tender feeling she might dare repeat
The same sad question. Meanwhile her poor hut

Sunk to decay, for he was gone whose hand,
At the first nippings of October frost,
Closed up each chink and with fresh bands of straw
Chequered the green-grown thatch. And so she sate
Through the long winter, reckless and alone,
Till this reft house by frost, and thaw, and rain
Was sapped; and when she slept the nightly damps
Did chill her breast, and in the stormy day   520
Her tattered clothes were ruffled by the wind
Even at the side of her own fire. – Yet still
She loved this wretched spot, nor would for worlds
Have parted hence; and still that length of road
And this rude bench one torturing hope endeared,
Fast rooted at her heart, and here, my friend,
In sickness she remained, and here she died,
Last human tenant of these ruined walls.'

A Night-Piece

           The sky is overspread
With a close veil of one continuous cloud
All whitened by the moon, that just appears,
A dim-seen orb, yet chequers not the ground
With any shadow – plant, or tower, or tree.
At last a pleasant instantaneous light
Startles the musing man whose eyes are bent
To earth. He looks around, the clouds are split
Asunder, and above his head he views
The clear moon and the glory of the heavens.   10
There in a black-blue vault she sails along
Followed by multitudes of stars, that small,
And bright, and sharp along the gloomy vault
Drive as she drives. How fast they wheel away!
Yet vanish not! The wind is in the trees;
But they are silent. Still they roll along
Immeasurably distant, and the vault

Built round by those white clouds, enormous clouds,
Still deepens its interminable depth.
20   At length the vision closes, and the mind
Not undisturbed by the deep joy it feels,
Which slowly settles into peaceful calm,
Is left to muse upon the solemn scene.

The Discharged Soldier

                              I love to walk
Along the public way when for the night,
Deserted in its silence, it assumes
A character of deeper quietness
Than pathless solitudes. At such a time
I slowly mounted up a steep ascent
Where the road's watry surface to the ridge
Of that sharp rising glittered in the moon
And seemed before my eyes another stream
10   Stealing with silent lapse to join the brook
That murmured in the valley. On I passed
Tranquil, receiving in my own despite
Amusement, as I slowly passed along,
From such near objects as from time to time
Perforce disturbed the slumber of the sense
Quiescent, and disposed to sympathy,
With an exhausted mind worn out by toil
And all unworthy of the deeper joy
Which waits on distant prospect, cliff or sea,
20   The dark blue vault, and universe of stars.
Thus did I steal along that silent road,
My body from the stillness drinking in
A restoration like the calm of sleep
But sweeter far. Above, before, behind,
Around me, all was peace and solitude:
I looked not round, nor did the solitude

Speak to my eye, but it was heard and felt.
Oh happy state! What beauteous pictures now
Rose in harmonious imagery – they rose
As from some distant region of my soul   30
And came along like dreams, yet such as left
Obscurely mingled with their passing forms
A consciousness of animal delight,
A self-possession felt in every pause
And every gentle movement of my frame.
  While thus I wandered step by step led on,
It chanced a sudden turning of the road
Presented to my view an uncouth shape
So near that, stepping back into the shade
Of a thick hawthorn, I could mark him well,   40
Myself unseen. He was in stature tall,
A foot above man's common measure tall,
And lank, and upright. There was in his form
A meagre stiffness. You might almost think
That his bones wounded him. His legs were long,
So long and shapeless that I looked at them
Forgetful of the body they sustained.
His arms were long and lean; his hands were bare;
His visage, wasted though it seemed, was large
In feature; his cheeks sunken; and his mouth   50
Shewed ghastly in the moonlight. From behind
A mile-stone propped him, and his figure seemed
Half-sitting and half-standing. I could mark
That he was clad in military garb,
Though faded yet entire. His face was turned
Towards the road, yet not as if he sought
For any living thing. He appeared
Forlorn and desolate, a man cut off
From all his kind, and more than half detached
From his own nature.
                        He was alone,   60
Had no attendant, neither dog, nor staff,
Nor knapsack – in his very dress appeared
A desolation, a simplicity

That appertained to solitude. I think
If but a glove had dangled in his hand
It would have made him more akin to man.
Long time I scanned him with a mingled sense
Of fear and sorrow. From his lips meanwhile
There issued murmuring sounds as if of pain
70 Or of uneasy thought; yet still his form
Kept the same fearful steadiness. His shadow
Lay at his feet and moved not. In a glen
Hard by a village stood, whose silent doors
Were visible among the scattered trees,
Scarce distant from the spot an arrow's flight.
I wished to see him move, but he remained
Fixed to his place, and still from time to time
Sent forth a murmuring voice of dead complaint,
A groan scarce audible. Yet all the while
80 The chained mastiff in his wooden house
Was vexed, and from among the village trees
Howled never ceasing. Not without reproach
Had I prolonged my watch, and now confirmed,
And my heart's specious cowardice subdued,
I left the shady nook where I had stood
And hailed the Stranger. From his resting-place
He rose, and with his lean and wasted arm
In measured gesture lifted to his head
Returned my salutation. A short while
90 I held discourse on things indifferent
And casual matter. He meanwhile had ceased
From all complaint – his station had resumed,
Propped by the mile stone as before; and when erelong
I asked his history, he in reply
Was neither slow nor eager, but unmoved,
And with a quiet uncomplaining voice,
A stately air of mild indifference,
He told a simple fact: that he had been
A Soldier, to the tropic isles had gone,
100 Whence he had landed now some ten days past;
That on his landing he had been dismissed,

And with the little strength he yet had left
Was travelling to regain his native home.
At this I turned and through the trees looked down
Into the village – all were gone to rest,
Nor smoke nor any taper light appeared,
But every silent window to the moon
Shone with a yellow glitter. 'No one there,'
Said I, 'is waking; we must measure back
The way which we have come. Behind yon wood   110
A labourer dwells, an honest man and kind;
He will not murmur should we break his rest,
And he will give you food if food you need,
And lodging for the night.' At this he stooped,
And from the ground took up an oaken staff
By me yet unobserved, a traveller's staff,
Which I suppose from his slack hand had dropped,
And, such the languor of the weary man,
Had lain till now neglected in the grass,
But not forgotten. Back we turned and shaped   120
Our course toward the cottage. He appeared
To travel without pain, and I beheld
With ill-suppressed astonishment his tall
And ghostly figure moving at my side.
As we advanced I asked him for what cause
He tarried there, nor had demanded rest
At inn or cottage. He replied, 'In truth
My weakness made me loth to move, and here
I felt myself at ease and much relieved,
But that the village mastiff fretted me,   130
And every second moment rang a peal
Felt at my very heart. There was no noise,
Nor any foot abroad – I do not know
What ailed him, but it seemed as if the dog
Were howling to the murmur of the stream.'
While thus we travelled on I did not fail
To question him of what he had endured
From war and battle and the pestilence.
He all the while was in demeanor calm,

140 Concise in answer: solemn and sublime
He might have seemed, but that in all he said
There was a strange half-absence and a tone
Of weakness and indifference, as of one
Remembering the importance of his theme,
But feeling it no longer. We advanced
Slowly, and ere we to the wood were come
Discourse had ceased. Together on we passed
In silence through the shades gloomy and dark,
Then turning up along an open field
150 We gained the cottage. At the door I knocked,
And called aloud, 'My Friend, here is a man
By sickness overcome; beneath your roof
This night let him find rest, and give him food –
The service if need be I will requite.'
Assured that now my comrade would repose
In comfort, I entreated that henceforth
He would not linger in the public ways
But at the door of cottage or of inn
Demand the succour which his state required,
160 And told him feeble as he was, 'twere fit
He asked relief or alms. At this reproof
With the same ghastly mildness in his look
He said, 'My trust is in the God of heaven,
And in the eye of him that passes me.'
By this the labourer had unlocked the door,
And now my comrade touched his hat again
With his lean hand, and in a voice that seemed
To speak with a reviving interest
Till then unfelt, he thanked me. I returned
170 The blessing of the poor unhappy man,
And so we parted.

The Old Cumberland Beggar,

A Description

The class of Beggars to which the old man here
described belongs, will probably soon be extinct. It
consisted of poor, and, mostly, old and infirm persons,
who confined themselves to a stated round in their
neighbourhood, and had certain fixed days, on which, at
different houses, they regularly received charity;
sometimes in money, but mostly in provisions.

I saw an aged Beggar in my walk,
And he was seated by the highway side
On a low structure of rude masonry
Built at the foot of a huge hill, that they
Who lead their horses down the steep rough road
May thence remount at ease. The aged man
Had placed his staff across the broad smooth stone
That overlays the pile, and from a bag
All white with flour the dole of village dames,
He drew his scraps and fragments, one by one,   10
And scanned them with a fixed and serious look
Of idle computation. In the sun,
Upon the second step of that small pile,
Surrounded by those wild unpeopled hills,
He sate, and eat his food in solitude;
And ever, scattered from his palsied hand,
That still attempting to prevent the waste,
Was baffled still, the crumbs in little showers
Fell on the ground, and the small mountain birds,
Not venturing yet to peck their destined meal,   20
Approached within the length of half his staff.

Him from my childhood have I known, and then
He was so old, he seems not older now;
He travels on, a solitary man,
So helpless in appearance, that for him
The sauntering horseman-traveller does not throw

With careless hand his alms upon the ground,
But stops, that he may safely lodge the coin
Within the old Man's hat; nor quits him so,
30   But still when he has given his horse the rein
Towards the aged Beggar turns a look,
Sidelong and half-reverted. She who tends
The toll-gate, when in summer at her door
She turns her wheel, if on the road she sees
The aged Beggar coming, quits her work,
And lifts the latch for him that he may pass.
The Post-boy when his rattling wheels o'ertake
The aged Beggar, in the woody lane,
Shouts to him from behind, and, if perchance
40   The old Man does not change his course, the Boy
Turns with less noisy wheels to the road-side,
And passes gently by, without a curse
Upon his lips, or anger at his heart.
He travels on, a solitary Man,
His age has no companion. On the ground
His eyes are turned, and, as he moves along,
They move along the ground; and evermore,
Instead of common and habitual sight
Of fields with rural works, of hill and dale,
50   And the blue sky, one little span of earth
Is all his prospect. Thus, from day to day,
Bowbent, his eyes for ever on the ground,
He plies his weary journey, seeing still,
And never knowing that he sees, some straw,
Some scattered leaf, or marks which, in one track,
The nails of cart or chariot wheel have left
Impressed on the white road, in the same line,
At distance still the same. Poor Traveller!
His staff trails with him, scarcely do his feet
60   Disturb the summer dust, he is so still
In look and motion that the cottage curs,
Ere he have passed the door, will turn away
Weary of barking at him. Boys and girls,
The vacant and the busy, maids and youths,

And urchins newly breeched all pass him by:
Him even the slow-paced waggon leaves behind.

But deem not this man useless. – Statesmen! ye
Who are so restless in your wisdom, ye
Who have a broom still ready in your hands
To rid the world of nuisances; ye proud,   70
Heart-swoln, while in your pride ye contemplate
Your talents, power, and wisdom, deem him not
A burthen of the earth. 'Tis Nature's law
That none, the meanest of created things,
Of forms created the most vile and brute,
The dullest or most noxious, should exist
Divorced from good, a spirit and pulse of good,
A life and soul to every mode of being
Inseparably linked. While thus he creeps
From door to door, the Villagers in him   80
Behold a record which together binds
Past deeds and offices of charity
Else unremembered, and so keeps alive
The kindly mood in hearts which lapse of years,
And that half-wisdom half-experience gives
Make slow to feel, and by sure steps resign
To selfishness and cold oblivious cares.
Among the farms and solitary huts
Hamlets, and thinly-scattered villages,
Where'er the aged Beggar takes his rounds,   90
The mild necessity of use compels
To acts of love; and habit does the work
Of reason, yet prepares that after joy
Which reason cherishes. And thus the soul,
By that sweet taste of pleasure unpursued
Doth find itself insensibly disposed
To virtue and true goodness. Some there are,
By their good works exalted, lofty minds
And meditative, authors of delight
And happiness, which to the end of time   100
Will live, and spread, and kindle; minds like these,

In childhood, from this solitary being,
This helpless wanderer, have perchance received,
(A thing more precious far than all that books
Or the solicitudes of love can do!)
That first mild touch of sympathy and thought,
In which they found their kindred with a world
Where want and sorrow were. The easy man
Who sits at his own door, and like the pear
Which overhangs his head from the green wall,
Feeds in the sunshine; the robust and young,
The prosperous and unthinking, they who live
Sheltered, and flourish in a little grove
Of their own kindred, all behold in him
A silent monitor, which on their minds
Must needs impress a transitory thought
Of self-congratulation, to the heart
Of each recalling his peculiar boons,
His charters and exemptions; and perchance,
Though he to no one give the fortitude
And circumspection needful to preserve
His present blessings, and to husband up
The respite of the season, he, at least,
And 'tis no vulgar service, makes them felt.
Yet further. – Many, I believe, there are
Who live a life of virtuous decency,
Men who can hear the Decalogue and feel
No self-reproach, who of the moral law
Established in the land where they abide
Are strict observers, and not negligent,
Meanwhile, in any tenderness of heart
Or act of love to those with whom they dwell,
Their kindred, and the children of their blood.
Praise be to such, and to their slumbers peace!
– But of the poor man ask, the abject poor,
Go and demand of him, if there be here,
In this cold abstinence from evil deeds,
And these inevitable charities,
Wherewith to satisfy the human soul.

No – man is dear to man: the poorest poor   140
Long for some moments in a weary life
When they can know and feel that they have been
Themselves the fathers and the dealers out
Of some small blessings, have been kind to such
As needed kindness, for this single cause,
That we have all of us one human heart.
– Such pleasure is to one kind Being known
My Neighbour, when with punctual care, each week
Duly as Friday comes, though pressed herself
By her own wants, she from her chest of meal   150
Takes one unsparing handful for the scrip
Of this old Mendicant, and, from her door
Returning with exhilarated heart,
Sits by her fire and builds her hope in heav'n.

Then let him pass, a blessing on his head!
And while, in that vast solitude to which
The tide of things has led him, he appears
To breathe and live but for himself alone,
Unblamed, uninjured, let him bear about
The good which the benignant law of heaven   160
Has hung around him, and, while life is his,
Still let him prompt the unlettered Villagers
To tender offices and pensive thoughts.
Then let him pass, a blessing on his head!
And, long as he can wander, let him breathe
The freshness of the vallies, let his blood
Struggle with frosty air and winter snows,
And let the chartered wind that sweeps the heath
Beat his grey locks against his withered face.
Reverence the hope whose vital anxiousness   170
Gives the last human interest to his heart.
May never House, misnamed of industry,
Make him a captive; for that pent-up din,
Those life-consuming sounds that clog the air,
Be his the natural silence of old age.
Let him be free of mountain solitudes,

And have around him, whether heard or not,
The pleasant melody of woodland birds.
Few are his pleasures; if his eyes, which now
180 Have been so long familiar with the earth,
No more behold the horizontal sun
Rising or setting, let the light at least
Find a free entrance to their languid orbs.
And let him, *where* and *when* he will, sit down
Beneath the trees, or by the grassy bank
Of high-way side, and with the little birds
Share his chance-gathered meal, and, finally,
As in the eye of Nature he has lived,
So in the eye of Nature let him die.

Goody Blake and Harry Gill,

A True Story

Oh! what's the matter? what's the matter?
What is't that ails young Harry Gill?
That evermore his teeth they chatter,
Chatter, chatter, chatter still.
Of waistcoats Harry has no lack,
Good duffle grey, and flannel fine;
He has a blanket on his back,
And coats enough to smother nine.

In March, December, and in July,
10 'Tis all the same with Harry Gill;
The neighbours tell, and tell you truly,
His teeth they chatter, chatter still.
At night, at morning, and at noon,
'Tis all the same with Harry Gill;
Beneath the sun, beneath the moon,
His teeth they chatter, chatter still.

Young Harry was a lusty drover,
And who so stout of limb as he?
His cheeks were red as ruddy clover,
His voice was like the voice of three.   20
Auld Goody Blake was old and poor,
Ill fed she was, and thinly clad;
And any man who passed her door,
Might see how poor a hut she had.

All day she spun in her poor dwelling,
And then her three hours' work at night!
Alas! 'twas hardly worth the telling,
It would not pay for candle-light.
– This woman dwelt in Dorsetshire,
Her hut was on a cold hill-side,   30
And in that country coals are dear,
For they come far by wind and tide.

By the same fire to boil their pottage,
Two poor old dames, as I have known,
Will often live in one small cottage,
But she, poor woman, dwelt alone.
'Twas well enough when summer came,
The long, warm, lightsome summer-day,
Then at her door the *canty* dame
Would sit, as any linnet gay.   40

But when the ice our streams did fetter,
Oh! then how her old bones would shake!
You would have said, if you had met her,
'Twas a hard time for Goody Blake.
Her evenings then were dull and dead;
Sad case it was, as you may think,
For very cold to go to bed,
And then for cold not sleep a wink.

Oh joy for her! when e'er in winter
50   The winds at night had made a rout,
And scattered many a lusty splinter,
And many a rotten bough about.
Yet never had she, well or sick,
As every man who knew her says,
A pile before-hand, wood or stick,
Enough to warm her for three days.

Now, when the frost was past enduring,
And made her poor old bones to ache,
Could any thing be more alluring,
60   Than an old hedge to Goody Blake?
And now and then, it must be said,
When her old bones were cold and chill,
She left her fire, or left her bed,
To seek the hedge of Harry Gill.

Now Harry he had long suspected
This trespass of old Goody Blake,
And vowed that she should be detected,
And he on her would vengeance take.
And oft from his warm fire he'd go,
70   And to the fields his road would take,
And there, at night, in frost and snow,
He watched to seize old Goody Blake.

And once, behind a rick of barley,
Thus looking out did Harry stand;
The moon was full and shining clearly,
And crisp with frost the stubble-land.
– He hears a noise – he's all awake –
Again? – on tip-toe down the hill
He softly creeps – 'Tis Goody Blake,
80   She's at the hedge of Harry Gill.

Right glad was he when he beheld her:
Stick after stick did Goody pull,
He stood behind a bush of elder,
Till she had filled her apron full.
When with her load she turned about,
The bye-road back again to take,
He started forward with a shout,
And sprang upon poor Goody Blake.

And fiercely by the arm he took her,
And by the arm he held her fast,   90
And fiercely by the arm he shook her,
And cried, 'I've caught you then at last!'
Then Goody, who had nothing said,
Her bundle from her lap let fall;
And kneeling on the sticks, she prayed
To God that is the judge of all

She prayed, her withered hand uprearing,
While Harry held her by the arm –
'God! who art never out of hearing,
O may he never more be warm!'   100
The cold, cold moon above her head,
Thus on her knees did Goody pray,
Young Harry heard what she had said,
And icy-cold he turned away.

He went complaining all the morrow
That he was cold and very chill:
His face was gloom, his heart was sorrow,
Alas! that day for Harry Gill!
That day he wore a riding-coat,
But not a whit the warmer he: 110
Another was on Thursday brought,
And ere the Sabbath he had three.

'Twas all in vain, a useless matter,
And blankets were about him pinned;
Yet still his jaws and teeth they clatter,
Like a loose casement in the wind.
And Harry's flesh it fell away;
And all who see him say 'tis plain,
That, live as long as live he may,
He never will be warm again.

No word to any man he utters,
A-bed or up, to young or old;
But ever to himself he mutters,
'Poor Harry Gill is very cold.'
A-bed or up, by night or day;
His teeth they chatter, chatter still.
Now think, ye farmers all, I pray,
Of Goody Blake and Harry Gill.

Lines

*Written at a Small Distance from My House, and Sent by My
Little Boy to the Person to Whom They are Addressed*

It is the first mild day of March:
Each minute sweeter than before,
The red-breast sings from the tall larch
That stands beside our door.

There is a blessing in the air,
Which seems a sense of joy to yield
To the bare trees, and mountains bare,
And grass in the green field.

My Sister! ('tis a wish of mine)
Now that our morning meal is done,
Make haste, your morning task resign;
Come forth and feel the sun.

Edward will come with you, and pray,
Put on with speed your woodland dress,
And bring no book, for this one day
We'll give to idleness.

No joyless forms shall regulate
Our living Calendar:
We from to-day, my friend, will date
The opening of the year.   20

Love, now an universal birth,
From heart to heart is stealing,
From earth to man, from man to earth,
– It is the hour of feeling.

One moment now may give us more
Than fifty years of reason;
Our minds shall drink at every pore
The spirit of the season.

Some silent laws our hearts may make,
Which they shall long obey;   30
We for the year to come may take
Our temper from to-day.

And from the blessed power that rolls
About, below, above;
We'll frame the measure of our souls,
They shall be tuned to love.

Then come, my sister! come, I pray,
With speed put on your woodland dress,
And bring no book; for this one day
We'll give to idleness.   40

The Thorn

I.

There is a thorn; it looks so old,
In truth you'd find it hard to say,
How it could ever have been young,
It looks so old and grey.
Not higher than a two–years' child,
It stands erect this aged thorn;
No leaves it has, no thorny points;
It is a mass of knotted joints,
A wretched thing forlorn.
It stands erect, and like a stone
With lichens it is overgrown.

II.

Like rock or stone, it is o'ergrown
With lichens to the very top,
And hung with heavy tufts of moss,
A melancholy crop:
Up from the earth these mosses creep,
And this poor thorn they clasp it round
So close, you'd say that they were bent
With plain and manifest intent,
To drag it to the ground;
And all had joined in one endeavour
To bury this poor thorn for ever.

III.

High on a mountain's highest ridge,
Where oft the stormy winter gale
Cuts like a scythe, while through the clouds
It sweeps from vale to vale;

Not five yards from the mountain-path,
This thorn you on your left espy;
And to the left, three yards beyond,
You see a little muddy pond   30
Of water, never dry;
I've measured it from side to side:
'Tis three feet long, and two feet wide.

IV.

And close beside this aged thorn,
There is a fresh and lovely sight,
A beauteous heap, a hill of moss,
Just half a foot in height.
All lovely colours there you see,
All colours that were ever seen,
And mossy network too is there,   40
As if by hand of lady fair
The work had woven been,
And cups, the darlings of the eye,
So deep is their vermilion dye.

V.

Ah me! what lovely tints are there!
Of olive-green and scarlet bright,
In spikes, in branches, and in stars,
Green, red, and pearly white.
This heap of earth o'ergrown with moss,
Which close beside the thorn you see,   50
So fresh in all its beauteous dyes,
Is like an infant's grave in size
As like as like can be:
But never, never any where,
An infant's grave was half so fair.

VI.

Now would you see this aged thorn,
This pond and beauteous hill of moss,
You must take care and chuse your time
The mountain when to cross.
For oft there sits, between the heap
That's like an infant's grave in size,
And that same pond of which I spoke,
A woman in a scarlet cloak,
And to herself she cries,
'Oh misery! oh misery!
Oh woe is me! oh misery!'

VII.

At all times of the day and night
This wretched woman thither goes,
And she is known to every star,
And every wind that blows;
And there beside the thorn she sits
When the blue day-light's in the skies,
And when the whirlwind's on the hill,
Or frosty air is keen and still,
And to herself she cries,
'Oh misery! oh misery!
Oh woe is me! oh misery!'

VIII.

'Now wherefore thus, by day and night,
In rain, in tempest, and in snow,
Thus to the dreary mountain-top
Does this poor woman go?

And why sits she beside the thorn
When the blue day-light's in the sky,
Or when the whirlwind's on the hill,
Or frosty air is keen and still,
And wherefore does she cry? –
Oh wherefore? wherefore? tell me why
Does she repeat that doleful cry?'

IX.

I cannot tell; I wish I could;
For the true reason no one knows,   90
But if you'd gladly view the spot,
The spot to which she goes;
The heap that's like an infant's grave,
The pond – and thorn, so old and grey,
Pass by her door – tis seldom shut –
And if you see her in her hut,
Then to the spot away! –
I never heard of such as dare
Approach the spot when she is there.

X.

'But wherefore to the mountain-top   100
Can this unhappy woman go,
Whatever star is in the skies,
Whatever wind may blow?'
Nay rack your brain – 'tis all in vain,
I'll tell you every thing I know;
But to the thorn, and to the pond
Which is a little step beyond,
I wish that you would go:
Perhaps when you are at the place
You something of her tale may trace.   110

XI.

I'll give you the best help I can:
Before you up the mountain go,
Up to the dreary mountain-top,
I'll tell you all I know.
'Tis now some two and twenty years,
Since she (her name is Martha Ray)
Gave with a maiden's true good will
Her company to Stephen Hill;
And she was blithe and gay,
And she was happy, happy still
Whene'er she thought of Stephen Hill.

XII.

And they had fixed the wedding-day,
The morning that must wed them both;
But Stephen to another maid
Had sworn another oath;
And with this other maid to church
Unthinking Stephen went –
Poor Martha! on that woful day
A cruel, cruel fire, they say,
Into her bones was sent:
It dried her body like a cinder,
And almost turned her brain to tinder.

XIII.

They say, full six months after this,
While yet the summer-leaves were green,
She to the mountain-top would go,
And there was often seen.

120

130

'Tis said, a child was in her womb,
As now to any eye was plain;
She was with child, and she was mad,
Yet often she was sober sad   140
From her exceeding pain.
Oh me! ten thousand times I'd rather
That he had died, that cruel father!

XIV.

Sad case for such a brain to hold
Communion with a stirring child!
Sad case, as you may think, for one
Who had a brain so wild!
Last Christmas when we talked of this,
Old Farmer Simpson did maintain,
That in her womb the infant wrought   150
About its mother's heart, and brought
Her senses back again:
And when at last her time drew near,
Her looks were calm, her senses clear.

XV.

No more I know, I wish I did,
And I would tell it all to you;
For what became of this poor child
There's none that ever knew:
And if a child was born or no,
There's no one that could ever tell;   160
And if 'twas born alive or dead,
There's no one knows, as I have said,
But some remember well,
That Martha Ray about this time
Would up the mountain often climb.

XVI.

And all that winter, when at night
The wind blew from the mountain-peak,
'Twas worth your while, though in the dark,
The church-yard path to seek:
170   For many a time and oft were heard
Cries coming from the mountain-head,
Some plainly living voices were,
And others, I've heard many swear,
Were voices of the dead:
I cannot think, whate'er they say,
They had to do with Martha Ray.

XVII.

But that she goes to this old thorn,
The thorn which I've described to you,
And there sits in a scarlet cloak,
180   I will be sworn is true.
For one day with my telescope,
To view the ocean wide and bright,
When to this country first I came,
Ere I had heard of Martha's name,
I climbed the mountain's height:
A storm came on, and I could see
No object higher than my knee.

XVIII.

'Twas mist and rain, and storm and rain,
No screen, no fence could I discover,
190   And then the wind! in faith, it was
A wind full ten times over.

I looked around, I thought I saw
A jutting crag, and off I ran,
Head-foremost, through the driving rain,
The shelter of the crag to gain,
And, as I am a man,
Instead of jutting crag, I found
A woman seated on the ground.

XIX.

I did not speak – I saw her face,
Her face it was enough for me;   200
I turned about and heard her cry,
'O misery! O misery!'
And there she sits, until the moon
Through half the clear blue sky will go,
And when the little breezes make
The waters of the pond to shake,
As all the country know,
She shudders and you hear her cry,
'Oh misery! oh misery!'

XX.

'But what's the thorn? and what's the pond? 210
And what's the hill of moss to her?
And what's the creeping breeze that comes
The little pond to stir?'
I cannot tell; but some will say
She hanged her baby on the tree,
Some say she drowned it in the pond,
Which is a little step beyond,
But all and each agree,
The little babe was buried there,
Beneath that hill of moss so fair.   220

XXI.

I've heard the scarlet moss is red
With drops of that poor infant's blood;
But kill a new-born infant thus!
I do not think she could.
Some say, if to the pond you go,
And fix on it a steady view,
The shadow of a babe you trace,
A baby and a baby's face,
And that it looks at you;
230   Whene'er you look on it, 'tis plain
The baby looks at you again.

XXII.

And some had sworn an oath that she
Should be to public justice brought;
And for the little infant's bones
With spades they would have sought.
But then the beauteous hill of moss
Before their eyes began to stir;
And for full fifty yards around,
The grass it shook upon the ground;
240   But all do still aver
The little babe is buried there,
Beneath that hill of moss so fair.

XXIII.

I cannot tell how this may be,
But plain it is, the thorn is bound
With heavy tufts of moss, that strive
To drag it to the ground.
And this I know, full many a time,
When she was on the mountain high,
By day, and in the silent night,

44

When all the stars shone clear and bright,   250
That I have heard her cry,
'Oh misery! oh misery!
O woe is me! oh misery!'

'A whirl-blast from behind the hill'

A whirl-blast from behind the hill
Rushed o'er the wood with startling sound:
Then all at once the air was still,
And showers of hail-stones pattered round.
Where leafless Oaks towered high above,
I sate within an undergrove
Of tallest hollies, tall and green,
A fairer bower was never seen.
From year to year the spacious floor
With withered leaves is covered o'er,   10
You could not lay a hair between:
And all the year the bower is green.
But see! where'er the hailstones drop
The withered leaves all skip and hop,
There's not a breeze – no breath of air –
Yet here, and there, and every where
Along the floor, beneath the shade
By those embowering hollies made,
The leaves in myriads jump and spring,
As if with pipes and music rare   20
Some Robin Good-fellow were there,
And all those leaves, that jump and spring,
Were each a joyous, living thing.

Oh! grant me Heaven a heart at ease
That I may never cease to find,
Even in appearances like these
Enough to nourish and to stir my mind!

45

The Idiot Boy

'Tis eight o'clock, – a clear March night,
The moon is up – the sky is blue,
The owlet in the moonlight air,
He shouts from nobody knows where;
He lengthens out his lonely shout,
Halloo! halloo! a long halloo!

– Why bustle thus about your door,
What means this bustle, Betty Foy?
Why are you in this mighty fret?
And why on horseback have you set
Him whom you love, your idiot boy?

Beneath the moon that shines so bright,
Till she is tired, let Betty Foy
With girt and stirrup fiddle-faddle;
But wherefore set upon a saddle
Him whom she loves, her idiot boy?

There's scarce a soul that's out of bed;
Good Betty! put him down again;
His lips with joy they burr at you,
But, Betty! what has he to do
With stirrup, saddle, or with rein?

The world will say 'tis very idle,
Bethink you of the time of night;
There's not a mother, no not one,
But when she hears what you have done,
Oh! Betty she'll be in a fright.

But Betty's bent on her intent,
For her good neighbour, Susan Gale,
Old Susan, she who dwells alone,
Is sick, and makes a piteous moan,   30
As if her very life would fail.

There's not a house within a mile,
No hand to help them in distress:
Old Susan lies a-bed in pain,
And sorely puzzled are the twain,
For what she ails they cannot guess.

And Betty's husband's at the wood,
Where by the week he doth abide,
A woodman in the distant vale;
There's none to help poor Susan Gale,   40
What must be done? what will betide?

And Betty from the lane has fetched
Her pony, that is mild and good,
Whether he be in joy or pain,
Feeding at will along the lane,
Or bringing faggots from the wood.

And he is all in travelling trim,
And by the moonlight, Betty Foy
Has up upon the saddle set,
The like was never heard of yet,   50
Him whom she loves, her idiot boy.

And he must post without delay
Across the bridge that's in the dale,
And by the church, and o'er the down,
To bring a doctor from the town,
Or she will die, old Susan Gale.

There is no need of boot or spur,
There is no need of whip or wand,
For Johnny has his holly-bough,
60 And with a hurly-burly now
He shakes the green bough in his hand.

And Betty o'er and o'er has told
The boy who is her best delight,
Both what to follow, what to shun,
What do, and what to leave undone,
How turn to left, and how to right.

And Betty's most especial charge,
Was, 'Johnny! Johnny! mind that you
Come home again, nor stop at all,
70 Come home again, what'er befal,
My Johnny do, I pray you do.'

To this did Johnny answer make,
Both with his head, and with his hand,
And proudly shook the bridle too,
And then! his words were not a few,
Which Betty well could understand.

And now that Johnny is just going,
Though Betty's in a mighty flurry,
She gently pats the pony's side,
80 On which her idiot boy must ride,
And seems no longer in a hurry.

But when the pony moved his legs,
Oh! then for the poor idiot boy!
For joy he cannot hold the bridle,
For joy his head and heels are idle,
He's idle all for very joy.

And while the pony moves his legs,
In Johnny's left-hand you may see,
The green bough's motionless and dead;
The moon that shines above his head   90
Is not more still and mute than he.

His heart it was so full of glee,
That till full fifty yards were gone,
He quite forgot his holly whip,
And all his skill in horsemanship,
Oh! happy, happy, happy John.

And Betty's standing at the door,
And Betty's face with joy o'erflows,
Proud of herself, and proud of him,
She sees him in his travelling trim;   100
How quietly her Johnny goes.

The silence of her idiot boy,
What hopes it sends to Betty's heart!
He's at the guide-post – he turns right,
She watches till he's out of sight,
And Betty will not then depart.

Burr, burr – now Johnny's lips they burr,
As loud as any mill, or near it,
Meek as a lamb the pony moves,
And Johnny makes the noise he loves,   110
And Betty listens, glad to hear it.

Away she hies to Susan Gale:
And Johnny's in a merry tune,
The owlets hoot, the owlets curr,
And Johnny's lips they burr, burr, burr,
And on he goes beneath the moon.

His steed and he right well agree,
For of this pony there's a rumour,
That should he lose his eyes and ears,
120 And should he live a thousand years,
He never will be out of humour.

But then he is a horse that thinks!
And when he thinks his pace is slack;
Now, though he knows poor Johnny well,
Yet for his life he cannot tell
What he has got upon his back.

So through the moonlight lanes they go,
And far into the moonlight dale,
And by the church, and o'er the down,
130 To bring a doctor from the town,
To comfort poor old Susan Gale.

And Betty, now at Susan's side,
Is in the middle of her story,
What comfort Johnny soon will bring,
With many a most diverting thing,
Of Johnny's wit and Johnny's glory.

And Betty's still at Susan's side:
By this time she's not quite so flurried;
Demure with porringer and plate
140 She sits, as if in Susan's fate
Her life and soul were buried.

But Betty, poor good woman! she,
You plainly in her face may read it,
Could lend out of that moment's store
Five years of happiness or more,
To any that might need it.

But yet I guess that now and then
With Betty all was not so well,
And to the road she turns her ears,
And thence full many a sound she hears,   150
Which she to Susan will not tell.

Poor Susan moans, poor Susan groans,
'As sure as there's a moon in heaven,'
Cries Betty, 'he'll be back again;
They'll both be here, 'tis almost ten,
They'll both be here before eleven.'

Poor Susan moans, poor Susan groans,
The clock gives warning for eleven;
'Tis on the stroke – 'If Johnny's near,'
Quoth Betty 'he will soon be here,   160
As sure as there's a moon in heaven.'

The clock is on the stroke of twelve,
And Johnny is not yet in sight,
The moon's in heaven, as Betty sees,
But Betty is not quite at ease;
And Susan has a dreadful night.

And Betty, half an hour ago,
On Johnny vile reflections cast;
'A little idle sauntering thing!'
With other names, an endless string,   170
But now that time is gone and past.

And Betty's drooping at the heart,
That happy time all past and gone,
'How can it be he is so late?
The doctor he has made him wait,
Susan! they'll both be here anon.'

And Susan's growing worse and worse,
And Betty's in a sad quandary;
And then there's nobody to say
180   If she must go or she must stay:
 – She's in a sad quandary.

The clock is on the stroke of one;
But neither Doctor nor his guide
Appear along the moonlight road,
There's neither horse nor man abroad,
And Betty's still at Susan's side.

And Susan she begins to fear
Of sad mischances not a few,
That Johnny may perhaps be drowned,
190   Or lost perhaps, and never found;
Which they must both for ever rue.

She prefaced half a hint of this
With, 'God forbid it should be true!'
At the first word that Susan said
Cried Betty, rising from the bed,
'Susan, I'd gladly stay with you.

'I must be gone, I must away,
Consider, Johnny's but half-wise;
Susan, we must take care of him,
200   If he is hurt in life or limb' –
'Oh God forbid!' poor Susan cries.

'What can I do?' says Betty, going,
'What can I do to ease your pain?
Good Susan tell me, and I'll stay;
I fear you're in a dreadful way,
But I shall soon be back again.'

'Good Betty go, good Betty go,
There's nothing that can ease my pain.'
Then off she hies, but with a prayer
That God poor Susan's life would spare,   210
Till she comes back again.

So, through the moonlight lane she goes,
And far into the moonlight dale;
And how she ran, and how she walked,
And all that to herself she talked,
Would surely be a tedious tale.

In high and low, above, below,
In great and small, in round and square,
In tree and tower was Johnny seen,
In bush and brake, in black and green,   220
'Twas Johnny, Johnny, every where.

She's past the bridge that's in the dale,
And now the thought torments her sore,
Johnny perhaps his horse forsook,
To hunt the moon that's in the brook,
And never will be heard of more.

And now she's high upon the down,
Alone amid a prospect wide;
There's neither Johnny nor his horse,
Among the fern or in the gorse;   230
There's neither doctor nor his guide.

'Oh saints! what is become of him?
Perhaps he's climbed into an oak,
Where he will stay till he is dead;
Or sadly he has been misled,
And joined the wandering gypsey-folk.

'Or him that wicked pony's carried
To the dark cave, the goblins' hall,
Or in the castle he's pursuing,
Among the ghosts, his own undoing;
Or playing with the waterfall.'

At poor old Susan then she railed,
While to the town she posts away;
'If Susan had not been so ill,
Alas! I should have had him still,
My Johnny, till my dying day.'

Poor Betty! in this sad distemper,
The doctor's self would hardly spare,
Unworthy things she talked and wild,
Even he, of cattle the most mild,
The pony had his share.

And now she's got into the town,
And to the doctor's door she hies;
'Tis silence all on every side;
The town so long, the town so wide,
Is silent as the skies.

And now she's at the doctor's door,
She lifts the knocker, rap, rap, rap,
The doctor at the casement shews,
His glimmering eyes that peep and doze;
And one hand rubs his old night-cap.

'Oh Doctor! Doctor! where's my Johnny?'
'I'm here, what is't you want with me?'
'Oh Sir! you know I'm Betty Foy,
And I have lost my poor dear boy,
You know him – him you often see;

240

250

260

'He's not so wise as some folks be,'
'The devil take his wisdom!' said
The Doctor, looking somewhat grim,
'What, woman! should I know of him?'   270
And, grumbling, he went back to bed.

'O woe is me! O woe is me!
Here will I die; here will I die;
I thought to find my Johnny here,
But he is neither far nor near,
Oh! what a wretched mother I!'

She stops, she stands, she looks about,
Which way to turn she cannot tell.
Poor Betty! it would ease her pain
If she had heart to knock again;   280
– The clock strikes three – a dismal knell!

Then up along the town she hies,
No wonder if her senses fail,
This piteous news so much it shocked her,
She quite forgot to send the Doctor,
To comfort poor old Susan Gale.

And now she's high upon the down,
And she can see a mile of road,
'Oh cruel! I'm almost three-score;
Such night as this was ne'er before,   290
There's not a single soul abroad.'

She listens, but she cannot hear
The foot of horse, the voice of man;
The streams with softest sound are flowing,
The grass you almost hear it growing,
You hear it now if e'er you can.

The owlets through the long blue night
Are shouting to each other still:
Fond lovers, yet not quite hob nob,
They lengthen out the tremulous sob,
That echoes far from hill to hill.

Poor Betty now has lost all hope,
Her thoughts are bent on deadly sin;
A green-grown pond she just has passed,
And from the brink she hurries fast,
Lest she should drown herself therein.

And now she sits her down and weeps;
Such tears she never shed before;
'Oh dear, dear pony! my sweet joy!
Oh carry back my idiot boy!
And we will ne'er o'erload thee more.'

A thought is come into her head;
'The pony he is mild and good,
And we have always used him well;
Perhaps he's gone along the dell,
And carried Johnny to the wood.'

Then up she springs as if on wings;
She thinks no more of deadly sin;
If Betty fifty ponds should see,
The last of all her thoughts would be,
To drown herself therein.

Oh reader! now that I might tell
What Johnny and his horse are doing!
What they've been doing all this time,
Oh could I put it into rhyme,
A most delightful tale pursuing!

Perhaps, and no unlikely thought!
He with his pony now doth roam
The cliffs and peaks so high that are,
To lay his hands upon a star,   330
And in his pocket bring it home.

Perhaps he's turned himself about,
His face unto his horse's tail,
And still and mute, in wonder lost,
All like a silent horseman-ghost,
He travels on along the vale.

And now, perhaps, he's hunting sheep,
A fierce and dreadful hunter he!
Yon valley, that's so trim and green,
In five months' time, should he be seen,   340
A desart wilderness will be.

Perhaps, with head and heels on fire,
And like the very soul of evil,
He's galloping away, away,
And so he'll gallop on for aye,
The bane of all that dread the devil.

I to the muses have been bound,
These fourteen years, by strong indentures;
Oh gentle muses! let me tell
But half of what to him befel,   350
For sure he met with strange adventures.

Oh gentle muses! is this kind?
Why will ye thus my suit repel?
Why of your further aid bereave me?
And can ye thus unfriended leave me?
Ye muses! whom I love so well.

Who's yon, that, near the waterfall,
Which thunders down with headlong force,
Beneath the moon, yet shining fair,
360   As careless as if nothing were,
Sits upright on a feeding horse?

Unto his horse, that's feeding free,
He seems, I think, the rein to give;
Of moon or stars he takes no heed;
Of such we in romances read,
– 'Tis Johnny! Johnny! as I live.

And that's the very pony too.
Where is she, where is Betty Foy?
She hardly can sustain her fears;
370   The roaring water-fall she hears,
And cannot find her idiot boy.

Your pony's worth his weight in gold,
Then calm your terrors, Betty Foy!
She's coming from among the trees,
And now, all full in view, she sees
Him whom she loves, her idiot boy.

And Betty sees the pony too:
Why stand you thus Good Betty Foy?
It is no goblin, 'tis no ghost,
380   'Tis he whom you so long have lost,
He whom you love, your idiot boy.

She looks again – her arms are up –
She screams – she cannot move for joy;
She darts as with a torrent's force,
She almost has o'erturned the horse,
And fast she holds her idiot boy.

And Johnny burrs and laughs aloud,
Whether in cunning or in joy,
I cannot tell; but while he laughs,
Betty a drunken pleasure quaffs,   390
To hear again her idiot boy.

And now she's at the pony's tail,
And now she's at the pony's head,
On that side now, and now on this,
And almost stifled with her bliss,
A few sad tears does Betty shed.

She kisses o'er and o'er again,
Him whom she loves, her idiot boy,
She's happy here, she's happy there,
She is uneasy every where;   400
Her limbs are all alive with joy.

She pats the pony, where or when
She knows not, happy Betty Foy!
The little pony glad may be,
But he is milder far than she,
You hardly can perceive his joy.

'Oh! Johnny, never mind the Doctor;
You've done your best, and that is all.'
She took the reins, when this was said,
And gently turned the pony's head   410
From the loud water-fall.

By this the stars were almost gone,
The moon was setting on the hill,
So pale you scarcely looked at her:
The little birds began to stir,
Though yet their tongues were still.

The pony, Betty, and her boy,
Wind slowly through the woody dale:
And who is she, be-times abroad,
420   That hobbles up the steep rough road?
Who is it, but old Susan Gale?

Long Susan lay deep lost in thought,
And many dreadful fears beset her,
Both for her messenger and nurse;
And as her mind grew worse and worse,
Her body it grew better.

She turned, she tossed herself in bed,
On all sides doubts and terrors met her;
Point after point did she discuss;
430   And while her mind was fighting thus,
Her body still grew better.

'Alas! what is become of them?
These fears can never be endured,
I'll to the wood.' – The word scarce said,
Did Susan rise up from her bed,
As if by magic cured.

Away she posts up hill and down,
And to the wood at length is come,
She spies her friends, she shouts a greeting;
440   Oh me! it is a merry meeting,
As ever was in Christendom.

The owls have hardly sung their last,
While our four travellers homeward wend;
The owls have hooted all night long,
And with the owls began my song,
And with the owls must end.

For while they all were travelling home,
Cried Betty, 'Tell us Johnny, do,
Where all this long night you have been,
What you have heard, what you have seen,   450
And Johnny, mind you tell us true.'

Now Johnny all night long had heard
The owls in tuneful concert strive;
No doubt too he the moon had seen;
For in the moonlight he had been
From eight o'clock till five.

And thus to Betty's question, he
Made answer, like a traveller bold,
(His very words I give to you,)
'The cocks did crow to-whoo, to-whoo,   460
And the sun did shine so cold.'
– Thus answered Johnny in his glory,
And that was all his travel's story.

Lines

Written in Early Spring

I heard a thousand blended notes,
While in a grove I sate reclined,
In that sweet mood when pleasant thoughts
Bring sad thoughts to the mind.

To her fair works did nature link
The human soul that through me ran;
And much it grieved my heart to think
What man has made of man.

Through primrose-tufts, in that sweet bower,
10   The periwinkle trailed its wreathes;
And 'tis my faith that every flower
Enjoys the air it breathes.

The birds around me hopped and played:
Their thoughts I cannot measure,
But the least motion which they made,
It seemed a thrill of pleasure.

The budding twigs spread out their fan,
To catch the breezy air;
And I must think, do all I can,
20   That there was pleasure there.

If I these thoughts may not prevent,
If such be of my creed the plan,
Have I not reason to lament
What man has made of man?

Anecdote for Fathers,

Shewing how the Art of Lying May be Taught

I have a boy of five years old,
His face is fair and fresh to see;
His limbs are cast in beauty's mould,
And dearly he loves me.

One morn we strolled on our dry walk,
Our quiet house all full in view,
And held such intermitted talk
As we are wont to do.

My thoughts on former pleasures ran;
I thought of Kilve's delightful shore,
My pleasant home, when spring began,
A long, long year before.

A day it was when I could bear
To think, and think, and think again;
With so much happiness to spare,
I could not feel a pain.

My boy was by my side, so slim
And graceful in his rustic dress!
And oftentimes I talked to him,
In very idleness.

The young lambs ran a pretty race;
The morning sun shone bright and warm;
'Kilve,' said I, 'was a pleasant place,
And so is Liswyn farm.

'My little boy, which like you more,'
I said and took him by the arm —
'Our home by Kilve's delightful shore,
Or here at Liswyn farm?

'And tell me, had you rather be,'
I said and held him by the arm,
'At Kilve's smooth shore by the green sea,
Or here at Liswyn farm?'

In careless mood he looked at me,
While still I held him by the arm,
And said, 'At Kilve I'd rather be
Than here at Liswyn farm.'

'Now, little Edward, say why so;
My little Edward, tell me why;'
'I cannot tell, I do not know.'
'Why this is strange,' said I.

'For, here are woods and green-hills warm;
There surely must some reason be
Why you would change sweet Liswyn farm
For Kilve by the green sea.'

At this, my boy, so fair and slim,
Hung down his head, nor made reply;
And five times did I say to him,
'Why? Edward, tell me why?'

His head he raised – there was in sight,
It caught his eye, he saw it plain –
Upon the house-top, glittering bright,
A broad and gilded vane.

Then did the boy his tongue unlock,
And thus to me he made reply;
'At Kilve there was no weather-cock,
And that's the reason why.'

Oh dearest, dearest boy! my heart
For better lore would seldom yearn,
Could I but teach the hundredth part
Of what from thee I learn.

We are Seven

A simple child, dear brother Jim,
That lightly draws its breath,
And feels its life in every limb,
What should it know of death?

I met a little cottage girl,
She was eight years old, she said;
Her hair was thick with many a curl
That clustered round her head.

She had a rustic, woodland air,
And she was wildly clad;   10
Her eyes were fair, and very fair,
– Her beauty made me glad.

'Sisters and brothers, little maid,
How many may you be?'
'How many? seven in all,' she said,
And wondering looked at me.

'And where are they, I pray you tell?'
She answered, 'Seven are we,
And two of us at Conway dwell,
And two are gone to sea.   20

'Two of us in the church-yard lie,
My sister and my brother,
And in the church-yard cottage, I
Dwell near them with my mother.'

'You say that two at Conway dwell,
And two are gone to sea,
Yet you are seven; I pray you tell
Sweet Maid, how this may be?'

65

Then did the little Maid reply,
'Seven boys and girls are we;
Two of us in the church-yard lie,
Beneath the church-yard tree.'

'You run about, my little maid,
Your limbs they are alive;
If two are in the church-yard laid,
Then ye are only five.'

'Their graves are green, they may be seen,'
The little Maid replied,
'Twelve steps or more from my mother's door,
And they are side by side.

'My stockings there I often knit,
My 'kerchief there I hem;
And there upon the ground I sit –
I sit and sing to them.

'And often after sunset, Sir,
When it is light and fair,
I take my little porringer,
And eat my supper there.

'The first that died was little Jane;
In bed she moaning lay,
Till God released her of her pain,
And then she went away.

'So in the church-yard she was laid,
And all the summer dry,
Together round her grave we played,
My brother John and I.

'And when the ground was white with snow,
And I could run and slide,
My brother John was forced to go,
And he lies by her side.'

60

'How many are you then,' said I,
'If they two are in Heaven?'
The little Maiden did reply,
'O Master! we are seven.'

'But they are dead; those two are dead!
Their spirits are in heaven!'
'Twas throwing words away; for still
The little Maid would have her will,
And said, 'Nay, we are seven!'

Simon Lee, the Old Huntsman,

with an Incident in Which He was Concerned

In the sweet shire of Cardigan,
Not far from pleasant Ivor-hall,
An old man dwells, a little man,
I've heard he once was tall.
Of years he has upon his back,
No doubt, a burthen weighty;
He says he is three score and ten,
But others say he's eighty.

A long blue livery-coat has he,
That's fair behind, and fair before;
Yet, meet him where you will, you see
At once that he is poor.

10

Full five and twenty years he lived
A running huntsman merry;
And, though he has but one eye left,
His cheek is like a cherry.

No man like him the horn could sound,
And no man was so full of glee;
To say the least, four counties round
Had heard of Simon Lee;
His master's dead, and no one now
Dwells in the hall of Ivor;
Men, dogs, and horses, all are dead;
He is the sole survivor.

His hunting feats have him bereft
Of his right eye, as you may see:
And then, what limbs those feats have left
To poor old Simon Lee!
He has no son, he has no child,
His wife, an aged woman,
Lives with him, near the waterfall,
Upon the village common.

And he is lean and he is sick,
His little body's half awry
His ancles they are swoln and thick;
His legs are thin and dry.
When he was young he little knew
Of husbandry or tillage;
And now he's forced to work, though weak,
–The weakest in the village.

He all the country could outrun,
Could leave both man and horse behind;
And often, ere the race was done,
He reeled and was stone-blind.

And still there's something in the world
At which his heart rejoices;
For when the chiming hounds are out,
He dearly loves their voices!

Old Ruth works out of doors with him,
And does what Simon cannot do;   50
For she, not over stout of limb,
Is stouter of the two.
And though you with your utmost skill
From labour could not wean them,
Alas! 'tis very little, all
Which they can do between them.

Beside their moss-grown hut of clay,
Not twenty paces from the door,
A scrap of land they have, but they
Are poorest of the poor.   60
This scrap of land he from the heath
Enclosed when he was stronger;
But what avails the land to them,
Which they can till no longer?

Few months of life has he in store,
As he to you will tell,
For still, the more he works, the more
His poor old ancles swell.
My gentle reader, I perceive
How patiently you've waited,   70
And I'm afraid that you expect
Some tale will be related.

O reader! had you in your mind
Such stores as silent thought can bring,
O gentle reader! you would find
A tale in every thing.

What more I have to say is short,
I hope you'll kindly take it;
It is no tale; but should you think,
Perhaps a tale you'll make it.

One summer-day I chanced to see
This old man doing all he could
About the root of an old tree,
A stump of rotten wood.
The mattock tottered in his hand;
So vain was his endeavour
That at the root of the old tree
He might have worked for ever.

'You're overtasked, good Simon Lee,
Give me your tool' to him I said;
And at the word right gladly he
Received my proffered aid.
I struck, and with a single blow
The tangled root I severed,
At which the poor old man so long
And vainly had endeavoured.

The tears into his eyes were brought,
And thanks and praises seemed to run
So fast out of his heart, I thought
They never would have done.
— I've heard of hearts unkind, kind deeds
With coldness still returning.
Alas! the gratitude of men
Has oftner left me mourning.

The Last of the Flock

In distant countries I have been,
And yet I have not often seen
A healthy man, a man full grown,
Weep in the public roads alone.
But such a one, on English ground,
And in the broad high-way, I met;
Along the broad high-way he came,
His cheeks with tears were wet.
Sturdy he seemed, though he was sad;
And in his arms a lamb he had.   10

He saw me, and he turned aside,
As if he wished himself to hide:
Then with his coat he made essay
To wipe those briny tears away.
I followed him, and said, 'My friend
What ails you? wherefore weep you so?'
– 'Shame on me, Sir! this lusty lamb,
He makes my tears to flow.
To-day I fetched him from the rock;
He is the last of all my flock.   20

'When I was young, a single man,
And after youthful follies ran,
Though little given to care and thought,
Yet, so it was, a ewe I bought;
And other sheep from her I raised,
As healthy sheep as you might see,
And then I married, and was rich
As I could wish to be;
Of sheep I numbered a full score,
And every year encreased my store.   30

71

'Year after year my stock it grew,
And from this one, this single ewe,
Full fifty comely sheep I raised,
As sweet a flock as ever grazed!
Upon the mountain did they feed;
They throve, and we at home did thrive.
– This lusty lamb of all my store
Is all that is alive:
And now I care not if we die,
And perish all of poverty.

'Ten children, Sir! had I to feed,
Hard labour in a time of need!
My pride was tamed, and in our grief,
I of the parish asked relief.
They said I was a wealthy man;
My sheep upon the mountain fed,
And it was fit that thence I took
Whereof to buy us bread:
"Do this; how can we give to you,"
They cried, "what to the poor is due?"

'I sold a sheep as they had said,
And bought my little children bread,
And they were healthy with their food;
For me it never did me good.
A woeful time it was for me,
To see the end of all my gains,
The pretty flock which I had reared
With all my care and pains,
To see it melt like snow away!
For me it was a woeful day.

'Another still! and still another!
A little lamb, and then its mother!
It was a vein that never stopped,
Like blood-drops from my heart they dropped.
Till thirty were not left alive

72

They dwindled, dwindled, one by one,
And I may say that many a time
I wished they all were gone:
They dwindled one by one away;
For me it was a woeful day.   70

'To wicked deeds I was inclined,
And wicked fancies crossed my mind,
And every man I chanced to see,
I thought he knew some ill of me.
No peace, no comfort could I find,
No ease, within doors or without,
And crazily, and wearily,
I went my work about.
Oft-times I thought to run away;
For me it was a woeful day.   80

'Sir! 'twas a precious flock to me,
As dear as my own children be;
For daily with my growing store
I loved my children more and more.
Alas! it was an evil time;
God cursed me in my sore distress,
I prayed, yet every day I thought
I loved my children less;
And every week, and every day,
My flock, it seemed to melt away.   90

'They dwindled, Sir, sad sight to see!
From ten to five, from five to three,
A lamb, a weather, and a ewe;
And then at last, from three to two;
And of my fifty, yesterday
I had but only one,
And here it lies upon my arm,
Alas! and I have none;
To-day I fetched it from the rock;
It is the last of all my flock.'   100

Expostulation and Reply

'Why William, on that old grey stone,
Thus for the length of half a day,
Why William, sit you thus alone,
And dream your time away?

'Where are your books? that light bequeathed
To beings else forlorn and blind!
Up! Up! and drink the spirit breathed
From dead men to their kind.

'You look round on your mother earth,
As if she for no purpose bore you;
As if you were her first-born birth,
And none had lived before you!'

One morning thus, by Esthwaite lake,
When life was sweet I knew not why,
To me my good friend Matthew spake,
And thus I made reply.

'The eye it cannot chuse but see,
We cannot bid the ear be still;
Our bodies feel, where'er they be,
Against, or with our will.

'Nor less I deem that there are powers,
Which of themselves our minds impress,
That we can feed this mind of ours,
In a wise passiveness.

'Think you, mid all this mighty sum
Of things for ever speaking,
That nothing of itself will come,
But we must still be seeking?

' – Then ask not wherefore, here, alone,
Conversing as I may,
I sit upon this old grey stone,
And dream my time away.'   30

The Tables Turned;

an Evening Scene, on the Same Subject

Up! up! my friend, and clear your looks,
Why all this toil and trouble?
Up! up! my friend, and quit your books,
Or surely you'll grow double.

The sun above the mountain's head,
A freshening lustre mellow,
Through all the long green fields has spread,
His first sweet evening yellow.

Books! 'tis a dull and endless strife,
Come, hear the woodland linnet,   10
How sweet his music; on my life
There's more of wisdom in it.

And hark! how blithe the throstle sings!
And he is no mean preacher;
Come forth into the light of things,
Let Nature be your teacher.

She has a world of ready wealth,
Our minds and hearts to bless –
Spontaneous wisdom breathed by health,
Truth breathed by cheerfulness.   20

One impulse from a vernal wood
May teach you more of man;
Of moral evil and of good,
Than all the sages can.

Sweet is the lore which nature brings;
Our meddling intellect
Mishapes the beauteous forms of things;
– We murder to dissect.

Enough of science and of art;
30   Close up these barren leaves;
Come forth, and bring with you a heart
That watches and receives.

Lines Written a Few Miles above Tintern Abbey,

on Revisiting the Banks of the Wye during a Tour, July 13, 1798

Five years have passed; five summers, with the length
Of five long winters! and again I hear
These waters, rolling from their mountain-springs
With a sweet inland murmur. – Once again
Do I behold these steep and lofty cliffs,
Which on a wild secluded scene impress
Thoughts of more deep seclusion; and connect
The landscape with the quiet of the sky.
The day is come when I again repose
10   Here, under this dark sycamore, and view
These plots of cottage-ground, these orchard-tufts,
Which, at this season, with their unripe fruits,
Among the woods and copses lose themselves,
Nor, with their green and simple hue, disturb

The wild green landscape. Once again I see
These hedge-rows, hardly hedge-rows, little lines
Of sportive wood run wild; these pastoral farms
Green to the very door; and wreathes of smoke
Sent up, in silence, from among the trees,
With some uncertain notice, as might seem,   20
Of vagrant dwellers in the houseless woods,
Or of some hermit's cave, where by his fire
The hermit sits alone.

                Though absent long,
These forms of beauty have not been to me,
As is a landscape to a blind man's eye:
But oft, in lonely rooms, and mid the din
Of towns and cities, I have owed to them,
In hours of weariness, sensations sweet,
Felt in the blood, and felt along the heart,
And passing even into my purer mind   30
With tranquil restoration: – feelings too
Of unremembered pleasure; such, perhaps,
As may have had no trivial influence
On that best portion of a good man's life;
His little, nameless, unremembered acts
Of kindness and of love. Nor less, I trust,
To them I may have owed another gift,
Of aspect more sublime; that blessed mood,
In which the burthen of the mystery,
In which the heavy and the weary weight   40
Of all this unintelligible world
Is lightened: – that serene and blessed mood,
In which the affections gently lead us on,
Until, the breath of this corporeal frame,
And even the motion of our human blood
Almost suspended, we are laid asleep
In body, and become a living soul:
While with an eye made quiet by the power
Of harmony, and the deep power of joy,
We see into the life of things.
         . .

50   If this
Be but a vain belief, yet, oh! how oft,
In darkness, and amid the many shapes
Of joyless day-light; when the fretful stir
Unprofitable, and the fever of the world,
Have hung upon the beatings of my heart,
How oft, in spirit, have I turned to thee
O sylvan Wye! Thou wanderer through the wood
How often has my spirit turned to thee!

And now, with gleams of half-extinguished thought,
60   With many recognitions dim and faint,
And somewhat of a sad perplexity,
The picture of the mind revives again:
While here I stand, not only with the sense
Of present pleasure, but with pleasing thoughts
That in this moment there is life and food
For future years. And so I dare to hope
Though changed, no doubt, from what I was, when first
I came among these hills; when like a roe
I bounded o'er the mountains, by the sides
70   Of the deep rivers, and the lonely streams,
Wherever nature led; more like a man
Flying from something that he dreads, than one
Who sought the thing he loved. For nature then
(The coarser pleasures of my boyish days,
And their glad animal movements all gone by,)
To me was all in all. – I cannot paint
What then I was. The sounding cataract
Haunted me like a passion: the tall rock,
The mountain, and the deep and gloomy wood,
80   Their colours and their forms, were then to me
An appetite: a feeling and a love,
That had no need of a remoter charm,
By thought supplied, or any interest
Unborrowed from the eye. – That time is past,
And all its aching joys are now no more,
And all its dizzy raptures. Not for this

Faint I, nor mourn nor murmur: other gifts
Have followed, for such loss, I would believe,
Abundant recompence. For I have learned
To look on nature, not as in the hour   90
Of thoughtless youth, but hearing oftentimes
The still, sad music of humanity,
Not harsh nor grating, though of ample power
To chasten and subdue. And I have felt
A presence that disturbs me with the joy
Of elevated thoughts; a sense sublime
Of something far more deeply interfused,
Whose dwelling is the light of setting suns,
And the round ocean, and the living air,
And the blue sky, and in the mind of man,   100
A motion and a spirit, that impels
All thinking things, all objects of all thought,
And rolls through all things. Therefore am I still
A lover of the meadows and the woods,
And mountains; and of all that we behold
From this green earth; of all the mighty world
Of eye and ear, both what they half-create,
And what perceive; well pleased to recognize
In nature and the language of the sense,
The anchor of my purest thoughts, the nurse,   110
The guide, the guardian of my heart, and soul
Of all my moral being.

                Nor, perchance,
If I were not thus taught, should I the more
Suffer my genial spirits to decay:
For thou art with me, here, upon the banks
Of this fair river; thou, my dearest Friend,
My dear, dear Friend, and in thy voice I catch
The language of my former heart, and read
My former pleasures in the shooting lights
Of thy wild eyes. Oh! yet a little while   120
May I behold in thee what I was once,
My dear, dear Sister! And this prayer I make,

Knowing that Nature never did betray
The heart that loved her; 'tis her privilege,
Through all the years of this our life, to lead
From joy to joy: for she can so inform
The mind that is within us, so impress
With quietness and beauty, and so feed
With lofty thoughts, that neither evil tongues,
130 Rash judgments, nor the sneers of selfish men,
Nor greetings where no kindness is, nor all
The dreary intercourse of daily life,
Shall e'er prevail against us, or disturb
Our cheerful faith that all which we behold
Is full of blessings. Therefore let the moon
Shine on thee in thy solitary walk;
And let the misty mountain winds be free
To blow against thee: and in after years,
When these wild ecstasies shall be matured
140 Into a sober pleasure, when thy mind
Shall be a mansion for all lovely forms,
Thy memory be as a dwelling-place
For all sweet sounds and harmonies; Oh! then,
If solitude, or fear, or pain, or grief,
Should be thy portion, with what healing thoughts
Of tender joy wilt thou remember me,
And these my exhortations! Nor, perchance,
If I should be, where I no more can hear
Thy voice, nor catch from thy wild eyes these gleams
150 Of past existence, wilt thou then forget
That on the banks of this delightful stream
We stood together; and that I, so long
A worshipper of Nature, hither came,
Unwearied in that service: rather say
With warmer love, oh! with far deeper zeal
Of holier love. Nor wilt thou then forget,
That after many wanderings, many years
Of absence, these steep woods and lofty cliffs,
And this green pastoral landscape, were to me
160 More dear, both for themselves, and for thy sake.

'There was a Boy'

There was a Boy, ye knew him well, ye Cliffs
And Islands of Winander! many a time,
At evening, when the stars had just begun
To move along the edges of the hills,
Rising or setting, would he stand alone,
Beneath the trees, or by the glimmering lake,
And there, with fingers interwoven, both hands
Pressed closely palm to palm and to his mouth
Uplifted, he, as through an instrument,
Blew mimic hootings to the silent owls   10
That they might answer him. And they would shout
Across the wat'ry vale and shout again
Responsive to his call, with quivering peals,
And long halloos, and screams, and echoes loud
Redoubled and redoubled, a wild scene
Of mirth and jocund din. And, when it chanced
That pauses of deep silence mocked his skill,
Then, sometimes, in that silence, while he hung
Listening, a gentle shock of mild surprize
Has carried far into his heart the voice   20
Of mountain torrents, or the visible scene
Would enter unawares into his mind
With all its solemn imagery, its rocks,
Its woods, and that uncertain heaven, received
Into the bosom of the steady lake.

    Fair are the woods, and beauteous is the spot,
The vale where he was born: the Church-yard hangs
Upon a slope above the village school,
And there along that bank when I have passed
At evening, I believe, that near his grave   30
A full half-hour together I have stood,
Mute – for he died when he was ten years old.

'If Nature, for a favorite Child'

In the School of ——— is a tablet on which are
inscribed, in gilt letters, the names of the several persons
who have been Schoolmasters there since the foundation
of the School, with the time at which they entered upon
and quitted their office. Opposite one of those names
the Author wrote the following lines.

If Nature, for a favorite Child
In thee hath tempered so her clay,
That every hour thy heart runs wild
Yet never once doth go astray,

Read o'er these lines; and then review
This tablet, that thus humbly rears
In such diversity of hue
Its history of two hundred years.

– When through this little wreck of fame,
Cypher and syllable, thine eye
Has travelled down to Matthew's name,
Pause with no common sympathy.

And if a sleeping tear should wake
Then be it neither checked nor stayed:
For Matthew a request I make
Which for himself he had not made.

Poor Matthew, all his frolics o'er,
Is silent as a standing pool,
Far from the chimney's merry roar,
And murmur of the village school.

The sighs which Matthew heaved were sighs
Of one tired out with fun and madness;
The tears which came to Matthew's eyes
Were tears of light, the oil of gladness.

Yet sometimes when the secret cup
Of still and serious thought went round
It seemed as if he drank it up,
He felt with spirit so profound.

– Thou soul of God's best earthly mould,
Thou happy soul, and can it be   30
That these two words of glittering gold
Are all that must remain of thee?

The Fountain,

A Conversation

We talked with open heart, and tongue
Affectionate and true,
A pair of Friends, though I was young,
And Matthew seventy-two.

We lay beneath a spreading oak,
Beside a mossy seat,
And from the turf a fountain broke,
And gurgled at our feet.

Now, Matthew, let us try to match
This water's pleasant tune   10
With some old Border-song, or catch
That suits a summer's noon.

Or of the Church-clock and the chimes
Sing here beneath the shade,
That half-mad thing of witty rhymes
Which you last April made!

In silence Matthew lay, and eyed
The spring beneath the tree;
And thus the dear old Man replied,
The grey-haired Man of glee.

'Down to the vale this water steers,
How merrily it goes!
'Twill murmur on a thousand years,
And flow as now it flows.

'And here, on this delightful day,
I cannot chuse but think
How oft, a vigorous Man, I lay
Beside this Fountain's brink.

'My eyes are dim with childish tears,
My heart is idly stirred,
For the same sound is in my ears,
Which in those days I heard.

'Thus fares it still in our decay:
And yet the wiser mind
Mourns less for what age takes away
Than what it leaves behind.

'The blackbird in the summer trees,
The lark upon the hill,
Let loose their carols when they please,
Are quiet when they will.

'With Nature never do *they* wage
A foolish strife; they see
A happy youth, and their old age
Is beautiful and free:

'But we are pressed by heavy laws,
And often, glad no more,
We wear a face of joy, because
We have been glad of yore.

'If there is one who need bemoan
His kindred laid in earth,   50
The household hearts that were his own,
It is the man of mirth.

'My days, my Friend, are almost gone,
My life has been approved,
And many love me, but by none
Am I enough beloved.'

'Now both himself and me he wrongs,
The man who thus complains!
I live and sing my idle songs
Upon these happy plains,   60

'And, Matthew, for thy Children dead
I'll be a son to thee!'
At this he grasped his hands, and said,
'Alas! that cannot be.'

We rose up from the fountain-side,
And down the smooth descent
Of the green sheep-track did we glide,
And through the wood we went,

And, ere we came to Leonard's Rock
He sang those witty rhymes   70
About the crazy old church-clock
And the bewildered chimes.

The Two April Mornings

We walked along, while bright and red
Uprose the morning sun,
And Matthew stopped, he looked, and said,
'The will of God be done!'

A village Schoolmaster was he,
With hair of glittering grey;
As blithe a man as you could see
On a spring holiday.

And on that morning, through the grass,
And by the steaming rills,
We travelled merrily to pass
A day among the hills.

'Our work,' said I, 'was well begun;
Then, from thy breast what thought,
Beneath so beautiful a sun,
So sad a sigh has brought?'

A second time did Matthew stop,
And fixing still his eye
Upon the eastern mountain-top
To me he made reply.

'Yon cloud with that long purple cleft
Brings fresh into my mind
A day like this which I have left
Full thirty years behind.

'And on that slope of springing corn
The self-same crimson hue
Fell from the sky that April morn,
The same which now I view!

86

'With rod and line my silent sport
I plied by Derwent's wave,   30
And, coming to the church, stopped short
Beside my Daughter's grave.

'Nine summers had she scarcely seen
The pride of all the vale;
And then she sang! – she would have been
A very nightingale.

'Six feet in earth my Emma lay,
And yet I loved her more,
For so it seemed, than till that day
I e'er had loved before.   40

'And, turning from her grave, I met
Beside the church-yard Yew
A blooming Girl, whose hair was wet
With points of morning dew.

'A basket on her head she bare,
Her brow was smooth and white,
To see a Child so very fair,
It was a pure delight!

'No fountain from its rocky cave
E'er tripped with foot so free,   50
She seemed as happy as a wave
That dances on the sea.

'There came from me a sigh of pain
Which I could ill confine;
I looked at her and looked again;
– And did not wish her mine.'

Matthew is in his grave, yet now
Methinks I see him stand,
As at that moment, with his bough
Of wilding in his hand.

'*A slumber did my spirit seal*'

A slumber did my spirit seal,
  I had no human fears:
She seemed a thing that could not feel
  The touch of earthly years.

No motion has she now, no force
  She neither hears nor sees
Rolled round in earth's diurnal course
  With rocks and stones and trees!

Song

She dwelt among th' untrodden ways
  Beside the springs of Dove,
A Maid whom there were none to praise
  And very few to love.

A Violet by a mossy stone
  Half-hidden from the Eye!
– Fair, as a star when only one
  Is shining in the sky!

She *lived* unknown, and few could know
  When Lucy ceased to be;
But she is in her Grave, and Oh!
  The difference to me.

'Strange fits of passion I have known'

Strange fits of passion I have known,
And I will dare to tell,
But in the lover's ear alone,
What once to me befel.

When she I loved, was strong and gay
And like a rose in June,
I to her cottage bent my way,
Beneath the evening moon.

Upon the moon I fixed my eye,
All over the wide lea;   10
My horse trudged on, and we drew nigh
Those paths so dear to me.

And now we reached the orchard plot,
And, as we climbed the hill,
Towards the roof of Lucy's cot
The moon descended still.

In one of those sweet dreams I slept,
Kind Nature's gentlest boon!
And, all the while, my eyes I kept
On the descending moon.

                                                          20

My horse moved on; hoof after hoof
He raised and never stopped:
When down behind the cottage roof
At once the planet dropped.

What fond and wayward thoughts will slide
Into a Lover's head –
'O mercy!' to myself I cried,
'If Lucy should be dead!'

Lucy Gray

Oft I had heard of Lucy Gray,
And when I crossed the Wild,
I chanced to see at break of day
The solitary Child.

No Mate, no comrade Lucy knew;
She dwelt on a wild Moor,
The sweetest Thing that ever grew
Beside a human door!

You yet may spy the Fawn at play,
10   The Hare upon the Green;
But the sweet face of Lucy Gray
Will never more be seen.

'To-night will be a stormy night,
You to the Town must go,
And take a lantern, Child, to light
Your Mother thro' the snow.'

'That, Father! will I gladly do;
'Tis scarcely afternoon –
The Minster-clock has just struck two,
20   And yonder is the Moon.'

At this the Father raised his hook
And snapped a faggot-band;
He plied his work, and Lucy took
The lantern in her hand.

Not blither is the mountain roe,
With many a wanton stroke
Her feet disperse the powd'ry snow
That rises up like smoke.

The storm came on before its time,
She wandered up and down, 30
And many a hill did Lucy climb
But never reached the Town.

The wretched Parents all that night
Went shouting far and wide;
But there was neither sound nor sight
To serve them for a guide.

At day-break on a hill they stood
That overlooked the Moor;
And thence they saw the Bridge of Wood
A furlong from their door. 40

And now they homeward turned, and cried
'In Heaven we all shall meet!'
When in the snow the Mother spied
The print of Lucy's feet.

Then downward from the steep hill's edge
They tracked the footmarks small;
And through the broken hawthorn-hedge,
And by the long stone-wall;

And then an open field they crossed,
The marks were still the same; 50
They tracked them on, nor ever lost,
And to the Bridge they came.

They followed from the snowy bank
The footmarks, one by one,
Into the middle of the plank,
And further there were none.

Yet some maintain that to this day
She is a living Child,
That you may see sweet Lucy Gray
Upon the lonesome Wild.

O'er rough and smooth she trips along,
And never looks behind;
And sings a solitary song
That whistles in the wind.

A Poet's Epitaph

Art thou a Statesman, in the van
Of public business trained and bred,
– First learn to love one living man;
Then may'st thou think upon the dead.

A Lawyer art thou? – draw not nigh;
Go, carry to some other place
The hardness of thy coward eye,
The falshood of thy sallow face.

Art thou a man of purple cheer?
A rosy man, right plump to see?
Approach; yet Doctor, not too near:
This grave no cushion is for thee.

Art thou a man of gallant pride,
A Soldier, and no man of chaff?
Welcome! – but lay thy sword aside,
And lean upon a Peasant's staff.

Physician art thou? One, all eyes,
Philosopher! a fingering slave,
One that would peep and botanize
Upon his mother's grave?   20

Wrapped closely in thy sensual fleece
O turn aside, and take, I pray,
That he below may rest in peace,
Thy pin-point of a soul away!

– A Moralist perchance appears;
Led, Heaven knows how! to this poor sod:
And He has neither eyes nor ears;
Himself his world, and his own God;

One to whose smooth-rubbed soul can cling
Nor form nor feeling great nor small,   30
A reasoning, self-sufficing thing,
An intellectual All in All!

Shut close the door! press down the latch:
Sleep in thy intellectual crust,
Nor lose ten tickings of thy watch,
Near this unprofitable dust.

But who is He with modest looks,
And clad in homely russet brown?
He murmurs near the running brooks
A music sweeter than their own.   40

He is retired as noontide dew,
Or fountain in a noonday grove;
And you must love him, ere to you
He will seem worthy of your love.

The outward shews of sky and earth,
Of hill and valley he has viewed;
And impulses of deeper birth
Have come to him in solitude.

In common things that round us lie
50   Some random truths he can impart
The harvest of a quiet eye
That broods and sleeps on his own heart.

But he is weak, both man and boy,
Hath been an idler in the land;
Contented if he might enjoy
The things which others understand.

– Come hither in thy hour of strength,
Come, weak as is a breaking wave!
Here stretch thy body at full length;
60   Or build thy house upon this grave. –

Nutting

—————————— It seems a day,
One of those heavenly days which cannot die,
When forth I sallied from our cottage-door,
And with a wallet o'er my shoulder slung,
A nutting crook in hand, I turned my steps
Towards the distant woods, a Figure quaint,
Tricked out in proud disguise of Beggar's weeds
Put on for the occasion, by advice
And exhortation of my frugal Dame.
10   Motley accoutrements! of power to smile
At thorns, and brakes, and brambles, and, in truth,
More ragged than need was. Among the woods,
And o'er the pathless rocks, I forced my way

Until, at length, I came to one dear nook
Unvisited, where not a broken bough
Drooped with its withered leaves, ungracious sign
Of devastation, but the hazels rose
Tall and erect, with milk-white clusters hung,
A virgin scene! – A little while I stood,
Breathing with such suppression of the heart   20
As joy delights in; and with wise restraint
Voluptuous, fearless of a rival, eyed
The banquet, or beneath the trees I sate
Among the flowers, and with the flowers I played;
A temper known to those, who, after long
And weary expectation, have been blessed
With sudden happiness beyond all hope. –
– Perhaps it was a bower beneath whose leaves
The violets of five seasons re-appear
And fade, unseen by any human eye,   30
Where fairy water-breaks do murmur on
For ever, and I saw the sparkling foam,
And with my cheek on one of those green stones
That, fleeced with moss, beneath the shady trees,
Lay round me scattered like a flock of sheep,
I heard the murmur and the murmuring sound,
In that sweet mood when pleasure loves to pay
Tribute to ease, and, of its joy secure
The heart luxuriates with indifferent things,
Wasting its kindliness on stocks and stones,   40
And on the vacant air. Then up I rose,
And dragged to earth both branch and bough, with crash
And merciless ravage; and the shady nook
Of hazels, and the green and mossy bower
Deformed and sullied, patiently gave up
Their quiet being: and unless I now
Confound my present feelings with the past,
Even then, when from the bower I turned away,
Exulting, rich beyond the wealth of kings
I felt a sense of pain when I beheld   50
The silent trees and the intruding sky. –

. .

Then, dearest Maiden! move along these shades
In gentleness of heart; with gentle hand
Touch,—— for there is a Spirit in the woods.

Written in Germany,

on One of the Coldest Days of the Century

I must apprize the Reader that the stoves in North
Germany generally have the impression of a galloping
Horse upon them, this being part of the Brunswick
Arms.

A fig for your languages, German and Norse,
Let me have the song of the Kettle,
And the tongs and the poker, instead of that horse
That gallops away with such fury and force
On this dreary dull plate of black metal.

Our earth is no doubt made of excellent stuff,
But her pulses beat slower and slower,
The weather in Forty was cutting and rough,
And then, as Heaven knows, the glass stood low enough,
And *now* it is four degrees lower.

Here's a Fly, a disconsolate creature perhaps,
A child of the field, or the grove,
And sorrow for him! this dull treacherous heat
Has seduced the poor fool from his winter retreat,
And he creeps to the edge of my stove.

Alas! how he fumbles about the domains
Which this comfortless oven environ,
He cannot find out in what track he must crawl,
Now back to the tiles, and now back to the wall,
And now on the brink of the iron.

Stock-still there he stands like a traveller bemazed,
The best of his skill he has tried;
His feelers methinks I can see him put forth
To the East and the West, and the South and the North,
But he finds neither guide-post nor guide.

See! his spindles sink under him, foot, leg and thigh,
His eyesight and hearing are lost,
Between life and death his blood freezes and thaws,
And his two pretty pinions of blue dusky gauze
Are glued to his sides by the frost.   30

No Brother, no Friend has he near him, while I
Can draw warmth from the cheek of my Love,
As blest and as glad in this desolate gloom,
As if green summer grass were the floor of my room,
And woodbines were hanging above.

Yet, God is my witness, thou small helpless Thing,
Thy life I would gladly sustain
Till summer comes up from the South, and with crowds
Of thy brethren a march thou should'st sound through the clouds,
And back to the forests again.   40

'Three years she grew'

Three years she grew in sun and shower,
Then Nature said, 'A lovelier flower
On earth was never sown;
This Child I to myself will take,
She shall be mine, and I will make
A Lady of my own.

'Myself will to my darling be
Both law and impulse, and with me
The Girl in rock and plain,

In earth and heaven, in glade and bower,
Shall feel an overseeing power
To kindle or restrain.

'She shall be sportive as the fawn
That wild with glee across the lawn
Or up the mountain springs,
And hers shall be the breathing balm,
And hers the silence and the calm
Of mute insensate things.

'The floating clouds their state shall lend
To her, for her the willow bend,
Nor shall she fail to see
Even in the motions of the storm
A beauty that shall mould her form
By silent sympathy.

'The stars of midnight shall be dear
To her, and she shall lean her ear
In many a secret place
Where rivulets dance their wayward round,
And beauty born of murmuring sound
Shall pass into her face.

'And vital feelings of delight
Shall rear her form to stately height,
Her virgin bosom swell,
Such thoughts to Lucy I will give
While she and I together live
Here in this happy dell.'

Thus Nature spake – The work was done –
How soon my Lucy's race was run!
She died and left to me
This heath, this calm and quiet scene,
The memory of what has been,
And never more will be.

The Two-Part Prelude

FIRST PART

Was it for this
That one, the fairest of all rivers, loved
To blend his murmurs with my nurse's song,
And from his alder shades and rocky falls,
And from his fords and shallows, sent a voice
That flowed along my dreams? For this didst thou,
O Derwent, travelling over the green plains
Near my 'sweet birthplace', didst thou, beauteous stream,
Make ceaseless music through the night and day,
Which with its steady cadence tempering   10
Our human waywardness, composed my thoughts
To more than infant softness, giving me
Among the fretful dwellings of mankind
A knowledge, a dim earnest, of the calm
Which Nature breathes among the fields and groves?
Beloved Derwent, fairest of all streams,
Was it for this that I, a four years' child,
A naked boy, among thy silent pools
Made one long bathing of a summer's day,
Basked in the sun, or plunged into thy streams,   20
Alternate, all a summer's day, or coursed
Over the sandy fields, and dashed the flowers
Of yellow grunsel; or, when crag and hill,
The woods, and distant Skiddaw's lofty height,
Were bronzed with a deep radiance, stood alone
A naked savage in the thunder-shower?
        And afterwards ('twas in a later day,
Though early), when upon the mountain slope
The frost and breath of frosty wind had snapped
The last autumnal crocus, 'twas my joy   30
To wander half the night among the cliffs
And the smooth hollows where the woodcocks ran
Along the moonlight turf. In thought and wish

That time, my shoulder all with springes hung,
I was a fell destroyer. Gentle powers,
Who give us happiness and call it peace,
When scudding on from snare to snare I plied
My anxious visitation, hurrying on,
Still hurrying, hurrying onward, how my heart
40   Panted! – among the scattered yew-trees and the crags
That looked upon me, how my bosom beat
With expectation! Sometimes strong desire
Resistless overpowered me, and the bird
Which was the captive of another's toils
Became my prey; and when the deed was done
I heard among the solitary hills
Low breathings coming after me, and sounds
Of undistinguishable motion, steps
Almost as silent as the turf they trod.

50   Nor less in springtime, when on southern banks
The shining sun had from his knot of leaves
Decoyed the primrose flower, and when the vales
And woods were warm, was I a rover then
In the high places, on the lonesome peaks,
Among the mountains and the winds. Though mean
And though inglorious were my views, the end
Was not ignoble. Oh, when I have hung
Above the raven's nest, by knots of grass
Or half-inch fissures in the slippery rock
60   But ill sustained, and almost, as it seemed,
Suspended by the blast which blew amain,
Shouldering the naked crag, oh, at that time,
While on the perilous ridge I hung alone,
With what strange utterance did the loud dry wind
Blow through my ears; the sky seemed not a sky
Of earth, and with what motion moved the clouds!

       The mind of man is fashioned and built up
Even as a strain of music. I believe
That there are spirits which, when they would form
70   A favored being, from his very dawn
Of infancy do open out the clouds

As at the touch of lightning, seeking him
With gentle visitation – quiet powers,
Retired, and seldom recognized, yet kind,
And to the very meanest not unknown –
With me, though rarely, in my boyish days
They communed. Others too there are, who use,
Yet haply aiming at the self-same end,
Severer interventions, ministry
More palpable – and of their school was I.   80
        They guided me: one evening led by them
I went alone into a shepherd's boat,
A skiff, that to a willow-tree was tied
Within a rocky cave, its usual home.
The moon was up, the lake was shining clear
Among the hoary mountains; from the shore
I pushed, and struck the oars, and struck again
In cadence, and my little boat moved on
Just like a man who walks with stately step
Though bent on speed. It was an act of stealth   90
And troubled pleasure. Not without the voice
Of mountain echoes did my boat move on,
Leaving behind her still on either side
Small circles glittering idly in the moon,
Until they melted all into one track
Of sparkling light. A rocky steep uprose
Above the cavern of the willow-tree,
And now, as suited one who proudly rowed
With his best skill, I fixed a steady view
Upon the top of that same craggy ridge,   100
The bound of the horizon – for behind
Was nothing but the stars and the grey sky.
She was an elfin pinnace; twenty times
I dipped my oars into the silent lake,
And as I rose upon the stroke my boat
Went heaving through the water like a swan –
When from behind that rocky steep, till then
The bound of the horizon, a huge cliff,
As if with voluntary power instinct,

110   Upreared its head. I struck, and struck again,
       And, growing still in stature, the huge cliff
       Rose up between me and the stars, and still,
       With measured motion, like a living thing
       Strode after me. With trembling hands I turned,
       And through the silent water stole my way
       Back to the cavern of the willow-tree.
       There in her mooring-place I left my bark,
       And through the meadows homeward went with grave
       And serious thoughts; and after I had seen
120   That spectacle, for many days my brain
       Worked with a dim and undetermined sense
       Of unknown modes of being. In my thoughts
       There was a darkness – call it solitude,
       Or blank desertion – no familiar shapes
       Of hourly objects, images of trees,
       Of sea or sky, no colours of green fields,
       But huge and mighty forms that do not live
       Like living men moved slowly through my mind
       By day, and were the trouble of my dreams.
130   Ah, not in vain ye beings of the hills,
       And ye that walk the woods and open heaths
       By moon or star-light, thus, from my first dawn
       Of childhood, did ye love to intertwine
       The passions that build up our human soul
       Not with the mean and vulgar works of man,
       But with high objects, with eternal things,
       With life and Nature, purifying thus
       The elements of feeling and of thought,
       And sanctifying by such discipline
140   Both pain and fear, until we recognise
       A grandeur in the beatings of the heart.
       Nor was this fellowship vouchsafed to me
       With stinted kindness. In November days,
       When vapours rolling down the valleys made
       A lonely scene more lonesome, among woods
       At noon, and mid the calm of summer nights
       When by the margin of the trembling lake

Beneath the gloomy hills I homeward went
In solitude, such intercourse was mine.
     And in the frosty season, when the sun   150
Was set, and visible for many a mile
The cottage windows through the twilight blazed,
I heeded not the summons. Clear and loud
The village clock tolled six; I wheeled about
Proud and exulting, like an untired horse
That cares not for its home. All shod with steel
We hissed along the polished ice in games
Confederate, imitative of the chace
And woodland pleasures, the resounding horn,
The pack loud bellowing, and the hunted hare.   160
So through the darkness and the cold we flew,
And not a voice was idle. With the din,
Meanwhile, the precipices rang aloud;
The leafless trees and every icy crag
Tinkled like iron; while the distant hills
Into the tumult sent an alien sound
Of melancholy, not unnoticed; while the stars,
Eastward, were sparkling clear, and in the west
The orange sky of evening died away.
     Not seldom from the uproar I retired   170
Into a silent bay, or sportively
Glanced sideway, leaving the tumultuous throng,
To cut across the shadow of a star
That gleamed upon the ice. And oftentimes
When we had given our bodies to the wind,
And all the shadowy banks on either side
Came sweeping through the darkness, spinning still
The rapid line of motion, then at once
Have I, reclining back upon my heels,
Stopped short – yet still the solitary cliffs   180
Wheeled by me, even as if the earth had rolled
With visible motion her diurnal round.
Behind me did they stretch in solemn train,
Feebler and feebler, and I stood and watched
Till all was tranquil as a summer sea.

Ye powers of earth, ye genii of the springs,
And ye that have your voices in the clouds,
And ye that are familiars of the lakes
And of the standing pools, I may not think
190   A vulgar hope was yours when you employed
Such ministry – when ye through many a year
Thus by the agency of boyish sports,
On caves and trees, upon the woods and hills,
Impressed upon all forms the characters
Of danger or desire, and thus did make
The surface of the universal earth
With meanings of delight, of hope and fear,
Work like a sea.

                Not uselessly employed,
I might pursue this theme through every change
200   Of exercise and sport to which the year
Did summon us in its delightful round.
We were a noisy crew; the sun in heaven
Beheld not vales more beautiful than ours,
Nor saw a race in happiness and joy
More worthy of the fields where they were sown.
I would record with no reluctant voice
Our home amusements by the warm peat fire
At evening, when with pencil and with slate,
In square divisions parcelled out, and all
210   With crosses and with cyphers scribbled o'er,
We schemed and puzzled, head opposed to head,
In strife too humble to be named in verse;
Or round the naked table, snow-white deal,
Cherry, or maple, sate in close array,
And to the combat – lu or whist – led on
A thick-ribbed army, not as in the world
Discarded and ungratefully thrown by
Even for the very service they had wrought,
But husbanded through many a long campaign.
220   Oh, with what echoes on the board they fell –
Ironic diamonds, hearts of sable hue,
Queens gleaming through their splendour's last decay,

Knaves wrapt in one assimilating gloom,
And kings indignant at the shame incurred
By royal visages. Meanwhile abroad
The heavy rain was falling, or the frost
Raged bitterly with keen and silent tooth,
And, interrupting the impassioned game,
Oft from the neighbouring lake the splitting ice,
While it sank down towards the water, sent   230
Among the meadows and the hills its long
And frequent yellings, imitative some
Of wolves that howl along the Bothnic main.

     Nor with less willing heart would I rehearse
The woods of autumn, and their hidden bowers
With milk-white clusters hung; the rod and line –
True symbol of the foolishness of hope –
Which with its strong enchantment led me on
By rocks and pools, where never summer star
Impressed its shadow, to forlorn cascades   240
Among the windings of the mountain-brooks;
The kite in sultry calms from some high hill
Sent up, ascending thence till it was lost
Among the fleecy clouds – in gusty days
Launched from the lower grounds, and suddenly
Dashed headlong and rejected by the storm.
All these, and more, with rival claims demand
Grateful acknowledgement. It were a song
Venial, and such as – if I rightly judge –
I might protract unblamed, but I perceive   250
That much is overlooked, and we should ill
Attain our object if, from delicate fears
Of breaking in upon the unity
Of this my argument, I should omit
To speak of such effects as cannot here
Be regularly classed, yet tend no less
To the same point, the growth of mental power
And love of Nature's works.
                        Ere I had seen
Eight summers – and 'twas in the very week

260   When I was first transplanted to thy vale,
       Beloved Hawkshead; when thy paths, thy shores
       And brooks, were like a dream of novelty
       To my half-infant mind – I chanced to cross
       One of those open fields which, shaped like ears,
       Make green peninsulas on Esthwaite's lake.
       Twilight was coming on, yet through the gloom
       I saw distinctly on the opposite shore,
       Beneath a tree and close by the lake side,
       A heap of garments, as if left by one
270   Who there was bathing. Half an hour I watched
       And no one owned them; meanwhile the calm lake
       Grew dark with all the shadows on its breast,
       And now and then a leaping fish disturbed
       The breathless stillness. The succeeding day
       There came a company, and in their boat
       Sounded with iron hooks and with long poles.
       At length the dead man, mid that beauteous scene
       Of trees and hills and water, bolt upright
       Rose with his ghastly face. I might advert
280   To numerous accidents in flood or field,
       Quarry or moor, or mid the winter snows,
       Distresses and disasters, tragic facts
       Of rural history that impressed my mind
       With images to which in following years
       Far other feelings were attached – with forms
       That yet exist with independent life,
       And, like their archetypes, know no decay.
              There are in our existence spots of time
       Which with distinct pre-eminence retain
290   A fructifying virtue, whence, depressed
       By trivial occupations and the round
       Of ordinary intercourse, our minds –
       Especially the imaginative power –
       Are nourished and invisibly repaired.
       Such moments chiefly seem to have their date
       In our first childhood. I remember well
       ('Tis of an early season that I speak,

The twilight of rememberable life),
While I was yet an urchin, one who scarce
Could hold a bridle, with ambitious hopes   300
I mounted, and we rode towards the hills.
We were a pair of horsemen: honest James
Was with me, my encourager and guide.
We had not travelled long ere some mischance
Disjoined me from my comrade, and, through fear
Dismounting, down the rough and stony moor
I led my horse, and stumbling on, at length
Came to a bottom where in former times
A man, the murderer of his wife, was hung
In irons. Mouldered was the gibbet-mast;   310
The bones were gone, the iron and the wood;
Only a long green ridge of turf remained
Whose shape was like a grave. I left the spot,
And reascending the bare slope I saw
A naked pool that lay beneath the hills,
The beacon on the summit, and more near
A girl who bore a pitcher on her head
And seemed with difficult steps to force her way
Against the blowing wind. It was in truth
An ordinary sight, but I should need   320
Colours and words that are unknown to man
To paint the visionary dreariness
Which, while I looked all round for my lost guide,
Did at that time invest the naked pool,
The beacon on the lonely eminence,
The woman and her garments vexed and tossed
By the strong wind.
            Nor less I recollect –
Long after, though my childhood had not ceased –
Another scene which left a kindred power
Implanted in my mind. One Christmas time,   330
The day before the holidays began,
Feverish, and tired, and restless, I went forth
Into the fields, impatient for the sight
Of those three horses which should bear us home,

My brothers and myself. There was a crag,
An eminence, which from the meeting-point
Of two highways ascending overlooked
At least a long half-mile of those two roads,
By each of which the expected steeds might come –
340   The choice uncertain. Thither I repaired
Up to the highest summit. 'Twas a day
Stormy, and rough, and wild, and on the grass
I sate half sheltered by a naked wall.
Upon my right hand was a single sheep,
A whistling hawthorn on my left, and there,
Those two companions at my side, I watched
With eyes intensely straining, as the mist
Gave intermitting prospects of the wood
And plain beneath. Ere I to school returned
350   That dreary time, ere I had been ten days
A dweller in my father's house, he died,
And I and my two brothers, orphans then,
Followed his body to the grave. The event,
With all the sorrow which it brought, appeared
A chastisement; and when I called to mind
That day so lately passed, when from the crag
I looked in such anxiety of hope,
With trite reflections of morality,
Yet with the deepest passion, I bowed low
360   To God who thus corrected my desires.
And afterwards the wind and sleety rain,
And all the business of the elements,
The single sheep, and the one blasted tree,
And the bleak music of that old stone wall,
The noise of wood and water, and the mist
Which on the line of each of those two roads
Advanced in such indisputable shapes –
All these were spectacles and sounds to which
I often would repair, and thence would drink
370   As at a fountain. And I do not doubt
That in this later time, when storm and rain
Beat on my roof at midnight, or by day

When I am in the woods, unknown to me
The workings of my spirit thence are brought.
    Nor, sedulous as I have been to trace
How Nature by collateral interest,
And by extrinsic passion, peopled first
My mind with forms or beautiful or grand
And made me love them, may I well forget
How other pleasures have been mine, and joys   380
Of subtler origin – how I have felt
Not seldom, even in that tempestuous time,
Those hallowed and pure motions of the sense
Which seem in their simplicity to own
An intellectual charm, that calm delight
Which, if I err not, surely must belong
To those first-born affinities that fit
Our new existence to existing things,
And, in our dawn of being, constitute
The bond of union betwixt life and joy.   390
    Yes, I remember when the changeful earth
And twice five seasons on my mind had stamped
The faces of the moving year, even then,
A child, I held unconscious intercourse
With the eternal beauty, drinking in
A pure organic pleasure from the lines
Of curling mist, or from the level plain
Of waters coloured by the steady clouds.
The sands of Westmoreland, the creeks and bays
Of Cumbria's rocky limits, they can tell   400
How when the sea threw off his evening shade
And to the shepherd's hut beneath the crags
Did send sweet notice of the rising moon,
How I have stood, to images like these
A stranger, linking with the spectacle
No body of associated forms,
And bringing with me no peculiar sense
Of quietness or peace – yet I have stood
Even while my eye has moved o'er three long leagues
Of shining water, gathering, as it seemed,   410

Through the wide surface of that field of light
New pleasure, like a bee among the flowers.
   Thus often in those fits of vulgar joy
Which through all seasons on a child's pursuits
Are prompt attendants, mid that giddy bliss
Which like a tempest works along the blood
And is forgotten, even then I felt
Gleams like the flashing of a shield. The earth
And common face of Nature spake to me
Rememberable things – sometimes, 'tis true,
By quaint associations, yet not vain
Nor profitless, if haply they impressed
Collateral objects and appearances,
Albeit lifeless then, and doomed to sleep
Until maturer seasons called them forth
To impregnate and to elevate the mind.
And if the vulgar joy by its own weight
Wearied itself out of the memory,
The scenes which were a witness of that joy
Remained, in their substantial lineaments
Depicted on the brain, and to the eye
Were visible, a daily sight. And thus
By the impressive agency of fear,
By pleasure and repeated happiness –
So frequently repeated – and by force
Of obscure feelings representative
Of joys that were forgotten, these same scenes,
So beauteous and majestic in themselves,
Though yet the day was distant, did at length
Become habitually dear, and all
Their hues and forms were by invisible links
Allied to the affections.
      I began
My story early, feeling, as I fear,
The weakness of a human love for days
Disowned by memory – ere the birth of spring
Planting my snowdrops among winter snows.
Nor will it seem to thee, my friend, so prompt

420

430

440

In sympathy, that I have lengthened out
With fond and feeble tongue a tedious tale.
Meanwhile my hope has been that I might fetch   450
Reproaches from my former years, whose power
May spur me on, in manhood now mature,
To honourable toil. Yet should it be
That this is but an impotent desire –
That I by such inquiry am not taught
To understand myself, nor thou to know
With better knowledge how the heart was framed
Of him thou lovest – need I dread from thee
Harsh judgments if I am so loth to quit
Those recollected hours that have the charm   460
Of visionary things, and lovely forms
And sweet sensations, that throw back our life
And make our infancy a visible scene
On which the sun is shining?

SECOND PART

Thus far, my friend, have we retraced the way
Through which I travelled when I first began
To love the woods and fields. The passion yet
Was in its birth, sustained, as might befal,
By nourishment that came unsought – for still
From week to week, from month to month, we lived
A round of tumult. Duly were our games
Prolonged in summer till the daylight failed:
No chair remained before the doors, the bench
And threshold steps were empty, fast asleep   10
The labourer and the old man who had sate
A later lingerer, yet the revelry
Continued and the loud uproar. At last,
When all the ground was dark and the huge clouds
Were edged with twinkling stars, to bed we went
With weary joints and with a beating mind.
Ah, is there one who ever has been young
And needs a monitory voice to tame

The pride of virtue and of intellect?
20 And is there one, the wisest and the best
Of all mankind, who does not sometimes wish
For things which cannot be, who would not give,
If so he might, to duty and to truth
The eagerness of infantine desire?
A tranquillizing spirit presses now
On my corporeal frame, so wide appears
The vacancy between me and those days,
Which yet have such self-presence in my heart
That sometimes when I think of them I seem
30 Two consciousnesses – conscious of myself,
And of some other being.

               A grey stone
Of native rock, left midway in the square
Of our small market-village, was the home
And centre of these joys; and when, returned
After long absence thither I repaired,
I found that it was split and gone to build
A smart assembly-room that perked and flared
With wash and rough-cast, elbowing the ground
Which had been ours. But let the fiddle scream,
40 And be ye happy! Yet I know, my friends,
That more than one of you will think with me
Of those soft starry nights, and that old dame
From whom the stone was named, who there had sate
And watched her table with its huckster's wares,
Assiduous, for the length of sixty years.

    We ran a boisterous race, the year span round
With giddy motion; but the time approached
That brought with it a regular desire
For calmer pleasures – when the beauteous scenes
50 Of Nature were collaterally attached
To every scheme of holiday delight,
And every boyish sport, less grateful else
And languidly pursued. When summer came
It was the pastime of our afternoons
To beat along the plain of Windermere

With rival oars; and the selected bourn
Was now an island musical with birds
That sang for ever, now a sister isle
Beneath the oak's umbrageous covert, sown
With lilies-of-the-valley like a field,   60
And now a third small island where remained
An old stone table and one mouldered cave –
A hermit's history. In such a race,
So ended, disappointment could be none,
Uneasiness, or pain, or jealousy;
We rested in the shade, all pleased alike,
Conquered or conqueror. Thus our selfishness
Was mellowed down, and thus the pride of strength
And the vainglory of superior skill
Were interfused with objects which subdued   70
And tempered them, and gradually produced
A quiet independence of the heart.
And to my friend who knows me I may add,
Unapprehensive of reproof, that hence
Ensued a diffidence and modesty,
And I was taught to feel – perhaps too much –
The self-sufficing power of solitude.
         No delicate viands sapped our bodily strength:
More than we wished we knew the blessing then
Of vigorous hunger, for our daily meals   80
Were frugal, Sabine fare – and then, exclude
A little weekly stipend, and we lived
Through three divisions of the quartered year
In pennyless poverty. But now, to school
Returned from the half-yearly holidays,
We came with purses more profusely filled,
Allowance which abundantly sufficed
To gratify the palate with repasts
More costly than the dame of whom I spake,
That ancient woman, and her board, supplied.   90
Hence inroads into distant vales, and long
Excursions far away among the hills,
Hence rustic dinners on the cool green ground –

Or in the woods, or by a river-side
Or fountain – festive banquets, that provoked
The languid action of a natural scene
By pleasure of corporeal appetite.
     Nor is my aim neglected if I tell
How twice in the long length of those half-years
100 We from our funds perhaps with bolder hand
Drew largely, anxious for one day at least
To feel the motion of the galloping steed;
And with the good old innkeeper, in truth
I needs must say, that sometimes we have used
Sly subterfuge, for the intended bound
Of the day's journey was too distant far
For any cautious man: a structure famed
Beyond its neighbourhood, the antique walls
Of a large abbey, with its fractured arch,
110 Belfry, and images, and living trees –
A holy scene. Along the smooth green turf
Our horses grazed. In more than inland peace,
Left by the winds that overpass the vale,
In that sequestered ruin trees and towers –
Both silent and both motionless alike –
Hear all day long the murmuring sea that beats
Incessantly upon a craggy shore.
     Our steeds remounted, and the summons given,
With whip and spur we by the chantry flew
120 In uncouth race, and left the cross-legged knight
And the stone abbot, and that single wren
Which one day sang so sweetly in the nave
Of the old church that, though from recent showers
The earth was comfortless, and, touched by faint
Internal breezes, from the roofless walls
The shuddering ivy dripped large drops, yet still
So sweetly mid the gloom the invisible bird
Sang to itself that there I could have made
My dwelling-place, and lived for ever there,
130 To hear such music. Through the walls we flew
And down the valley, and, a circuit made

In wantonness of heart, through rough and smooth
We scampered homeward. O, ye rocks and streams,
And that still spirit of the evening air,
Even in this joyous time I sometimes felt
Your presence, when, with slackened step, we breathed
Along the sides of the steep hills, or when,
Lightened by gleams of moonlight from the sea,
We beat with thundering hoofs the level sand.
      There was a row of ancient trees, since fallen,   140
That on the margin of a jutting land
Stood near the lake of Coniston, and made,
With its long boughs above the water stretched,
A gloom through which a boat might sail along
As in a cloister. An old hall was near,
Grotesque and beautiful, its gavel-end
And huge round chimneys to the top o'ergrown
With fields of ivy. Thither we repaired –
'Twas even a custom with us – to the shore,
And to that cool piazza. They who dwelt   150
In the neglected mansion-house supplied
Fresh butter, tea-kettle and earthernware,
And chafing-dish with smoking coals; and so
Beneath the trees we sate in our small boat,
And in the covert eat our delicate meal
Upon the calm smooth lake. It was a joy
Worthy the heart of one who is full grown
To rest beneath those horizontal boughs
And mark the radiance of the setting sun,
Himself unseen, reposing on the top   160
Of the high eastern hills. And there I said,
That beauteous sight before me, there I said
(Then first beginning in my thoughts to mark
That sense of dim similitude which links
Our moral feelings with external forms)
That in whatever region I should close
My mortal life I would remember you,
Fair scenes – that dying I would think on you,
My soul would send a longing look to you,

170 Even as that setting sun, while all the vale
 Could nowhere catch one faint memorial gleam,
 Yet with the last remains of his last light
 Still lingered, and a farewell lustre threw
 On the dear mountain-tops where first he rose.
 'Twas then my fourteenth summer, and these words
 Were uttered in a casual access
 Of sentiment, a momentary trance
 That far outran the habit of my mind.
    Upon the eastern shore of Windermere
180 Above the crescent of a pleasant bay
 There was an inn, no homely-featured shed,
 Brother of the surrounding cottages,
 But 'twas a splendid place, the door beset
 With chaises, grooms, and liveries, and within
 Decanters, glasses and the blood-red wine.
 In ancient times, or ere the hall was built
 On the large island, had the dwelling been
 More worthy of a poet's love, a hut
 Proud of its one bright fire and sycamore shade;
190 But though the rhymes were gone which once inscribed
 The threshold, and large golden characters
 On the blue-frosted signboard had usurped
 The place of the old lion, in contempt
 And mockery of the rustic painter's hand,
 Yet to this hour the spot to me is dear
 With all its foolish pomp. The garden lay
 Upon a slope surmounted by the plain
 Of a small bowling-green; beneath us stood
 A grove, with gleams of water through the trees
200 And over the tree-tops – nor did we want
 Refreshment, strawberries and mellow cream –
 And there through half an afternoon we played
 On the smooth platform, and the shouts we sent
 Made all the mountains ring. But ere the fall
 Of night, when in our pinnace we returned
 Over the dusky lake, and to the beach
 Of some small island steered our course, with one,

The minstrel of our troop, and left him there,
And rowed off gently, while he blew his flute
Alone upon the rock, oh, then the calm   210
And dead still water lay upon my mind
Even with a weight of pleasure, and the sky,
Never before so beautiful, sank down
Into my heart and held me like a dream.
       Thus day by day my sympathies increased,
And thus the common range of visible things
Grew dear to me. Already I began
To love the sun – a boy I loved the sun
Not as I since have loved him (as a pledge
And surety of my earthly life, a light   220
Which while I view I feel I am alive),
But for this cause, that I had seen him lay
His beauty on the morning hills, had seen
The western mountain touch his setting orb
In many a thoughtless hour, when from excess
Of happiness my blood appeared to flow
With its own pleasure, and I breathed with joy.
And from like feelings, humble though intense,
To patriotic and domestic love
Analogous, the moon to me was dear: 230
For I would dream away my purposes
Standing to look upon her, while she hung
Midway between the hills as if she knew
No other region but belonged to thee,
Yea appertained by a peculiar right
To thee and thy grey huts, my native vale.
       Those incidental charms which first attached
My heart to rural objects, day by day
Grew weaker, and I hasten on to tell
How Nature, intervenient till this time   240
And secondary, now at length was sought
For her own sake. But who shall parcel out
His intellect by geometric rules
Split like a province into round and square?
Who knows the individual hour in which

His habits were first sown even as a seed?
Who that shall point as with a wand, and say
'This portion of the river of my mind
Came from yon fountain'? Thou, my friend, art one
250 More deeply read in thy own thoughts, no slave
Of that false secondary power by which
In weakness we create distinctions, then
Believe our puny boundaries are things
Which we perceive, and not which we have made.
To thee, unblinded by these outward shews,
The unity of all has been revealed;
And thou wilt doubt with me, less aptly skilled
Than many are to class the cabinet
Of their sensations, and in voluble phrase
260 Run through the history and birth of each
As of a single independent thing.
Hard task to analyse a soul, in which
Not only general habits and desires,
But each most obvious and particular thought –
Not in a mystical and idle sense,
But in the words of reason deeply weighed –
Hath no beginning.
                Blessed the infant babe –
For with my best conjectures I would trace
The progress of our being – blest the babe
270 Nursed in his mother's arms, the babe who sleeps
Upon his mother's breast, who, when his soul
Claims manifest kindred with an earthly soul,
Doth gather passion from his mother's eye.
Such feelings pass into his torpid life
Like an awakening breeze, and hence his mind,
Even in the first trial of its powers,
Is prompt and watchful, eager to combine
In one appearance all the elements
And parts of the same object, else detached
280 And loth to coalesce. Thus day by day,
Subjected to the discipline of love,
His organs and recipient faculties

Are quickened, are more vigorous; his mind spreads,
Tenacious of the forms which it receives.
In one beloved presence – nay and more,
In that most apprehensive habitude
And those sensations which have been derived
From this beloved presence – there exists
A virtue which irradiates and exalts
All objects through all intercourse of sense.   290
No outcast he, bewildered and depressed;
Along his infant veins are interfused
The gravitation and the filial bond
Of Nature that connect him with the world.
Emphatically such a being lives,
An inmate of this *active* universe.
From Nature largely he receives, nor so
Is satisfied, but largely gives again;
For feeling has to him imparted strength,
And – powerful in all sentiments of grief,   300
Of exultation, fear and joy – his mind,
Even as an agent of the one great mind,
Creates, creator and receiver both,
Working but in alliance with the works
Which it beholds. Such, verily, is the first
Poetic spirit of our human life –
By uniform control of after years
In most abated and suppressed, in some
Through every change of growth or of decay
Preeminent till death.
               From early days,   310
Beginning not long after that first time
In which, a babe, by intercourse of touch
I held mute dialogues with my mother's heart,
I have endeavoured to display the means
Whereby this infant sensibility,
Great birthright of our being, was in me
Augmented and sustained. Yet is a path
More difficult before me, and I fear
That in its broken windings we shall need

320 The chamois' sinews and the eagle's wing.
For now a trouble came into my mind
From obscure causes. I was left alone
Seeking this visible world, nor knowing why.
The props of my affections were removed,
And yet the building stood, as if sustained
By its own spirit. All that I beheld
Was dear to me, and from this cause it came
That now to Nature's finer influxes
My mind lay open – to that more exact
330 And intimate communion which our hearts
Maintain with the minuter properties
Of objects which already are beloved,
And of those only.
              Many are the joys
Of youth, but oh, what happiness to live
When every hour brings palpable access
Of knowledge, when all knowledge is delight,
And sorrow is not there. The seasons came,
And every season brought a countless store
Of modes and temporary qualities
340 Which but for this most watchful power of love
Had been neglected, left a register
Of permanent relations else unknown.
Hence life, and change, and beauty, solitude
More active even than 'best society',
Society made sweet as solitude
By silent inobtrusive sympathies,
And gentle agitations of the mind
From manifold distinctions – difference
Perceived in things where to the common eye
350 No difference is – and hence, from the same source,
Sublimer joy. For I would walk alone
In storm and tempest, or in starlight nights
Beneath the quiet heavens, and at that time
Would feel whate'er there is of power in sound
To breathe an elevated mood, by form
Or image unprofaned; and I would stand

Beneath some rock, listening to sounds that are
The ghostly language of the ancient earth,
Or make their dim abode in distant winds.
Thence did I drink the visionary power.   360
I deem not profitless these fleeting moods
Of shadowy exaltation; not for this,
That they are kindred to our purer mind
And intellectual life, but that the soul –
Remembering how she felt, but what she felt
Remembering not – retains an obscure sense
Of possible sublimity, to which
With growing faculties she doth aspire,
With faculties still growing, feeling still
That whatsoever point they gain they still   370
Have something to pursue.
                              And not alone
In grandeur and in tumult, but no less
In tranquil scenes, that universal power
And fitness in the latent qualities
And essences of things, by which the mind
Is moved with feelings of delight, to me
Came strengthened with a superadded soul,
A virtue not its own. My morning walks
Were early: oft before the hours of school
I travelled round our little lake, five miles   380
Of pleasant wandering – happy time, more dear
For this, that one was by my side, a friend
Then passionately loved. With heart how full
Will he peruse these lines, this page – perhaps
A blank to other men – for many years
Have since flowed in between us, and, our minds
Both silent to each other, at this time
We live as if those hours had never been.
Nor seldom did I lift our cottage latch
Far earlier, and before the vernal thrush   390
Was audible, among the hills I sate
Alone upon some jutting eminence
At the first hour of morning, when the vale

Lay quiet in an utter solitude.
How shall I trace the history, where seek
The origin of what I then have felt?
Oft in those moments such a holy calm
Did overspread my soul that I forgot
The agency of sight, and what I saw
400   Appeared like something in myself, a dream,
A prospect in my mind.
               'Twere long to tell
What spring and autumn, what the winter snows,
And what the summer shade, what day and night,
The evening and the morning, what my dreams
And what my waking thoughts, supplied to nurse
That spirit of religious love in which
I walked with Nature. But let this at least
Be not forgotten, that I still retained
My first creative sensibility,
410   That by the regular action of the world
My soul was unsubdued. A plastic power
Abode with me, a forming hand, at times
Rebellious, acting in a devious mood,
A local spirit of its own, at war
With general tendency, but for the most
Subservient strictly to the external things
With which it communed. An auxiliar light
Came from my mind, which on the setting sun
Bestowed new splendour; the melodious birds,
420   The gentle breezes, fountains that ran on
Murmuring so sweetly in themselves, obeyed
A like dominion, and the midnight storm
Grew darker in the presence of my eye.
Hence my obeisance, my devotion hence,
And *hence* my transport.
             Nor should this, perchance,
Pass unrecorded, that I still had loved
The exercise and produce of a toil
Than analytic industry to me
More pleasing, and whose character I deem

Is more poetic, as resembling more 430
Creative agency – I mean to speak
Of that interminable building reared
By observation of affinities
In objects where no brotherhood exists
To common minds. My seventeenth year was come,
And, whether from this habit rooted now
So deeply in my mind, or from excess
Of the great social principle of life
Coercing all things into sympathy,
To unorganic natures I transferred 440
My own enjoyments, or, the power of truth
Coming in revelation, I conversed
With things that really are, I at this time
Saw blessings spread around me like a sea.
Thus did my days pass on, and now at length
From Nature and her overflowing soul
I had received so much that all my thoughts
Were steeped in feeling. I was only then
Contented when with bliss ineffable
I felt the sentiment of being spread 450
O'er all that moves, and all that seemeth still,
O'er all that, lost beyond the reach of thought
And human knowledge, to the human eye
Invisible, yet liveth to the heart,
O'er all that leaps, and runs, and shouts, and sings,
Or beats the gladsome air, o'er all that glides
Beneath the wave, yea, in the wave itself
And mighty depth of waters. Wonder not
If such my transports were, for in all things
I saw one life, and felt that it was joy; 460
One song they sang and it was audible –
Most audible then when the fleshly ear,
O'ercome by grosser prelude of that strain,
Forgot its functions and slept undisturbed.
    If this be error, and another faith
Find easier access to the pious mind,
Yet were I grossly destitute of all

Those human sentiments which make this earth
So dear if I should fail with grateful voice
470 To speak of you, ye mountains, and ye lakes
And sounding cataracts, ye mists and winds
That dwell among the hills where I was born.
If in my youth I have been pure in heart,
If, mingling with the world, I am content
With my own modest pleasures, and have lived
With God and Nature communing, removed
From little enmities and low desires,
The gift is yours; if in these times of fear,
This melancholy waste of hopes o'erthrown,
480 If, mid indifference and apathy
And wicked exultation, when good men
On every side fall off we know not how
To selfishness, disguised in gentle names
Of peace and quiet and domestic love –
Yet mingled, not unwillingly, with sneers
On visionary minds – if, in this time
Of dereliction and dismay, I yet
Despair not of our nature, but retain
A more than Roman confidence, a faith
490 That fails not, in all sorrow my support,
The blessing of my life, the gift is yours
Ye mountains, thine O Nature. Thou hast fed
My lofty speculations, and in thee
For this uneasy heart of ours I find
A never-failing principle of joy
And purest passion.
                  Thou, my friend, wast reared
In the great city, mid far other scenes,
But we by different roads at length have gained
The self-same bourne. And from this cause to thee
500 I speak unapprehensive of contempt,
The insinuated scoff of coward tongues,
And all that silent language which so oft
In conversation betwixt man and man
Blots from the human countenance all trace

Of beauty and of love. For thou hast sought
The truth in solitude, and thou art one
The most intense of Nature's worshippers,
In many things my brother, chiefly here
In this my deep devotion. Fare thee well:
Health and the quiet of a healthful mind   510
Attend thee, seeking oft the haunts of men –
But yet more often living with thyself,
And for thyself – so haply shall thy days
Be many, and a blessing to mankind.

The Brothers

These Tourists, Heaven preserve us! needs must live
A profitable life: some glance along,
Rapid and gay, as if the earth were air,
And they were butterflies to wheel about
Long as their summer lasted; some, as wise,
Upon the forehead of a jutting crag
Sit perched with book and pencil on their knee,
And look and scribble, scribble on and look,
Until a man might travel twelve stout miles,
Or reap an acre of his neighbour's corn.   10
But, for that moping son of Idleness
Why can he tarry *yonder?* – In our church-yard
Is neither epitaph nor monument,
Tomb-stone nor name, only the turf we tread
And a few natural graves. To Jane, his Wife,
Thus spake the homely Priest of Ennerdale.
It was a July evening, and he sate
Upon the long stone-seat beneath the eaves
Of his old cottage, as it chanced that day,
Employed in winter's work. Upon the stone   20
His Wife sate near him, teasing matted wool,
While, from the twin cards toothed with glittering wire,

125

He fed the spindle of his youngest child,
Who turned her large round wheel in the open air
With back and forward steps. Towards the field
In which the parish chapel stood alone,
Girt round with a bare ring of mossy wall,
While half an hour went by, the Priest had sent
Many a long look of wonder, and at last,
Risen from his seat, beside the snowy ridge
Of carded wool which the old Man had piled
He laid his implements with gentle care,
Each in the other locked; and, down the path
Which from his cottage to the church-yard led,
He took his way, impatient to accost
The Stranger, whom he saw still lingering there.

'Twas one well known to him in former days,
A Shepherd-lad: who ere his thirteenth year
Had changed his calling, with the mariners
A fellow-mariner, and so had fared
Through twenty seasons; but he had been reared
Among the mountains, and he in his heart
Was half a Shepherd on the stormy seas.
Oft in the piping shrouds had Leonard heard
The tones of waterfalls, and inland sounds
Of caves and trees; and when the regular wind
Between the tropics filled the steady sail
And blew with the same breath through days and weeks,
Lengthening invisibly its weary line
Along the cloudless main, he, in those hours
Of tiresome indolence would often hang
Over the vessel's side, and gaze and gaze,
And, while the broad green wave and sparkling foam
Flashed round him images and hues, that wrought
In union with the employment of his heart,
He, thus by feverish passion overcome,
Even with the organs of his bodily eye,
Below him, in the bosom of the deep
Saw mountains, saw the forms of sheep that grazed

30

40

50

On verdant hills, with dwellings among trees, 60
And Shepherds clad in the same country grey
Which he himself had worn.
                    And now at length,
From perils manifold, with some small wealth
Acquired by traffic in the Indian Isles,
To his paternal home he is returned,
With a determined purpose to resume
The life which he lived there, both for the sake
Of many darling pleasures, and the love
Which to an only brother he has borne
In all his hardships, since that happy time 70
When, whether it blew foul or fair, they two
Were brother Shepherds on their native hills.
—— They were the last of all their race; and now,
When Leonard had approached his home, his heart
Failed in him, and, not venturing to inquire
Tidings of one whom he so dearly loved,
Towards the church-yard he had turned aside,
That, as he knew in what particular spot
His family were laid, he thence might learn
If still his Brother lived, or to the file 80
Another grave was added. – He had found
Another grave, near which a full half hour
He had remained, but, as he gazed, there grew
Such a confusion in his memory,
That he began to doubt, and he had hopes
That he had seen this heap of turf before,
That it was not another grave, but one,
He had forgotten. He had lost his path,
As up the vale he came that afternoon,
Through fields which once had been well known to him. 90
And Oh! what joy the recollection now
Sent to his heart! he lifted up his eyes,
And looking round he thought that he perceived
Strange alteration wrought on every side
Among the woods and fields, and that the rocks,
And the eternal hills, themselves were changed.

                  . .

By this the Priest who down the field had come
Unseen by Leonard, at the church-yard gate
Stopped short, and thence, at leisure, limb by limb
100   He scanned him with a gay complacency.
Aye, thought the Vicar, smiling to himself,
'Tis one of those who needs must leave the path
Of the world's business, to go wild alone:
His arms have a perpetual holiday,
The happy man will creep about the fields
Following his fancies by the hour, to bring
Tears down his cheek, or solitary smiles
Into his face, until the setting sun
Write Fool upon his forehead. Planted thus
110   Beneath a shed that overarched the gate
Of this rude church-yard, till the stars appeared
The good man might have communed with himself
But that the Stranger, who had left the grave,
Approached; he recognized the Priest at once,
And after greetings interchanged, and given
By Leonard to the Vicar as to one
Unknown to him, this dialogue ensued.

LEONARD

You live, Sir, in these dales, a quiet life:
Your years make up one peaceful family;
120   And who would grieve and fret, if, welcome come
And welcome gone, they are so like each other,
They cannot be remembered. Scarce a funeral
Comes to this church-yard once in eighteen months;
And yet, some changes must take place among you.
And you, who dwell here, even among these rocks
Can trace the finger of mortality,
And see, that with our threescore years and ten
We are not all that perish.——I remember,
For many years ago I passed this road,
130   There was a foot-way all along the fields
By the brook-side – 'tis gone – and that dark cleft!
To me it does not seem to wear the face
Which then it had.

PRIEST

Why, Sir, for aught I know,
That chasm is much the same –

LEONARD

But, surely, yonder –

PRIEST

Aye, there indeed, your memory is a friend
That does not play you false.——On that tall pike,
(It is the loneliest place of all these hills)
There were two Springs which bubbled side by side,
As if they had been made that they might be
Companions for each other: ten years back,   140
Close to those brother fountains, the huge crag
Was rent with lightning – one is dead and gone,
The other, left behind, is flowing still.——
For accidents and changes such as these,
Why we have store of them! a water-spout
Will bring down half a mountain; what a feast
For folks that wander up and down like you,
To see an acre's breadth of that wide cliff
One roaring cataract – a sharp May storm
Will come with loads of January snow,   150
And in one night send twenty score of sheep
To feed the ravens, or a Shepherd dies
By some untoward death among the rocks:
The ice breaks up and sweeps away a bridge –
A wood is felled: – and then for our own homes!
A child is born or christened, a field ploughed,
A daughter sent to service, a web spun,
The old house cloth is decked with a new face;
And hence, so far from wanting facts or dates
To chronicle the time, we all have here   160
A pair of diaries, one serving, Sir,
For the whole dale, and one for each fire-side,
Your's was a stranger's judgment: for historians
Commend me to these vallies.

LEONARD

           Yet your church-yard
Seems, if such freedom may be used with you,
To say that you are heedless of the past.
Here's neither head nor foot-stone, plate of brass,
Cross-bones or skull, type of our earthly state
Or emblem of our hopes: the dead man's home
170   Is but a fellow to that pasture field.

PRIEST

Why there, Sir, is a thought that's new to me.
The Stone-cutters, 'tis true, might beg their bread
If every English church-yard were like ours:
Yet your conclusion wanders from the truth.
We have no need of names and epitaphs,
We talk about the dead by our fire-sides.
And then for our immortal part, *we* want
No symbols, Sir, to tell us that plain tale:
The thought of death sits easy on the man
180   Who has been born and dies among the mountains:

LEONARD

Your dalesmen, then, do in each other's thoughts
Possess a kind of second life: no doubt
You, Sir, could help me to the history
Of half these Graves?

PRIEST

With what I've witnessed, and with what I've heard,
Perhaps I might, and, on a winter's evening,
If you were seated at my chimney's nook
By turning o'er these hillocks one by one,
We two could travel, Sir, through a strange round,
190   Yet all in the broad high-way of the world.
Now there's a grave – your foot is half upon it,
It looks just like the rest, and yet that man
Died broken-hearted.

LEONARD
                'Tis a common case,
We'll take another: who is he that lies
Beneath yon ridge, the last of those three graves;–
It touches on that piece of native rock
Left in the church-yard wall.

PRIEST
                        That's Walter Ewbank.
He had as white a head and fresh a cheek
As ever were produced by youth and age
Engendering in the blood of hale fourscore.   200
For five long generations had the heart
Of Walter's forefathers o'erflowed the bounds
Of their inheritance, that single cottage,
You see it yonder, and those few green fields.
They toiled and wrought, and still, from sire to son,
Each struggled, and each yielded as before
A little – yet a little – and old Walter,
They left to him the family heart, and land
With other burthens than the crop it bore.
Year after year the old man still preserved   210
A cheerful mind, and buffeted with bond,
Interest and mortgages; at last he sank,
And went into his grave before his time.
Poor Walter! whether it was care that spurred him
God only knows, but to the very last
He had the lightest foot in Ennerdale:
His pace was never that of an old man:
I almost see him tripping down the path
With his two Grandsons after him – but you,
Unless our Landlord be your host to-night,   220
Have far to travel, and in these rough paths
Even in the longest day of midsummer –

LEONARD
But these two Orphans!

PRIEST
Orphans! such they were –
Yet not while Walter lived – for, though their Parents
Lay buried side by side as now they lie,
The old Man was a father to the boys,
Two fathers in one father: and if tears
Shed, when he talked of them where they were not,
And hauntings from the infirmity of love,
230   Are aught of what makes up a mother's heart,
This old Man in the day of his old age
Was half a mother to them. – If you weep, Sir,
To hear a stranger talking about strangers,
Heaven bless you when you are among your kindred!
Aye. You may turn that way – it is a grave
Which will bear looking at.

LEONARD
These Boys I hope
They loved this good old Man –

PRIEST
They did – and truly,
But that was what we almost overlooked,
They were such darlings of each other. For
240   Though from their cradles they had lived with Walter,
The only kinsman near them in the house,
Yet he being old, they had much love to spare,
And it all went into each other's hearts.
Leonard, the elder by just eighteen months,
Was two years taller: 'twas a joy to see,
To hear, to meet them! from their house the School
Was distant three short miles, and in the time
Of storm and thaw, when every water-course
And unbridged stream, such as you may have noticed
250   Crossing our roads at every hundred steps,
Was swoln into a noisy rivulet,
Would Leonard then, when elder boys perhaps
Remained at home, go staggering through the fords
Bearing his Brother on his back. – I've seen him,

On windy days, in one of those stray brooks,
Aye, more than once I've seen him mid-leg deep,
Their two books lying both on a dry stone
Upon the hither side: – and once I said,
As I remember, looking round these rocks
And hills on which we all of us were born,   260
That God who made the great book of the world
Would bless such piety –

LEONARD
                    It may be then –

PRIEST
Never did worthier lads break English bread:
The finest Sunday that the Autumn saw,
With all its mealy clusters of ripe nuts,
Could never keep these boys away from church,
Or tempt them to an hour of sabbath breach.
Leonard and James! I warrant, every corner
Among these rocks and every hollow place
Where foot could come, to one or both of them   270
Was known as well as to the flowers that grew there.
Like roe-bucks they went bounding o'er the hills:
They played like two young ravens on the crags:
Then they could write, aye and speak too, as well
As many of their betters – and for Leonard!
The very night before he went away,
In my own house I put into his hand
A Bible, and I'd wager twenty pounds,
That, if he is alive, he has it yet.

LEONARD
It seems, these Brothers have not lived to be   280
A comfort to each other. –

PRIEST
                    That they might
Live to that end, is what both old and young
In this our valley all of us have wished,
And what, for my part, I have often prayed:
But Leonard –

133

LEONARD
Then James still is left among you –

PRIEST
'Tis of the elder Brother I am speaking:
They had an Uncle, he was at that time
A thriving man, and trafficked on the seas:
And, but for this same Uncle, to this hour
Leonard had never handled rope or shroud.
For the Boy loved the life which we lead here;
And, though a very Stripling, twelve years old;
His soul was knit to this his native soil.
But, as I said, old Walter was too weak
To strive with such a torrent; when he died,
The estate and house were sold, and all their sheep,
A pretty flock, and which, for aught I know,
Had clothed the Ewbanks for a thousand years.
Well – all was gone, and they were destitute.
And Leonard, chiefly for his brother's sake,
Resolved to try his fortune on the seas.
'Tis now twelve years since we had tidings from him.
If there was one among us who had heard
That Leonard Ewbank was come home again,
From the great Gavel, down by Leeza's Banks,
And down the Enna, far as Egremont,
The day would be a very festival,
And those two bells of ours, which there you see
Hanging in the open air – but, O good Sir!
This is sad talk – they'll never sound for him
Living or dead – When last we heard of him
He was in slavery among the Moors
Upon the Barbary Coast – 'Twas not a little
That would bring down his spirit, and, no doubt,
Before it ended in his death, the Lad
Was sadly crossed – Poor Leonard! when we parted,
He took me by the hand and said to me,
If ever the day came when he was rich,
He would return, and on his Father's Land
He would grow old among us.

290

300

310

LEONARD

If that day 320

Should come, 'twould needs be a glad day for him;
He would himself, no doubt, be as happy then
As any that should meet him –

PRIEST

Happy, sir –

LEONARD

You said his kindred all were in their graves,
And that he had one Brother –

PRIEST

That is but

A fellow tale of sorrow. From his youth
James, though not sickly, yet was delicate,
And Leonard being always by his side
Had done so many offices about him,
That, though he was not of a timid nature, 330
Yet still the spirit of a mountain boy
In him was somewhat checked, and when his Brother
Was gone to sea and he was left alone
The little colour that he had was soon
Stolen from his cheek, he drooped, and pined and pined:

LEONARD

But these are all the graves of full grown men!

PRIEST

Aye, Sir, that passed away: we took him to us.
He was the child of all the dale – he lived
Three months with one, and six months with another:
And wanted neither food, nor clothes, nor love, 340
And many, many happy days were his.
But, whether blithe or sad, 'tis my belief
His absent Brother still was at his heart.
And, when he lived beneath our roof, we found
(A practice till this time unknown to him)
That often, rising from his bed at night,

He in his sleep would walk about, and sleeping
He sought his Brother Leonard – You are moved!
Forgive me, Sir: before I spoke to you,
I judged you most unkindly.

LEONARD

350   But this youth,
How did he die at last?

PRIEST

                        One sweet May morning,
It will be twelve years since, when Spring returns,
He had gone forth among the new-dropped lambs,
With two or three companions whom it chanced
Some further business summoned to a house
Which stands at the Dale-head. James, tired perhaps,
Or from some other cause remained behind.
You see yon precipice – it almost looks
Like some vast building made of many crags,
360 And in the midst is one particular rock
That rises like a column from the vale,
Whence by our Shepherds it is called, the Pillar.
James, pointing to its summit, over which
They all had purposed to return together,
Informed them that he there would wait for them:
They parted, and his comrades passed that way
Some two hours after, but they did not find him
At the appointed place, a circumstance
Of which they took no heed: but one of them,
370 Going by chance, at night, into the house
Which at this time was James's home, there learned
That nobody had seen him all that day:
The morning came, and still, he was unheard of:
The neighbours were alarmed, and to the Brook
Some went, and some towards the Lake; ere noon
They found him at the foot of that same Rock
Dead, and with mangled limbs. The third day after
I buried him, poor Lad, and there he lies.

LEONARD

And that then *is* his grave! – Before his death
You said that he saw many happy years?   380

PRIEST

Aye, that he did –

LEONARD

                    And all went well with him –

PRIEST

If he had one, the Lad had twenty homes.

LEONARD

And you believe then, that his mind was easy –

PRIEST

Yes, long before he died, he found that time
Is a true friend to sorrow, and unless
His thoughts were turned on Leonard's luckless fortune,
He talked about him with a cheerful love.

LEONARD

He could not come to an unhallowed end!

PRIEST

Nay, God forbid! You recollect I mentioned
A habit which disquietude and grief   390
Had brought upon him, and we all conjectured
That, as the day was warm, he had lain down
Upon the grass, and, waiting for his comrades
He there had fallen asleep, that in his sleep
He to the margin of the precipice
Had walked, and from the summit had fallen head-long,
And so no doubt he perished: at the time,
We guess, that in his hands he must have had
His Shepherd's staff; for midway in the cliff
It had been caught, and there for many years   400
It hung – and mouldered there.
                              The Priest here ended –
The Stranger would have thanked him, but he felt

Tears rushing in; both left the spot in silence,
And Leonard, when they reached the church-yard gate,
As the Priest lifted up the latch, turned round,
And, looking at the grave, he said, 'My Brother.'
The Vicar did not hear the words: and now,
Pointing towards the Cottage, he entreated
That Leonard would partake his homely fare:
The other thanked him with a fervent voice,
But added, that, the evening being calm,
He would pursue his journey. So they parted.

It was not long ere Leonard reached a grove
That overhung the road: he there stopped short,
And, sitting down beneath the trees, reviewed
All that the Priest had said: his early years
Were with him in his heart: his cherished hopes,
And thoughts which had been his an hour before,
All pressed on him with such a weight, that now,
This vale, where he had been so happy, seemed
A place in which he could not bear to live:
So he relinquished all his purposes.
He travelled on to Egremont; and thence,
That night, addressed a letter to the Priest
Reminding him of what had passed between them.
And adding, with a hope to be forgiven,
That it was from the weakness of his heart,
He had not dared to tell him, who he was.

This done, he went on shipboard, and is now
A Seaman, a grey headed Mariner.

Poems on the Naming of Places

I. 'IT WAS AN APRIL MORNING'

It was an April Morning: fresh and clear
The Rivulet, delighting in its strength,
Ran with a young man's speed, and yet the voice
Of waters which the winter had supplied
Was softened down into a vernal tone.
The spirit of enjoyment and desire,
And hopes and wishes, from all living things
Went circling, like a multitude of sounds.
The budding groves appeared as if in haste
To spur the steps of June; as if their shades   10
Of *various* green were hindrances that stood
Between them and their object: yet, meanwhile,
There was such deep contentment in the air
That every naked ash, and tardy tree
Yet leafless, seemed as though the countenance
With which it looked on this delightful day
Were native to the summer. – Up the brook
I roamed in the confusion of my heart,
Alive to all things and forgetting all.
At length I to a sudden turning came   20
In this continuous glen, where down a rock
The stream, so ardent in its course before,
Sent forth such sallies of glad sound, that all
Which I till then had heard, appeared the voice
Of common pleasure: beast and bird, the lamb,
The Shepherd's dog, the linnet and the thrush
Vied with this waterfall, and made a song
Which, while I listened, seemed like the wild growth
Or like some natural produce of the air
That could not cease to be. Green leaves were here,   30
But 'twas the foliage of the rocks, the birch,
The yew, the holly, and the bright green thorn,
With hanging islands of resplendent furze:

And on a summit, distant a short space,
By any who should look beyond the dell,
A single mountain Cottage might be seen.
I gazed and gazed, and to myself I said,
'Our thoughts at least are ours; and this wild nook,
My EMMA, I will dedicate to thee.'
40 ——Soon did the spot become my other home,
My dwelling, and my out-of-doors abode.
And, of the Shepherds who have seen me there,
To whom I sometimes in our idle talk
Have told this fancy, two or three, perhaps,
Years after we are gone and in our graves,
When they have cause to speak of this wild place,
May call it by the name of EMMA'S DELL.

II. TO JOANNA

Amid the smoke of cities did you pass
Your time of early youth, and there you learned,
From years of quiet industry, to love
The living Beings by your own fire-side,
With such a strong devotion, that your heart
Is slow towards the sympathies of them
Who look upon the hills with tenderness,
And make dear friendships with the streams and groves.
Yet we who are trangressors in this kind,
10 Dwelling retired in our simplicity
Among the woods and fields, we love you well,
Joanna! and I guess, since you have been
So distant from us now for two long years,
That you will gladly listen to discourse
However trivial, if you thence are taught
That they, with whom you once were happy, talk
Familiarly of you and of old times.

While I was seated, now some ten days past,
Beneath those lofty firs, that overtop
20 Their ancient neighbour, the old Steeple tower,

The Vicar from his gloomy house hard by
Came forth to greet me, and when he had asked,
'How fares Joanna, that wild-hearted Maid!
And when will she return to us?' he paused,
And after short exchange of village news,
He with grave looks demanded, for what cause,
Reviving obsolete Idolatry,
I like a Runic Priest, in characters
Of formidable size, had chiseled out
Some uncouth name upon the native rock,   30
Above the Rotha, by the forest side.
— Now, by those dear immunities of heart
Engendered betwixt malice and true love,
I was not loth to be so catechized,
And this was my reply. — 'As it befel,
One summer morning we had walked abroad
At break of day, Joanna and myself.
— 'Twas that delightful season, when the broom,
Full flowered, and visible on every steep,
Along the copses runs in veins of gold.   40
Our pathway led us on to Rotha's banks,
And when we came in front of that tall rock
Which looks towards the East, I there stopped short,
And traced the lofty barrier with my eye
From base to summit; such delight I found
To note in shrub and tree, in stone and flower,
That intermixture of delicious hues,
Along so vast a surface, all at once,
In one impression, by connecting force
Of their own beauty, imaged in the heart.   50
— When I had gazed perhaps two minutes' space,
Joanna, looking in my eyes, beheld
That ravishment of mine, and laughed aloud.
The rock, like something starting from a sleep,
Took up the Lady's voice, and laughed again:
That ancient Woman seated on Helm-crag
Was ready with her cavern; Hammar-Scar,
And the tall Steep of Silver-How sent forth

A noise of laughter; southern Loughrigg heard,
60 And Fairfield answered with a mountain tone:
Helvellyn far into the clear blue sky
Carried the Lady's voice, – old Skiddaw blew
His speaking trumpet; – back out of the clouds
Of Glaramara southward came the voice;
And Kirkstone tossed it from his misty head.
Now whether, (said I to our cordial Friend
Who in the hey-day of astonishment
Smiled in my face) this were in simple truth
A work accomplished by the brotherhood
70 Of ancient mountains, or my ear was touched
With dreams and visionary impulses,
Is not for me to tell; but sure I am
That there was a loud uproar in the hills.
And, while we both were listening, to my side
The fair Joanna drew, as if she wished
To shelter from some object of her fear.
– And hence, long afterwards, when eighteen moons
Were wasted, as I chanced to walk alone
Beneath this rock, at sun-rise, on a calm
80 And silent morning, I sate down, and there,
In memory of affections old and true,
I chiseled out in those rude characters
Joanna's name upon the living stone.
And I, and all who dwell by my fire-side
Have called the lovely rock, Joanna's Rock.'

III. 'THERE IS AN EMINENCE'

There is an Eminence, – of these our hills
The last that parleys with the setting sun.
We can behold it from our Orchard seat,
And, when at evening we pursue our walk
Along the public way, this Cliff, so high
Above us, and so distant in its height,
Is visible, and often seems to send
Its own deep quiet to restore our hearts.

142

The meteors make of it a favorite haunt:
The star of Jove, so beautiful and large   10
In the mid heav'ns, is never half so fair
As when he shines above it. 'Tis in truth
The loneliest place we have among the clouds.
And She who dwells with me, whom I have loved
With such communion, that no place on earth
Can ever be a solitude to me,
Hath said, this lonesome Peak shall bear my Name.

IV. 'A NARROW GIRDLE OF ROUGH STONES AND CRAGS'

A narrow girdle of rough stones and crags,
A rude and natural causeway, interposed
Between the water and a winding slope
Of copse and thicket, leaves the eastern shore
Of Grasmere safe in its own privacy.
And there, myself and two beloved Friends,
One calm September morning, ere the mist
Had altogether yielded to the sun,
Sauntered on this retired and difficult way.
——Ill suits the road with one in haste, but we   10
Played with our time; and, as we strolled along,
It was our occupation to observe
Such objects as the waves had tossed ashore,
Feather, or leaf, or weed, or withered bough,
Each on the other heaped along the line
Of the dry wreck. And in our vacant mood,
Not seldom did we stop to watch some tuft
Of dandelion seed or thistle's beard,
Which, seeming lifeless half, and half impelled
By some internal feeling, skimmed along   20
Close to the surface of the lake that lay
Asleep in a dead calm, ran closely on
Along the dead calm lake, now here, now there,
In all its sportive wanderings all the while
Making report of an invisible breeze
That was its wings, its chariot, and its horse,

Its very playmate, and its moving soul.
——And often, trifling with a privilege
Alike indulged to all, we paused, one now,
30   And now the other, to point out, perchance
To pluck, some flower or water-weed, too fair
Either to be divided from the place
On which it grew, or to be left alone
To its own beauty. Many such there are,
Fair ferns and flowers, and chiefly that tall plant
So stately, of the Queen Osmunda named,
Plant lovelier in its own retired abode
On Grasmere's beach, than Naiad by the side
Of Grecian brook, or Lady of the Mere
40   Sole-sitting by the shores of old Romance.
——So fared we that sweet morning: from the fields
Meanwhile, a noise was heard, the busy mirth
Of Reapers, Men and Women, Boys and Girls.
Delighted much to listen to those sounds,
And in the fashion which I have described,
Feeding unthinking fancies, we advanced
Along the indented shore; when suddenly,
Through a thin veil of glittering haze, we saw
Before us on a point of jutting land
50   The tall and upright figure of a Man
Attired in peasant's garb, who stood alone
Angling beside the margin of the lake.
That way we turned our steps; nor was it long,
Ere making ready comments on the sight
Which then we saw, with one and the same voice
We all cried out, that he must be indeed
An idle man, who thus could lose a day
Of the mid harvest, when the labourer's hire
Is ample, and some little might be stored
60   Wherewith to cheer him in the winter time.
Thus talking of that Peasant we approached
Close to the spot where with his rod and line
He stood alone; whereat he turned his head
To greet us – and we saw a man worn down

By sickness, gaunt and lean, with sunken cheeks
And wasted limbs, his legs so long and lean
That for my single self I looked at them,
Forgetful of the body they sustained.——
Too weak to labour in the harvest field,
The man was using his best skill to gain   70
A pittance from the dead unfeeling lake
That knew not of his wants. I will not say
What thoughts immediately were ours, nor how
The happy idleness of that sweet morn,
With all its lovely images, was changed
To serious musing and to self-reproach.
Nor did we fail to see within ourselves
What need there is to be reserved in speech,
And temper all our thoughts with charity.
——Therefore, unwilling to forget that day,   80
My Friend, Myself, and She who then received
The same admonishment, have called the place
By a memorial name, uncouth indeed
As e'er by Mariner was giv'n to Bay
Or Foreland on a new-discovered coast,
And, POINT RASH-JUDGMENT is the Name it bears.

V. TO M.H.

Our walk was far among the ancient trees:
There was no road, nor any wood-man's path,
But the thick umbrage, checking the wild growth
Of weed and sapling, on the soft green turf
Beneath the branches of itself had made
A track which brought us to a slip of lawn,
And a small bed of water in the woods.
All round this pool both flocks and herds might drink
On its firm margin, even as from a well
Or some stone-bason which the Herdsman's hand   10
Had shaped for their refreshment, nor did sun
Or wind from any quarter ever come
But as a blessing to this calm recess,

This glade of water and this one green field.
The spot was made by Nature for herself:
The travellers know it not, and 'twill remain
Unknown to them; but it is beautiful,
And if a man should plant his cottage near,
Should sleep beneath the shelter of its trees,
20 And blend its waters with his daily meal,
He would so love it that in his death-hour
Its image would survive among his thoughts,
And, therefore, my sweet MARY, this still nook
With all its beeches we have named from You.

''Tis said, that some have died for love'

'Tis said, that some have died for love:
And here and there a church-yard grave is found
In the cold North's unhallowed ground,
Because the wretched man himself had slain,
His love was such a grievous pain.
And there is one whom I five years have known;
He dwells alone
Upon Helvellyn's side.
He loved——The pretty Barbara died,
10 And thus he makes his moan:
Three years had Barbara in her grave been laid
When thus his moan he made.

'Oh! move thou Cottage from behind that oak
Or let the aged tree uprooted lie,
That in some other way yon smoke
May mount into the sky!
The clouds pass on; they from the Heavens depart:
I look – the sky is empty space;
I know not what I trace;
20 But when I cease to look, my hand is on my heart.

'O! what a weight is in these shades! Ye leaves,
When will that dying murmur be suppressed?
Your sound my heart of peace bereaves,
It robs my heart of rest.
Thou Thrush, that singest loud and loud and free,
Into yon row of willows flit,
Upon that alder sit;
Or sing another song, or chuse another tree.

'Roll back, sweet rill! back to thy mountain bounds,
And there for ever be thy waters chained!   30
For thou dost haunt the air with sounds
That cannot be sustained;
If still beneath that pine-tree's ragged bough
Headlong yon waterfall must come,
Oh let it then be dumb! –
Be any thing, sweet rill, but that which thou art now.

'Thou Eglantine whose arch so proudly towers
(Even like a rainbow spanning half the vale)
Thou one fair shrub, oh! shed thy flowers,
And stir not in the gale.   40
For thus to see thee nodding in the air,
To see thy arch thus stretch and bend,
Thus rise and thus descend,
Disturbs me, till the sight is more than I can bear.'

The man who makes this feverish complaint
Is one of giant stature, who could dance
Equipped from head to foot in iron mail.
Ah gentle Love! if ever thought was thine
To store up kindred hours for me, thy face
Turn from me, gentle Love, nor let me walk   50
Within the sound of Emma's voice, or know
Such happiness as I have known to-day.

147

Michael,

A Pastoral Poem

If from the public way you turn your steps
Up the tumultuous brook of Green-head Gill,
You will suppose that with an upright path
Your feet must struggle; in such bold ascent
The pastoral Mountains front you, face to face.
But, courage! for beside that boisterous Brook
The mountains have all opened out themselves,
And made a hidden valley of their own.
No habitation there is seen; but such
As journey thither find themselves alone
With a few sheep, with rocks and stones, and kites
That overhead are sailing in the sky.
It is in truth an utter solitude,
Nor should I have made mention of this Dell
But for one object which you might pass by,
Might see and notice not. Beside the brook
There is a straggling heap of unhewn stones!
And to that place a story appertains,
Which, though it be ungarnished with events,
Is not unfit, I deem, for the fire-side,
Or for the summer shade. It was the first,
The earliest of those tales that spake to me
Of Shepherds, dwellers in the vallies, men
Whom I already loved, not verily
For their own sakes, but for the fields and hills
Where was their occupation and abode.
And hence this Tale, while I was yet a boy
Careless of books, yet having felt the power
Of Nature, by the gentle agency
Of natural objects led me on to feel
For passions that were not my own, and think
At random and imperfectly indeed
On man; the heart of man and human life.

Therefore, although it be a history
Homely and rude, I will relate the same
For the delight of a few natural hearts,
And with yet fonder feeling, for the sake
Of youthful Poets, who among these Hills
Will be my second self when I am gone.

Upon the Forest-side in Grasmere Vale   40
There dwelt a Shepherd, Michael was his name,
An old man, stout of heart, and strong of limb.
His bodily frame had been from youth to age
Of an unusual strength: his mind was keen
Intense and frugal, apt for all affairs,
And in his Shepherd's calling he was prompt
And watchful more than ordinary men.
Hence he had learned the meaning of all winds,
Of blasts of every tone, and often-times
When others heeded not, he heard the South   50
Make subterraneous music, like the noise
Of Bagpipers on distant Highland hills;
The Shepherd, at such warning, of his flock
Bethought him, and he to himself would say
The winds are now devising work for me!
And truly at all times the storm, that drives
The Traveller to a shelter, summoned him
Up to the mountains: he had been alone
Amid the heart of many thousand mists
That came to him and left him on the heights.   60
So lived he till his eightieth year was passed.

And grossly that man errs, who should suppose
That the green Valleys, and the Streams and Rocks
Were things indifferent to the Shepherd's thoughts.
Fields, where with cheerful spirits he had breathed
The common air; the hills, which he so oft
Had climbed with vigorous steps; which had impressed
So many incidents upon his mind
Of hardship, skill or courage, joy or fear;

70 Which like a book preserved the memory
Of the dumb animals, whom he had saved,
Had fed or sheltered, linking to such acts,
So grateful in themselves, the certainty
Of honorable gains; these fields, these hills
Which were his living Being, even more
Than his own Blood – what could they less? had laid
Strong hold on his affections, were to him
A pleasurable feeling of blind love,
The pleasure which there is in life itself.

80 He had not passed his days in singleness.
He had a Wife, a comely Matron, old
Though younger than himself full twenty years.
She was a woman of a stirring life
Whose heart was in her house: two wheels she had
Of antique form, this large for spinning wool,
That small for flax, and if one wheel had rest,
It was because the other was at work.
The Pair had but one Inmate in their house,
An only Child, who had been born to them
90 When Michael telling o'er his years began
To deem that he was old, in Shepherd's phrase,
With one foot in the grave. This only son,
With two brave sheep dogs tried in many a storm,
The one of an inestimable worth,
Made all their Household. I may truly say,
That they were as a proverb in the vale
For endless industry. When day was gone,
And from their occupations out of doors
The Son and Father were come home, even then
100 Their labour did not cease, unless when all
Turned to their cleanly supper-board, and there
Each with a mess of pottage and skimmed milk,
Sate round their basket piled with oaten cakes,
And their plain home-made cheese. Yet when their meal
Was ended, LUKE (for so the Son was named)
And his old Father, both betook themselves

To such convenient work, as might employ
Their hands by the fire-side; perhaps to card
Wool for the House-wife's spindle, or repair
Some injury done to sickle, flail, or scythe,   110
Or other implement of house or field.

Down from the ceiling by the chimney's edge,
Which in our ancient uncouth country style
Did with a huge projection overbrow
Large space beneath, as duly as the light
Of day grew dim, the House-wife hung a lamp;
An aged utensil, which had performed
Service beyond all others of its kind.
Early at evening did it burn and late,
Surviving Comrade of uncounted Hours   120
Which going by from year to year had found
And left the Couple neither gay perhaps
Nor cheerful, yet with objects and with hopes
Living a life of eager industry.
And now, when LUKE was in his eighteenth year,
There by the light of this old lamp they sate,
Father and Son, while late into the night
The House-wife plied her own peculiar work,
Making the cottage thro' the silent hours
Murmur as with the sound of summer flies.   130
Not with a waste of words, but for the sake
Of pleasure, which I know that I shall give
To many living now, I of this Lamp
Speak thus minutely: for there are no few
Whose memories will bear witness to my tale.
The Light was famous in its neighbourhood,
And was a public Symbol of the life,
The thrifty Pair had lived. For, as it chanced,
Their Cottage on a plot of rising ground
Stood single, with large prospect North and South,   140
High into Easedale, up to Dunmal-Raise,
And Westward to the village near the Lake.
And from this constant light so regular

And so far seen, the House itself by all
Who dwelt within the limits of the vale,
Both old and young, was named The Evening Star.

Thus living on through such a length of years,
The Shepherd, if he loved himself, must needs
Have loved his Help-mate; but to Michael's heart
This Son of his old age was yet more dear –
Effect which might perhaps have been produced
By that instinctive tenderness, the same
Blind Spirit, which is in the blood of all,
Or that a child, more than all other gifts,
Brings hope with it, and forward-looking thoughts,
And stirrings of inquietude, when they
By tendency of nature needs must fail.
From such, and other causes, to the thoughts
Of the old Man his only Son was now
The dearest object that he knew on earth.
Exceeding was the love he bare to him,
His Heart and his Heart's joy! For oftentimes
Old Michael, while he was a babe in arms,
Had done him female service, not alone
For dalliance and delight, as is the use
Of Fathers, but with patient mind enforced
To acts of tenderness; and he had rocked
His cradle with a woman's gentle hand.

And in a later time, ere yet the Boy
Had put on Boy's attire, did Michael love,
Albeit of a stern unbending mind,
To have the young one in his sight, when he
Had work by his own door, or when he sate
With sheep before him on his Shepherd's stool,
Beneath that large old Oak, which near their door
Stood, and from its enormous breadth of shade
Chosen for the Shearer's covert from the sun,
Thence in our rustic dialect was called
The CLIPPING TREE, a name which yet it bears.

There, while they two were sitting in the shade,   180
With others round them, earnest all and blithe,
Would Michael exercise his heart with looks
Of fond correction and reproof bestowed
Upon the child, if he disturbed the sheep
By catching at their legs, or with his shouts
Scared them, while they lay still beneath the shears.

And when by Heaven's good grace the Boy grew up
A healthy Lad, and carried in his cheek
Two steady roses that were five years old,
Then Michael from a winter coppice cut   190
With his own hand a sapling, which he hooped
With iron, making it throughout in all
Due requisites a perfect Shepherd's Staff,
And gave it to the Boy; wherewith equipped
He as a Watchman oftentimes was placed
At gate or gap, to stem or turn the flock,
And to his office prematurely called
There stood the urchin, as you will divine,
Something between a hindrance and a help,
And for this cause not always, I believe,   200
Receiving from his Father hire of praise,
Though nought was left undone which staff or voice,
Or looks, or threatening gestures could perform.
But soon as Luke, full ten years old, could stand
Against the mountain blasts, and to the heights,
Not fearing toil, nor length of weary ways,
He with his Father daily went, and they
Were as companions, why should I relate
That objects which the Shepherd loved before
Were dearer now? that from the Boy there came   210
Feelings and emanations, things which were
Light to the sun and music to the wind;
And that the Old Man's heart seemed born again.
Thus in his Father's sight the Boy grew up:
And now when he had reached his eighteenth year,
He was his comfort and his daily hope.

While this good household thus were living on
From day to day, to Michael's ear there came
Distressful tidings. Long before the time
Of which I speak, the Shepherd had been bound
In surety for his Brother's Son, a man
Of an industrious life, and ample means,
But unforeseen misfortunes suddenly
Had pressed upon him, and old Michael now
Was summoned to discharge the forfeiture,
A grievous penalty, but little less
Than half his substance. This un-looked for claim
At the first hearing, for a moment took
More hope out of his life than he supposed
That any old man ever could have lost.
As soon as he had gathered so much strength
That he could look his trouble in the face,
It seemed that his sole refuge was to sell
A portion of his patrimonial fields.
Such was his first resolve; he thought again,
And his heart failed him. 'Isabel,' said he,
Two evenings after he had heard the news,
'I have been toiling more than seventy years,
And in the open sun-shine of God's love
Have we all lived, yet if these fields of ours
Should pass into a Stranger's hand, I think
That I could not lie quiet in my grave.
Our lot is a hard lot; the Sun itself
Has scarcely been more diligent than I,
And I have lived to be a fool at last
To my own family. An evil Man
That was, and made an evil choice, if he
Were false to us; and if he were not false,
There are ten thousand to whom loss like this
Had been no sorrow. I forgive him – but
'Twere better to be dumb than to talk thus.
When I began, my purpose was to speak
Of remedies and of a cheerful hope.
Our Luke shall leave us, Isabel; the land

Shall not go from us, and it shall be free,
He shall possess it, free as is the wind
That passes over it. We have, thou knowest,
Another Kinsman, he will be our friend
In this distress. He is a prosperous man,
Thriving in trade, and Luke to him shall go, 260
And with his Kinsman's help and his own thrift,
He quickly will repair this loss, and then
May come again to us. If here he stay,
What can be done? Where every one is poor
What can be gained?' At this, the old man paused,
And Isabel sate silent, for her mind
Was busy, looking back into past times.
There's Richard Bateman, thought she to herself,
He was a parish-boy – at the church-door
They made a gathering for him, shillings, pence, 270
And halfpennies, wherewith the Neighbours bought
A Basket, which they filled with Pedlar's wares,
And with this Basket on his arm, the Lad
Went up to London, found a Master there,
Who out of many chose the trusty Boy
To go and overlook his merchandise
Beyond the seas, where he grew wond'rous rich,
And left estates and monies to the poor,
And at his birth-place built a Chapel, floored
With Marble, which he sent from foreign lands. 280
These thoughts, and many others of like sort,
Passed quickly thro' the mind of Isabel,
And her face brightened. The Old Man was glad,
And thus resumed. 'Well! Isabel, this scheme
These two days has been meat and drink to me.
Far more than we have lost is left us yet.
– We have enough – I wish indeed that I
Were younger, but this hope is a good hope.
– Make ready Luke's best garments, of the best
Buy for him more, and let us send him forth 290
To-morrow, or the next day, or to-night:
– If he could go, the Boy should go to-night.'
                    . .

Here Michael ceased, and to the fields went forth
With a light heart. The House-wife for five days
Was restless morn and night, and all day long
Wrought on with her best fingers to prepare
Things needful for the journey of her Son.
But Isabel was glad when Sunday came
To stop her in her work; for, when she lay
By Michael's side, she for the two last nights
Heard him, how he was troubled in his sleep:
And when they rose at morning she could see
That all his hopes were gone. That day at noon
She said to Luke, while they two by themselves
Were sitting at the door, 'Thou must not go,
We have no other Child but thee to lose,
None to remember – do not go away,
For if thou leave thy Father he will die.'
The Lad made answer with a jocund voice,
And Isabel, when she had told her fears,
Recovered heart. That evening her best fare
Did she bring forth, and all together sate
Like happy people round a Christmas fire.

Next morning Isabel resumed her work,
And all the ensuing week the house appeared
As cheerful as a grove in Spring: at length
The expected letter from their Kinsman came,
With kind assurances that he would do
His utmost for the welfare of the Boy,
To which requests were added that forthwith
He might be sent to him. Ten times or more
The letter was read over; Isabel
Went forth to shew it to the neighbours round:
Nor was there at that time on English Land
A prouder heart than Luke's. When Isabel
Had to her house returned, the Old Man said,
'He shall depart to-morrow.' To this word
The House-wife answered, talking much of things

Which, if at such short notice he should go,
Would surely be forgotten. But at length 330
She gave consent, and Michael was at ease.

Near the tumultuous brook of Green-head Gill,
In that deep Valley, Michael had designed
To build a Sheep-fold, and, before he heard
The tidings of his melancholy loss,
For this same purpose he had gathered up
A heap of stones, which close to the brook side
Lay thrown together, ready for the work.
With Luke that evening thitherward he walked;
And soon as they had reached the place he stopped, 340
And thus the Old Man spake to him. 'My Son,
To-morrow thou wilt leave me; with full heart
I look upon thee, for thou art the same
That were a promise to me ere thy birth,
And all thy life hast been my daily joy.
I will relate to thee some little part
Of our two histories; 'twill do thee good
When thou art from me, even if I should speak
Of things thou canst not know of.——After thou
First cam'st into the world, as it befalls 350
To new-born infants, thou didst sleep away
Two days, and blessings from thy Father's tongue
Then fell upon thee. Day by day passed on,
And still I loved thee with encreasing love.
Never to living ear came sweeter sounds
Than when I heard thee by our own fire-side
First uttering without words a natural tune,
When thou, a feeding babe, didst in thy joy
Sing at thy Mother's breast. Month followed month,
And in the open fields my life was passed 360
And in the mountains, else I think that thou
Hadst been brought up upon thy father's knees.
– But we were playmates, Luke; among these hills,
As well thou know'st, in us the old and young

Have played together, nor with me didst thou
Lack any pleasure which a boy can know.'
Luke had a manly heart; but at these words
He sobbed aloud; the Old Man grasped his hand,
And said, 'Nay do not take it so – I see
370   That these are things of which I need not speak.
– Even to the utmost I have been to thee
A kind and a good Father; and herein
I but repay a gift which I myself
Receiv'd at others' hands, for, though now old
Beyond the common life of man, I still
Remember them who loved me in my youth.
Both of them sleep together: here they lived
As all their Forefathers had done, and when
At length their time was come, they were not loth
380   To give their bodies to the family mold.
I wished that thou should'st live the life they lived.
But 'tis a long time to look back, my Son,
And see so little gain from sixty years.
These fields were burthened when they came to me;
'Till I was forty years of age, not more
Than half of my inheritance was mine.
I toiled and toiled; God blessed me in my work,
And 'till these three weeks past the land was free.
– It looks as if it never could endure
390   Another Master. Heaven forgive me, Luke,
If I judge ill for thee, but it seems good
That thou should'st go.' At this the Old Man paused,
Then, pointing to the Stones near which they stood,
Thus, after a short silence, he resumed:
'This was a work for us, and now, my Son,
It is a work for me. But, lay one Stone –
Here, lay it for me, Luke, with thine own hands.
I for the purpose brought thee to this place.
Nay, Boy, be of good hope: – we both may live
400   To see a better day. At eighty-four
I still am strong and stout; – do thou thy part,
I will do mine. – I will begin again

With many tasks that were resigned to thee;
Up to the heights, and in among the storms,
Will I without thee go again, and do
All works which I was wont to do alone,
Before I knew thy face.——Heaven bless thee, Boy!
Thy heart these two weeks has been beating fast
With many hopes – it should be so – yes – yes –
I knew that thou could'st never have a wish   410
To leave me, Luke, thou hast been bound to me
Only by links of love, when thou art gone
What will be left to us! – But, I forget
My purposes. Lay now the corner-stone,
As I requested, and hereafter, Luke,
When thou art gone away, should evil men
Be thy companions, let this Sheep-fold be
Thy anchor and thy shield; amid all fear
And all temptation, let it be to thee
An emblem of the life thy Fathers lived,   420
Who, being innocent, did for that cause
Bestir them in good deeds. Now, fare thee well –
When thou return'st, thou in this place wilt see
A work which is not here, a covenant
'Twill be between us——but whatever fate
Befall thee, I shall love thee to the last,
And bear thy memory with me to the grave.'

The Shepherd ended here; and Luke stooped down,
And as his Father had requested, laid
The first stone of the Sheep-fold; at the sight   430
The Old Man's grief broke from him, to his heart
He pressed his Son, he kissed him and wept;
And to the House together they returned.

Next morning, as had been resolved, the Boy
Began his journey, and when he had reached
The public Way, he put on a bold face;
And all the Neighbours as he passed their doors
Came forth, with wishes and with farewell pray'rs,

That followed him 'till he was out of sight.
440 A good report did from their Kinsman come,
Of Luke and his well-doing; and the Boy
Wrote loving letters, full of wond'rous news,
Which, as the House-wife phrased it, were throughout
The prettiest letters that were ever seen.
Both parents read them with rejoicing hearts.
So, many months passed on: and once again
The Shepherd went about his daily work
With confident and cheerful thoughts; and now
Sometimes when he could find a leisure hour
450 He to that valley took his way, and there
Wrought at the Sheep-fold. Meantime Luke began
To slacken in his duty, and at length
He in the dissolute city gave himself
To evil courses: ignominy and shame
Fell on him, so that he was driven at last
To seek a hiding-place beyond the seas.

There is a comfort in the strength of love;
'Twill make a thing endurable, which else
Would break the heart: – Old Michael found it so.
460 I have conversed with more than one who well
Remember the Old Man, and what he was
Years after he had heard this heavy news.
His bodily frame had been from youth to age
Of an unusual strength. Among the rocks
He went, and still looked up upon the sun,
And listened to the wind; and as before
Performed all kinds of labour for his Sheep,
And for the land his small inheritance.
And to that hollow Dell from time to time
470 Did he repair, to build the Fold of which
His flock had need. 'Tis not forgotten yet
The pity which was then in every heart
For the Old Man – and 'tis believed by all
That many and many a day he thither went,
And never lifted up a single stone.
There, by the Sheep-fold, sometimes was he seen

Sitting alone, with that his faithful Dog,
Then old, beside him, lying at his feet.
The length of full seven years from time to time
He at the building of this Sheep-fold wrought,   480
And left the work unfinished when he died.

Three years, or little more, did Isabel,
Survive her Husband: at her death the estate
Was sold, and went into a Stranger's hand.
The Cottage which was named The Evening Star
Is gone, the ploughshare has been through the ground
On which it stood; great changes have been wrought
In all the neighbourhood, yet the Oak is left
That grew beside their Door; and the remains
Of the unfinished Sheep-fold may be seen   490
Beside the boisterous brook of Green-head Gill.

The Affliction of Margaret —— of —

Where art thou, my beloved Son,
Where art thou, worse to me than dead?
Oh find me prosperous or undone!
Or, if the grave be now thy bed,
Why am I ignorant of the same
That I may rest; and neither blame,
Nor sorrow may attend thy name?

Seven years, alas, to have received
No tidings of an only child;
To have despaired, and have believed,   10
And be for evermore beguiled;
Sometimes with thoughts of very bliss!
I catch at them, and then I miss;
Was ever darkness like to this?

He was among the prime in worth,
An object beauteous to behold;
Well born, well bred; I sent him forth
Ingenuous, innocent, and bold:
If things ensued that wanted grace,
As hath been said, they were not base;
And never blush was on my face.

Ah! little doth the Young One dream,
When full of play and childish cares,
What power hath even his wildest scream,
Heard by his Mother unawares!
He knows it not, he cannot guess:
Years to a Mother bring distress;
But do not make her love the less.

Neglect me! no I suffered long
From that ill thought; and being blind,
Said, 'Pride shall help me in my wrong;
Kind mother have I been, as kind
As ever breathed:' and that is true;
I've wet my path with tears like dew,
Weeping for him when no one knew.

My Son, if thou be humbled, poor,
Hopeless of honour and of gain,
Oh! do not dread thy mother's door;
Think not of me with grief and pain:
I now can see with better eyes;
And worldly grandeur I despise,
And fortune with her gifts and lies.

Alas! the fowls of Heaven have wings,
And blasts of Heaven will aid their flight;
They mount, how short a voyage brings
The Wanderers back to their delight!
Chains tie us down by land and sea;
And wishes, vain as mine, may be
All that is left to comfort thee.

Perhaps some dungeon hears thee groan,   50
Maimed, mangled by inhuman men;
Or thou upon a Desart thrown
Inheritest the Lion's Den;
Or hast been summoned to the Deep,
Thou, Thou and all thy mates, to keep
An incommunicable sleep.

I look for Ghosts; but none will force
Their way to me; 'tis falsely said
That there was ever intercourse
Betwixt the living and the dead;   60
For, surely, then I should have sight
Of Him I wait for day and night,
With love and longings infinite.

My apprehensions come in crowds;
I dread the rustling of the grass;
The very shadows of the clouds
Have power to shake me as they pass:
I question things, and do not find
One that will answer to my mind;
And all the world appears unkind.   70

Beyond participation lie
My troubles, and beyond relief:
If any chance to heave a sigh
They pity me, and not my grief.
Then come to me, my Son, or send
Some tidings that my woes may end;
I have no other earthly friend.

'I travelled among unknown Men'

I travelled among unknown Men,
   In Lands beyond the Sea;
Nor England! did I know till then
   What love I bore to thee.

'Tis past, that melancholy dream!
   Nor will I quit thy shore
A second time; for still I seem
   To love thee more and more.

Among thy mountains did I feel
   The joy of my desire;
And She I cherished turned her wheel
   Beside an English fire.

Thy mornings shewed – thy nights concealed
   The bowers where Lucy played;
And thine is, too, the last green field
   Which Lucy's eyes surveyed!

To a Sky-Lark

Up with me! up with me into the clouds!
    For thy song, Lark, is strong;
Up with me, up with me into the clouds!
    Singing, singing,
With all the heav'ns about thee ringing,
    Lift me, guide me, till I find
That spot which seems so to thy mind!

I have walked through wildernesses dreary,
    And today my heart is weary;
    Had I now the soul of a Faery,
      Up to thee would I fly.
There is madness about thee, and joy divine
    In that song of thine;
Up with me, up with me, high and high,
To thy banqueting-place in the sky!
    Joyous as Morning,
    Thou art laughing and scorning;
Thou hast a nest, for thy love and thy rest:
And, though little troubled with sloth,
Drunken Lark! thou would'st be loth
To be such a Traveller as I.
    Happy, happy Liver!
With a soul as strong as a mountain River,
Pouring out praise to the Almighty Giver,
    Joy and jollity be with us both!
    Hearing thee, or else some other,
    As merry a Brother,
I on the earth will go plodding on,
By myself, cheerfully, till the day is done.

The Sailor's Mother

One morning (raw it was and wet,
A foggy day in winter time)
A Woman in the road I met,
Not old, though something past her prime:
Majestic in her person, tall and straight;
And like a Roman matron's was her mien and gait.

The ancient Spirit is not dead;
Old times, thought I, are breathing there;
Proud was I that my country bred
Such strength, a dignity so fair:
She begged an alms, like one in poor estate;
I looked at her again, nor did my pride abate.

When from these lofty thoughts I woke,
With the first word I had to spare
I said to her, 'Beneath your Cloak
What's that which on your arm you bear?'
She answered soon as she the question heard,
'A simple burthen, Sir, a little Singing-bird.'

And, thus continuing, she said,
'I had a Son, who many a day
Sailed on the seas; but he is dead;
In Denmark he was cast away;
And I have been as far as Hull, to see
What clothes he might have left, or other property.

'The Bird and Cage they both were his;
'Twas my Son's Bird; and neat and trim
He kept it: many voyages
This Singing-bird hath gone with him;
When last he sailed he left the Bird behind;
As it might be, perhaps, from bodings of his mind.

'He to a Fellow-lodger's care
Had left it, to be watched and fed,
Till he came back again; and there
I found it when my Son was dead;
And now, God help me for my little wit!
I trail it with me, Sir! he took so much delight in it.'

Alice Fell

The Post-boy drove with fierce career,
For threat'ning clouds the moon had drowned;
When suddenly I seemed to hear
A moan, a lamentable sound.

As if the wind blew many ways
I heard the sound, and more and more:
It seemed to follow with the Chaise,
And still I heard it as before.

At length I to the Boy called out,
He stopped his horses at the word;   10
But neither cry, nor voice, nor shout,
Nor aught else like it could be heard.

The Boy then smacked his whip, and fast
The horses scampered through the rain;
And soon I heard upon the blast
The voice, and bade him halt again.

Said I, alighting on the ground,
'What can it be, this piteous moan?'
And there a little Girl I found,
Sitting behind the Chaise, alone.   20

'My Cloak!' the word was last and first,
And loud and bitterly she wept,
As if her very heart would burst;
And down from off the Chaise she leapt.

'What ails you, Child?' She sobbed, 'Look here!'
I saw it in the wheel entangled,
A weather beaten Rag as e'er
From any garden scare-crow dangled.

'Twas twisted betwixt nave and spoke;
30   Her help she lent, and with good heed
Together we released the Cloak;
A wretched, wretched rag indeed!

'And whither are you going, Child,
To night along these lonesome ways?'
'To Durham' answered she half wild –
'Then come with me into the chaise.'

She sate like one past all relief;
Sob after sob she forth did send
In wretchedness, as if her grief
40   Could never, never, have an end.

'My Child, in Durham do you dwell?'
She checked herself in her distress,
And said, 'My name is Alice Fell;
I'm fatherless and motherless.

'And I to Durham, Sir, belong.'
And then, as if the thought would choke
Her very heart, her grief grew strong;
And all was for her tattered Cloak.

The chaise drove on; our journey's end
Was nigh; and, sitting by my side,   50
As if she'd lost her only friend
She wept, nor would be pacified.

Up to the Tavern-door we post;
Of Alice and her grief I told;
And I gave money to the Host,
To buy a new Cloak for the old.

'And let it be of duffil grey,
As warm a cloak as man can sell!'
Proud Creature was she the next day,
The little Orphan, Alice Fell!   60

To a Butterfly

Stay near me – do not take thy flight!
A little longer stay in sight!
Much converse do I find in Thee,
Historian of my Infancy!
Float near me; do not yet depart!
Dead times revive in thee:
Thou bring'st, gay Creature as thou art!
A solemn image to my heart,
My Father's Family!

Oh! pleasant, pleasant were the days,   10
The time, when in our childish plays
My Sister Emmeline and I
Together chaced the Butterfly!
A very hunter did I rush
Upon the prey: – with leaps and springs
I followed on from brake to bush;
But She, God love her! feared to brush
The dust from off its wings.

The Sparrow's Nest

Look, five blue eggs are gleaming there!
Few visions have I seen more fair,
Nor many prospects of delight
More pleasing than that simple sight!
I started seeming to espy
The home and sheltered bed,
The Sparrow's dwelling, which, hard by
My Father's House, in wet or dry,
My Sister Emmeline and I
    Together visited.

She looked at it as if she feared it;
Still wishing, dreading to be near it:
Such heart was in her, being then
A little Prattler among men.
The Blessing of my later years
Was with me when a Boy;
She gave me eyes, she gave me ears;
And humble cares, and delicate fears;
A heart, the fountain of sweet tears;
    And love, and thought, and joy.

To the Cuckoo

O blithe New-comer! I have heard,
I hear thee and rejoice:
O Cuckoo! shall I call thee Bird,
Or but a wandering Voice?

While I am lying on the grass,
I hear thy restless shout:
From hill to hill it seems to pass,
About, and all about!

To me, no Babbler with a tale
Of sunshine and of flowers,   10
Thou tellest, Cuckoo! in the vale
Of visionary hours.

Thrice welcome, Darling of the Spring!
Even yet thou art to me
No Bird; but an invisible Thing,
A voice, a mystery.

The same whom in my School-boy days
I listened to; that Cry
Which made me look a thousand ways;
In bush, and tree, and sky.   20

To seek thee did I often rove
Through woods and on the green;
And thou wert still a hope, a love;
Still longed for, never seen!

And I can listen to thee yet;
Can lie upon the plain
And listen, till I do beget
That golden time again.

O blessed Bird! the earth we pace
Again appears to be   30
An unsubstantial, faery place;
That is fit home for Thee!

'My heart leaps up when I behold'

My heart leaps up when I behold
    A Rainbow in the sky:
So was it when my life began;
So is it now I am a Man;
So be it when I shall grow old,
    Or let me die!
The Child is Father of the Man;
And I could wish my days to be
Bound each to each by natural piety.

To H.C.,

Six Years Old

O Thou! whose fancies from afar are brought;
Who of thy words dost make a mock apparel,
And fittest to unutterable thought
The breeze-like motion and the self-born carol;
Thou Faery Voyager! that dost float
In such clear water, that thy Boat
May rather seem
To brood on air than on an earthly stream;
Suspended in a stream as clear as sky,
Where earth and heaven do make one imagery;
O blessed Vision! happy Child!
That art so exquisitely wild,
I think of thee with many fears
For what may be thy lot in future years.

I thought of times when Pain might be thy guest,
Lord of thy house and hospitality;
And grief, uneasy Lover! never rest
But when she sate within the touch of thee.

Oh! too industrious folly!
Oh! vain and causeless melancholy!   20
Nature will either end thee quite;
Or, lengthening out thy season of delight,
Preserve for thee, by individual right,
A young Lamb's heart among the full-grown flocks.
What hast Thou to do with sorrow,
Or the injuries of tomorrow?
Thou art a Dew-drop, which the morn brings forth,
Not doomed to jostle with unkindly shocks;
Or to be trailed along the soiling earth;
A Gem that glitters while it lives,   30
And no forewarning gives;
But, at the touch of wrong, without a strife
Slips in a moment out of life.

'Among all lovely things my Love had been'

Among all lovely things my Love had been;
Had noted well the stars, all flowers that grew
About her home; but she had never seen
A Glow-worm, never one, and this I knew.

While riding near her home one stormy night
A single Glow-worm did I chance to espy;
I gave a fervent welcome to the sight,
And from my Horse I leapt; great joy had I.

Upon a leaf the Glow-worm did I lay,
To bear it with me through the stormy night;   10
And, as before, it shone without dismay;
Albeit putting forth a fainter light.

When to the Dwelling of my Love I came,
I went into the Orchard quietly;
And left the Glow-worm, blessing it by name,
Laid safely by itself, beneath a Tree.

The whole next day, I hoped, and hoped with fear;
At night the Glow-worm shone beneath the Tree:
I led my Lucy to the spot, 'Look here!'
20   Oh! joy it was for her, and joy for me!

Written in March,

While Resting on the Bridge at the Foot of Brother's Water

The cock is crowing,
The stream is flowing,
The small birds twitter,
The lake doth glitter,
The green field sleeps in the sun;
The oldest and youngest
Are at work with the strongest;
The cattle are grazing,
Their heads never raising;
10   There are forty feeding like one!

Like an army defeated
The Snow hath retreated,
And now doth fare ill
On the top of the bare hill;
The Plough-boy is whooping – anon – anon:
There's joy in the mountains;
There's life in the fountains;
Small clouds are sailing,
Blue sky prevailing;
20   The rain is over and gone!

The Green Linnet

The May is come again: – how sweet
To sit upon my Orchard-seat!
And Birds and Flowers once more to greet,
    My last year's Friends together:
My thoughts they all by turns employ;
A whispering Leaf is now my joy,
And then a Bird will be the toy
    That doth my fancy tether.

One have I marked, the happiest Guest
In all this covert of the blest: 10
Hail to Thee, far above the rest
    In joy of voice and pinion,
Thou, Linnet! in thy green array,
Presiding Spirit here to-day,
Dost lead the revels of the May,
    And this is thy dominion.

While Birds, and Butterflies, and Flowers
Make all one Band of Paramours,
Thou, ranging up and down the bowers,
    Art sole in thy employment;   20
A Life, a Presence like the Air,
Scattering thy gladness without care,
Too blessed with any one to pair,
    Thyself thy own enjoyment.

Upon yon tuft of hazel trees,
That twinkle to the gusty breeze,
Behold him perched in ecstasies,
    Yet seeming still to hover;
There! where the flutter of his wings
Upon his back and body flings   30
Shadows and sunny glimmerings,
    That cover him all over.

While thus before my eyes he gleams,
A Brother of the Leaves he seems;
When in a moment forth he teems
    His little song in gushes:
As if it pleased him to disdain
And mock the Form which he did feign,
While he was dancing with the train
40   Of Leaves among the bushes.

To the Daisy

In youth from rock to rock I went,
From hill to hill, in discontent
Of pleasure high and turbulent,
    Most pleased when most uneasy;
But now my own delights I make,
My thirst at every rill can slake,
And gladly Nature's love partake
    Of thee, sweet Daisy!

When soothed a while by milder airs,
10 Thee Winter in the garland wears
That thinly shades his few grey hairs;
    Spring cannot shun thee;
Whole summer fields are thine by right;
And Autumn, melancholy Wight!
Doth in thy crimson head delight
    When rains are on thee.

In shoals and bands, a morrice train,
Thou greet'st the Traveller in the lane;
If welcome once thou count'st it gain;
20   Thou art not daunted,

Nor car'st if thou be set at naught;
And oft alone in nooks remote
We meet thee, like a pleasant thought,
    When such are wanted.

Be Violets in their secret mews
The flowers the wanton Zephyrs chuse;
Proud be the Rose, with rains and dews
    Her head impearling;
Thou liv'st with less ambitious aim,
Yet hast not gone without thy fame;   30
Thou art indeed by many a claim
    The Poet's darling.

If to a rock from rains he fly,
Or, some bright day of April sky,
Imprisoned by hot sunshine lie
    Near the green holly,
And wearily at length should fare;
He need but look about, and there
Thou art! a Friend at hand, to scare
    His melancholy.   40

A hundred times, by rock or bower,
Ere thus I have lain couched an hour,
Have I derived from thy sweet power
    Some apprehension;
Some steady love; some brief delight;
Some memory that had taken flight;
Some chime of fancy wrong or right;
    Or stray invention.

If stately passions in me burn,
And one chance look to Thee should turn,   50
I drink out of an humbler urn
    A lowlier pleasure;

The homely sympathy that heeds
The common life, our nature breeds;
A wisdom fitted to the needs
      Of hearts at leisure.

When, smitten by the morning ray,
I see thee rise alert and gay,
Then, cheerful Flower! my spirits play
60   With kindred motion:
At dusk, I've seldom marked thee press
The ground, as if in thankfulness
Without some feeling, more or less,
      Of true devotion.

And all day long I number yet,
All seasons through another debt,
Which I wherever thou art met,
      To thee am owing;
An instinct call it, a blind sense;
70   A happy, genial influence,
Coming one knows not how nor whence,
      Nor whither going.

Child of the Year! that round dost run
Thy course, bold lover of the sun,
And cheerful when the day's begun
      As morning Leveret,
Thou long the Poet's praise shalt gain;
Thou wilt be more beloved by men
In times to come; thou not in vain
80   Art Nature's Favorite.

To a Butterfly

I've watched you now a full half hour,
Self-poised upon that yellow flower;
And, little Butterfly! indeed
I know not if you sleep, or feed.
How motionless! not frozen seas
More motionless! and then
What joy awaits you, when the breeze
Hath found you out among the trees,
And calls you forth again!

This plot of Orchard-ground is ours;   10
My trees they are, my Sister's flowers;
Stop here whenever you are weary,
And rest as in a sanctuary!
Come often to us, fear no wrong;
Sit near us on the bough!
We'll talk of sunshine and of song;
And summer days, when we were young,
Sweet childish days, that were as long
        As twenty days are now!

'I have been here in the Moon-light'

I have been here in the Moon-light,
I have been here in the Day,
I have been here in the Dark Night,
And the Stream was still roaring away.

'These chairs they have no words to utter'

These chairs they have no words to utter,
No fire is in the grate to stir or flutter,
The ceiling and floor are mute as a stone,
My chamber is hushed and still,
  And I am alone,
  Happy and alone.

Oh, who would be afraid of life?
 The passion the sorrow and the strife,
  When he may lie
  Sheltered so easily?
May lie in peace on his bed,
Happy as they who are dead.

  Half an hour afterwards.
I have thoughts that are fed by the sun;
 The things which I see
 Are welcome to me,
 Welcome every one:
 I do not wish to lie
  Dead, dead,
Dead, without any company;
 Here alone on my bed,
With thoughts that are fed by the sun,
And hopes that are welcome every one,
 Happy am I.

O life, there is about thee
A deep delicious peace;
I would not be without thee,
 Stay, oh stay!
Yet be thou ever as now,
Sweetness and breath with the quiet of death,
 Peace, peace, peace.

10

20

30

180

To the Small Celandine

Pansies, Lilies, Kingcups, Daisies,
Let them live upon their praises;
Long as there's a sun that sets
Primroses will have their glory;
Long as there are Violets,
They will have a place in story;
There's a flower that shall be mine,
'Tis the little Celandine.

Eyes of some men travel far
For the finding of a star;   10
Up and down the heavens they go,
Men that keep a mighty rout!
I'm as great as they, I trow,
Since the day I found thee out,
Little flower! – I'll make a stir
Like a great Astronomer.

Modest, yet withal an Elf
Bold, and lavish of thyself,
Since we needs must first have met
I have seen thee, high and low,   20
Thirty years or more, and yet
'Twas a face I did not know;
Thou hast now, go where I may,
Fifty greetings in a day.

Ere a leaf is on a bush,
In the time before the Thrush
Has a thought about its nest,
Thou wilt come with half a call,
Spreading out thy glossy breast
Like a careless Prodigal;   30
Telling tales about the sun,
When we've little warmth, or none.

Poets, vain men in their mood!
Travel with the multitude;
Never heed them; I aver
That they all are wanton Wooers;
But the thrifty Cottager,
Who stirs little out of doors,
Joys to spy thee near her home,
40   Spring is coming, Thou art come!

Comfort have thou of thy merit,
Kindly, unassuming Spirit!
Careless of thy neighbourhood,
Thou dost shew thy pleasant face
On the moor, and in the wood,
In the lane – there's not a place,
Howsoever mean it be,
But 'tis good enough for thee.

Ill befal the yellow Flowers,
50   Children of the flaring hours!
Buttercups, that will be seen,
Whether we will see or no;
Others, too, of lofty mien;
They have done as worldlings do,
Taken praise that should be thine,
Little, humble Celandine!

Prophet of delight and mirth,
Scorned and slighted upon earth!
Herald of a mighty band,
60   Of a joyous train ensuing,
Singing at my heart's command,
In the lanes my thoughts pursuing.
I will sing, as doth behove,
Hymns in praise of what I love!

To the Same Flower

Pleasures newly found are sweet
When they lie about our feet:
February last my heart
First at sight of thee was glad;
All unheard of as thou art,
Thou must needs, I think, have had,
Celandine! and long ago,
Praise of which I nothing know.

I have not a doubt but he,
Whosoe'er the man might be,   10
Who the first with pointed rays,
(Workman worthy to be sainted)
Set the Sign-board in a blaze,
When the risen sun he painted,
Took the fancy from a glance
At thy glittering countenance.

Soon as gentle breezes bring
News of winter's vanishing,
And the children build their bowers,
Sticking 'kerchief-plots of mold   20
All about with full-blown flowers,
Thick as sheep in shepherd's fold!
With the proudest Thou art there,
Mantling in the tiny square.

Often have I sighed to measure
By myself a lonely pleasure,
Sighed to think, I read a book
Only read perhaps by me;
Yet I long could overlook
Thy bright coronet and Thee,   30
And thy arch and wily ways,
And thy store of other praise.

Blithe of heart, from week to week
Thou dost play at hide-and-seek;
While the patient Primrose sits
Like a Beggar in the cold,
Thou, a Flower of wiser wits,
Slipp'st into thy sheltered hold;
Bright as any of the train
When ye all are out again.

Thou art not beyond the moon,
But a thing 'beneath our shoon';
Let, as old Magellen did,
Others roam about the sea;
Build who will a pyramid;
Praise it is enough for me,
If there be but three or four
Who will love my little Flower.

Resolution and Independence

There was a roaring in the wind all night;
The rain came heavily and fell in floods;
But now the sun is rising calm and bright;
The birds are singing in the distant woods;
Over his own sweet voice the Stock-dove broods;
The Jay makes answer as the Magpie chatters;
And all the air is filled with pleasant noise of waters.

All things that love the sun are out of doors;
The sky rejoices in the morning's birth;
The grass is bright with rain-drops; on the moors
The Hare is running races in her mirth;
And with her feet she from the plashy earth
Raises a mist; which, glittering in the sun,
Runs with her all the way, wherever she doth run.

I was a Traveller then upon the moor;
I saw the Hare that raced about with joy;
I heard the woods, and distant waters, roar;
Or heard them not, as happy as a Boy:
The pleasant season did my heart employ:
My old remembrances went from me wholly;   20
And all the ways of men, so vain and melancholy.

But, as it sometimes chanceth, from the might
Of joy in minds that can no farther go,
As high as we have mounted in delight
In our dejection do we sink as low,
To me that morning did it happen so;
And fears, and fancies, thick upon me came;
Dim sadness, and blind thoughts I knew not nor could name.

I heard the Sky-lark singing in the sky;
And I bethought me of the playful Hare: 30
Even such a happy Child of earth am I;
Even as these blissful Creatures do I fare;
Far from the world I walk, and from all care;
But there may come another day to me,
Solitude, pain of heart, distress, and poverty.

My whole life I have lived in pleasant thought,
As if life's business were a summer mood;
As if all needful things would come unsought
To genial faith, still rich in genial good;
But how can He expect that others should   40
Build for him, sow for him, and at his call
Love him, who for himself will take no heed at all?

I thought of Chatterton, the marvellous Boy,
The sleepless Soul that perished in its pride;
Of Him who walked in glory and in joy
Behind his plough, upon the mountain-side:
By our own spirits are we deified;
We Poets in our youth begin in gladness;
But thereof comes in the end despondency and madness.

50   Now whether it were by peculiar grace,
A leading from above, a something given,
Yet it befel, that, in this lonely place,
When up and down my fancy thus was driven,
And I with these untoward thoughts had striven,
I saw a Man before me unawares:
The oldest Man he seemed that ever wore grey hairs.

My course I stopped as soon as I espied
The Old Man in that naked wilderness;
Close by a Pond, upon the further side,
60   He stood alone: a minute's space I guess
I watched him, he continuing motionless:
To the Pool's further margin then I drew:
He being all the while before me full in view.

As a huge Stone is sometimes seen to lie
Couched on the bald top of an eminence;
Wonder to all who do the same espy
By what means it could thither come, and whence;
So that it seems a thing endued with sense:
Like a Sea-beast crawled forth, which on a shelf
70   Of rock or sand reposeth, there to sun itself.

Such seemed this Man, not all alive nor dead,
Nor all asleep; in his extreme old age:
His body was bent double, feet and head
Coming together in their pilgrimage;
As if some dire constraint of pain, or rage
Of sickness felt by him in times long past,
A more than human weight upon his frame had cast.

Himself he propped, his body, limbs, and face,
Upon a long grey Staff of shaven wood:
And, still as I drew near with gentle pace,   80
Beside the little pond or moorish flood
Motionless as a Cloud the Old Man stood;
That heareth not the loud winds when they call;
And moveth altogether; if it move at all.

At length, himself unsettling, he the Pond
Stirred with his Staff, and fixedly did look
Upon the muddy water, which he conned,
As if he had been reading in a book:
And now such freedom as I could I took;
And, drawing to his side, to him did say,   90
'This morning gives us promise of a glorious day.'

A gentle answer did the Old Man make,
In courteous speech which forth he slowly drew:
And him with further words I thus bespake,
'What kind of work is that which you pursue?
This is a lonesome place for one like you.'
He answered me with pleasure and surprize;
And there was, while he spake, a fire about his eyes.

His words came feebly, from a feeble chest,
Yet each in solemn order followed each,
With something of a lofty utterance drest;
Choice word, and measured phrase; above the reach
Of ordinary men; a stately speech!
Such as grave Livers do in Scotland use,
Religious men, who give to God and Man their dues.

He told me that he to this pond had come
To gather Leeches, being old and poor:
Employment hazardous and wearisome!
And he had many hardships to endure:
From Pond to Pond he roamed, from moor to moor,
Housing, with God's good help, by choice or chance:
And in this way he gained an honest maintenance.

The Old Man still stood talking by my side;
But now his voice to me was like a stream
Scarce heard; nor word from word could I divide;
And the whole Body of the man did seem
Like one whom I had met with in a dream;
Or like a Man from some far region sent;
To give me human strength, and strong admonishment.

My former thoughts returned: the fear that kills;
The hope that is unwilling to be fed;
Cold, pain, and labour, and all fleshly ills;
And mighty Poets in their misery dead.
And now, not knowing what the Old Man had said,
My question eagerly did I renew,
'How is it that you live, and what is it you do?'

He with a smile did then his words repeat;
And said, that, gathering Leeches, far and wide
He travelled; stirring thus about his feet
The waters of the Ponds where they abide.   130
'Once I could meet with them on every side;
But they have dwindled long by slow decay;
Yet still I persevere, and find them where I may.'

While he was talking thus, the lonely place,
The Old Man's shape, and speech, all troubled me:
In my mind's eye I seemed to see him pace
About the weary moors continually,
Wandering about alone and silently.
While I these thoughts within myself pursued,
He, having made a pause, the same discourse renewed.   140

And soon with this he other matter blended,
Cheerfully uttered, with demeanour kind,
But stately in the main; and, when he ended,
I could have laughed myself to scorn, to find
In that decrepit Man so firm a mind.
'God', said I, 'be my help and stay secure;
I'll think of the Leech-gatherer on the lonely moor.'

Stanzas Written in my Pocket-Copy of Thomson's Castle of Indolence

Within our happy Castle there dwelt One
Whom without blame I may not overlook;
For never sun on living creature shone
Who more devout enjoyment with us took.

Here on his hours he hung as on a book;
On his own time here would he float away,
As doth a fly upon a summer brook;
But go to-morrow – or belike to-day –
Seek for him, – he is fled; and whither none can say.

Thus often would he leave our peaceful home
And find elsewhere his business or delight;
Out of our Valley's limits did he roam:
Full many time, upon a stormy night,
His voice came to us from the neighbouring height:
Oft did we see him driving full in view
At mid-day when the sun was shining bright;
What ill was on him, what he had to do,
A mighty wonder bred among our quiet crew.

Ah! piteous sight it was to see this man
When he came back to us, a withered flower, –
Or like a sinful creature, pale and wan.
Down would he sit; and without strength or power
Look at the common grass from hour to hour:
And oftentimes, how long I fear to say,
Where apple-trees in blossom made a bower,
Retired in that sunshiny shade he lay;
And, like a naked Indian, slept himself away.

Great wonder to our gentle Tribe it was
Whenever from our Valley he withdrew;
For happier soul no living creature has
Than he had, being here the long day through.
Some thought he was a lover, and did woo:
Some thought far worse of him, and judged him wrong:
But Verse was what he had been wedded to;
And his own mind did like a tempest strong
Come to him thus, and drove the weary Wight along.

With him there often walked in friendly guise
Or lay upon the moss by brook or tree
A noticeable Man with large grey eyes,
And a pale face that seemed undoubtedly 40
As if a blooming face it ought to be;
Heavy his low-hung lip did oft appear
Deprest by weight of musing Phantasy;
Profound his forehead was, though not severe;
Yet some did think that he had little business here:

Sweet heaven forefend! his was a lawful right;
Noisy he was, and gamesome as a boy;
His limbs would toss about him with delight
Like branches when strong winds the trees annoy.
Nor lacked his calmer hours device or toy 50
To banish listlessness and irksome care;
He would have taught you how you might employ
Yourself; and many did to him repair, –
And, certes, not in vain; he had inventions rare.

Expedients, too, of simplest sort he tried:
Long blades of grass, plucked round him as he lay,
Made – to his ear attentively applied –
A Pipe on which the wind would deftly play;
Glasses he had, that little things display, –
The beetle with his radiance manifold, 60
A mailed angel on a battle day;
And cups of flowers, and herbage green and gold;
And all the gorgeous sights which fairies do behold.

He would entice that other Man to hear
His music, and to view his imagery:
And, sooth, these two did love each other dear,
As far as love in such a place could be;
There did they dwell – from earthly labour free,

As happy spirits as were ever seen;
70   If but a bird, to keep them company,
Or butterfly sate down, they were, I ween,
As pleased as if the same had been a Maiden Queen.

'I grieved for Buonaparte'

I grieved for Buonaparte, with a vain
And an unthinking grief! the vital blood
Of that Man's mind what can it be? What food
Fed his first hopes? What knowledge could He gain?
'Tis not in battles that from youth we train
The Governor who must be wise and good,
And temper with the sternness of the brain
Thoughts motherly, and meek as womanhood.
Wisdom doth live with children round her knees:
10   Books, leisure, perfect freedom, and the talk
Man holds with week-day man in the hourly walk
Of the mind's business: these are the degrees
By which true Sway doth mount; this is the stalk
True Power doth grow on; and her rights are these.

'I am not One who much or oft delight'

I am not One who much or oft delight
To season my fireside with personal talk,
About Friends, who live within an easy walk,
Or Neighbours, daily, weekly, in my sight:
And, for my chance-acquaintance, Ladies bright,
Sons, Mothers, Maidens withering on the stalk,
These all wear out of me, like Forms, with chalk
Painted on rich men's floors, for one feast-night.

Better than such discourse doth silence long,
Long, barren silence, square with my desire;   10
To sit without emotion, hope, or aim,
By my half-kitchen my half-parlour fire,
And listen to the flapping of the flame,
Or kettle, whispering its faint undersong.

'Yet life,' you say, 'is life; we have seen and see,
And with a living pleasure we describe;
And fits of sprightly malice do but bribe
The languid mind into activity.
Sound sense, and love itself, and mirth and glee,
Are fostered by the comment and the gibe.'   20
Even be it so: yet still among your tribe,
Our daily world's true Worldlings, rank not me!
Children are blest, and powerful; their world lies
More justly balanced; partly at their feet,
And part far from them: – sweetest melodies
Are those that are by distance made more sweet;
Whose mind is but the mind of his own eyes
He is a Slave; the meanest we can meet!

Wings have we, and as far as we can go
We may find pleasure: wilderness and wood,   30
Blank ocean and mere sky, support that mood
Which with the lofty sanctifies the low:
Dreams, books, are each a world; and books, we know,
Are a substantial world, both pure and good:
Round these, with tendrils strong as flesh and blood,
Our pastime and our happiness will grow.
There do I find a never-failing store
Of personal themes, and such as I love best;
Matter wherein right voluble I am:
Two will I mention, dearer than the rest;   40
The gentle Lady, married to the Moor;
And heavenly Una with her milk-white Lamb.

Nor can I not believe but that hereby
Great gains are mine: for thus I live remote
From evil-speaking; rancour, never sought,
Comes to me not; malignant truth, or lie.
Hence have I genial seasons, hence have I
Smooth passions, smooth discourse, and joyous thought:
And thus from day to day my little Boat
50   Rocks in its harbour, lodging peaceably.
Blessings be with them, and eternal praise,
Who gave us nobler loves, and nobler cares,
The Poets, who on earth have made us Heirs
Of truth and pure delight by heavenly lays!
Oh! might my name be numbered among theirs,
Then gladly would I end my mortal days.

'The world is too much with us'

The world is too much with us; late and soon,
Getting and spending, we lay waste our powers:
Little we see in nature that is ours;
We have given our hearts away, a sordid boon!
This Sea that bares her bosom to the moon;
The Winds that will be howling at all hours
And are up-gathered now like sleeping flowers;
For this, for every thing, we are out of tune;
It moves us not – Great God! I'd rather be
10   A Pagan suckled in a creed outworn;
So might I, standing on this pleasant lea,
Have glimpses that would make me less forlorn
Have sight of Proteus coming from the sea;
Or hear old Triton blow his wreathed horn.

'The Sun has long been set'

The Sun has long been set:
The Stars are out by twos and threes;
The little Birds are piping yet
Among the bushes and trees;
There's a Cuckoo, and one or two thrushes;
And a noise of wind that rushes,
With a noise of water that gushes;
And the Cuckoo's sovereign cry
Fills all the hollow of the sky!

Who would go 'parading'   10
In London, and 'masquerading',
On such a night of June?
With that beautiful soft half-moon,
And all these innocent blisses,
On such a night as this is!

Calais,

August, 1802

Is it a Reed that's shaken by the wind,
Or what is it that ye go forth to see?
Lords, Lawyers, Statesmen, Squires of low degree,
Men known, and men unknown, Sick, Lame, and Blind,
Post forward all, like Creatures of one kind,
With first-fruit offerings crowd to bend the knee
In France, before the new-born Majesty.
'Tis ever thus. Ye Men of prostrate mind!
A seemly reverence may be paid to power;
But that's a loyal virtue, never sown   10

In haste, nor springing with a transient shower:
When truth, when sense, when liberty were flown
What hardship had it been to wait an hour?
Shame on you, feeble Heads, to slavery prone!

To a Friend,

Composed near Calais,
on the Road Leading to Ardres, August 7th, 1802

Jones! when from Calais southward you and I
Travelled on foot together; then this Way,
Which I am pacing now, was like the May
With festivals of new-born Liberty:
A homeless sound of joy was in the Sky;
The antiquated Earth, as one might say,
Beat like the heart of Man: songs, garlands, play,
Banners, and happy faces, far and nigh!
And now, sole register that these things were,
Two solitary greetings have I heard,
'*Good morrow, Citizen!*' a hollow word,
As if a dead Man spake it! Yet despair
I feel not: happy am I as a Bird:
Fair seasons yet will come, and hopes as fair.

10

'*It is a beauteous Evening, calm and free*'

It is a beauteous Evening, calm and free;
The holy time is quiet as a Nun
Breathless with adoration; the broad sun
Is sinking down in its tranquillity;
The gentleness of heaven is on the Sea:
Listen! the mighty Being is awake

And doth with his eternal motion make
A sound like thunder – everlastingly.
Dear Child! dear Girl! that walkest with me here,
If thou appear'st untouched by solemn thought,   10
Thy nature is not therefore less divine:
Thou liest in Abraham's bosom all the year;
And worshipp'st at the Temple's inner shrine,
God being with thee when we know it not.

Composed by the Sea-Side, near Calais,

August, 1802

Fair Star of Evening, Splendor of the West,
Star of my Country! on the horizon's brink
Thou hangest, stooping, as might seem, to sink
On England's bosom; yet well pleased to rest,
Meanwhile, and be to her a glorious crest
Conspicuous to the Nations. Thou, I think,
Should'st be my Country's emblem; and should'st wink,
Bright Star! with laughter on her banners, drest
In thy fresh beauty. There! that dusky spot
Beneath thee, it is England; there it lies.   10
Blessings be on you both! one hope, one lot,
One life, one glory! I, with many a fear
For my dear Country, many heartfelt sighs,
Among Men who do not love her linger here.

To Toussaint L'Ouverture

Toussaint, the most unhappy Man of Men!
Whether the rural Milk-maid by her Cow
Sing in thy hearing, or thou liest now
Alone in some deep dungeon's earless den,
O miserable chieftain! where and when
Wilt thou find patience? Yet die not; do thou
Wear rather in thy bonds a cheerful brow:
Though fallen Thyself, never to rise again,
Live, and take comfort. Thou hast left behind
Powers that will work for thee; air, earth, and skies;
There's not a breathing of the common wind
That will forget thee; thou hast great allies;
Thy friends are exultations, agonies,
And love, and Man's unconquerable mind.

Calais,

August 15th, 1802

Festivals have I seen that were not names:
This is young Buonaparte's natal day;
And his is henceforth an established sway,
Consul for life. With worship France proclaims
Her approbation, and with pomps and games.
Heaven grant that other Cities may be gay!
Calais is not: and I have bent my way
To the Sea-coast, noting that each man frames
His business as he likes. Another time
That was, when I was here long years ago:
The senselessness of joy was then sublime!
Happy is he, who, caring not for Pope,
Consul, or King, can sound himself to know
The destiny of Man, and live in hope.

198

September 1st, 1802

We had a fellow-Passenger who came
From Calais with us, gaudy in array,
A Negro Woman like a Lady gay,
Yet silent as a woman fearing blame;
Dejected, meek, yea pitiably tame,
She sate, from notice turning not away,
But on our proffered kindness still did lay
A weight of languid speech, or at the same
Was silent, motionless in eyes and face.
She was a Negro Woman driv'n from France,   10
Rejected like all others of that race,
Not one of whom may now find footing there;
This the poor Out-cast did to us declare,
Nor murmured at the unfeeling Ordinance.

Composed upon Westminster Bridge,

Sept. 3, 1802

Earth has not any thing to shew more fair:
Dull would he be of soul who could pass by
A sight so touching in its majesty:
This City now doth like a garment wear
The beauty of the morning; silent, bare,
Ships, towers, domes, theatres, and temples lie
Open unto the fields, and to the sky;
All bright and glittering in the smokeless air.
Never did sun more beautifully steep
In his first splendor valley, rock, or hill;   10
Ne'er saw I, never felt, a calm so deep!
The river glideth at his own sweet will:
Dear God! the very houses seem asleep;
And all that mighty heart is lying still!

'Great Men have been among us'

Great Men have been among us; hands that penned
And tongues that uttered wisdom, better none:
The later Sydney, Marvel, Harrington,
Young Vane, and others who called Milton Friend.
These Moralists could act and comprehend:
They knew how genuine glory was put on;
Taught us how rightfully a nation shone
In splendor: what strength was, that would not bend
But in magnanimous meekness. France, 'tis strange,
Hath brought forth no such souls as we had then.
Perpetual emptiness! unceasing change!
No single Volume paramount, no code,
No master spirit, no determined road;
But equally a want of Books and Men!

London,

1802

Milton! thou should'st be living at this hour:
England hath need of thee: she is a fen
Of stagnant waters: altar, sword and pen,
Fireside, the heroic wealth of hall and bower,
Have forfeited their ancient English dower
Of inward happiness. We are selfish men;
Oh! raise us up, return to us again;
And give us manners, virtue, freedom, power.
Thy soul was like a Star and dwelt apart:
Thou hadst a voice whose sound was like the sea;
Pure as the naked heavens, majestic, free,
So didst thou travel on life's common way,
In cheerful godliness; and yet thy heart
The lowliest duties on itself did lay.

'Nuns fret not at their Convent's narrow room'

Nuns fret not at their Convent's narrow room;
And Hermits are contented with their Cells;
And Students with their pensive Citadels:
Maids at the Wheel, the Weaver at his Loom,
Sit blithe and happy; Bees that soar for bloom,
High as the highest Peak of Furness Fells,
Will murmur by the hour in Foxglove bells:
In truth, the prison, unto which we doom
Ourselves, no prison is: and hence to me,
In sundry moods, 'twas pastime to be bound   10
Within the Sonnet's scanty plot of ground:
Pleased if some Souls (for such there needs must be)
Who have felt the weight of too much liberty,
Should find short solace there, as I have found.

Yarrow Unvisited

(See the various Poems the scene of which is laid upon
the Banks of the Yarrow; in particular, the exquisite
Ballad of Hamilton, beginning

'Busk ye, busk ye my bonny, bonny Bride,
Busk ye, busk ye my winsome Marrow!'–)

From Stirling Castle we had seen
The mazy Forth unravelled;
Had trod the banks of Clyde, and Tay,
And with the Tweed had travelled;
And, when we came to Clovenford,
Then said my 'winsome Marrow,'
'Whate'er betide, we'll turn aside,
And see the Braes of Yarrow.'

'Let Yarrow Folk, *frae* Selkirk Town,
Who have been buying, selling,
Go back to Yarrow, 'tis their own,
Each Maiden to her Dwelling!
On Yarrow's Banks let herons feed,
Hares couch, and rabbits burrow!
But we will downwards with the Tweed,
Nor turn aside to Yarrow.

'There's Galla Water, Leader Haughs,
Both lying right before us;
And Dryborough, where with chiming Tweed
The Lintwhites sing in chorus;
There's pleasant Tiviot Dale, a land
Made blithe with plough and harrow;
Why throw away a needful day
To go in search of Yarrow?

'What's Yarrow but a River bare
That glides the dark hills under?
There are a thousand such elsewhere
As worthy of your wonder.'
– Strange words they seemed of slight and scorn;
My True-love sighed for sorrow;
And looked me in the face, to think
I thus could speak of Yarrow!

'Oh! green,' said I, 'are Yarrow's Holms,
And sweet is Yarrow flowing!
Fair hangs the apple frae the rock,
But we will leave it growing.
O'er hilly path, and open Strath,
We'll wander Scotland thorough;
But, though so near, we will not turn
Into the Dale of Yarrow.

'Let Beeves and home-bred Kine partake
The sweets of Burn-mill meadow;
The Swan on still St Mary's Lake
Float double, Swan and Shadow!
We will not see them; will not go,
Today, nor yet tomorrow;
Enough if in our hearts we know,
There's such a place as Yarrow.

'Be Yarrow Stream unseen, unknown!
It must, or we shall rue it: 50
We have a vision of our own;
Ah! why should we undo it?
The treasured dreams of times long past
We'll keep them, *winsome Marrow*!
For when we're there although 'tis fair
'Twill be another Yarrow!

'If Care with freezing years should come,
And wandering seem but folly,
Should we be loth to stir from home,
And yet be melancholy;   60
Should life be dull, and spirits low,
'Twill soothe us in our sorrow
That earth has something yet to show,
The bonny Holms of Yarrow!'

'She was a Phantom of delight'

She was a Phantom of delight
When first she gleamed upon my sight;
A lovely Apparition, sent
To be a moment's ornament;
Her eyes as stars of Twilight fair;
Like Twilight's, too, her dusky hair;

But all things else about her drawn
From May-time and the cheerful Dawn;
A dancing Shape, an Image gay,
To haunt, to startle, and way-lay.

I saw her upon nearer view,
A Spirit, yet a Woman too!
Her household motions light and free,
And steps of virgin liberty;
A countenance in which did meet
Sweet records, promises as sweet;
A Creature not too bright or good
For human nature's daily food;
For transient sorrows, simple wiles,
Praise, blame, love, kisses, tears, and smiles.

And now I see with eye serene
The very pulse of the machine;
A Being breathing thoughtful breath;
A Traveller betwixt life and death;
The reason firm, the temperate will,
Endurance, foresight, strength and skill;
A perfect Woman; nobly planned,
To warn, to comfort, and command;
And yet a Spirit still, and bright
With something of an angel light.

The Small Celandine

There is a Flower, the Lesser Celandine,
That shrinks, like many more, from cold and rain;
And, the first moment that the sun may shine,
Bright as the sun itself, 'tis out again!

When hailstones have been falling swarm on swarm,
Or blasts the green field and the trees distressed,
Oft have I seen it muffled up from harm,
In close self-shelter, like a Thing at rest.

But lately, one rough day, this Flower I passed,
And recognized it, though an altered Form,   10
Now standing forth an offering to the Blast,
And buffetted at will by Rain and Storm.

I stopped, and said with inly muttered voice,
'It doth not love the shower, nor seek the cold:
This neither is its courage nor its choice,
But its necessity in being old.

'The sunshine may not bless it, nor the dew;
It cannot help itself in its decay;
Stiff in its members, withered, changed of hue.'
And, in my spleen, I smiled that it was grey.   20

To be a Prodigal's Favorite – then, worse truth,
A Miser's Pensioner – behold our lot!
O Man! that from thy fair and shining youth
Age might but take the things Youth needed not!

Ode to Duty

Stern Daughter of the Voice of God!
O Duty! if that name thou love
Who art a Light to guide, a Rod
To check the erring, and reprove;
Thou who art victory and law
When empty terrors overawe;
From vain temptations dost set free;
From strife and from despair; a glorious ministry.

There are who ask not if thine eye
Be on them; who, in love and truth,
Where no misgiving is, rely
Upon the genial sense of youth:
Glad Hearts! without reproach or blot;
Who do thy work, and know it not:
May joy be theirs while life shall last!
And Thou, if they should totter, teach them to stand fast!

Serene will be our days and bright,
And happy will our nature be,
When love is an unerring light,
And joy its own security.
And blessed are they who in the main
This faith, even now, do entertain:
Live in the spirit of this creed;
Yet find that other strength, according to their need.

I, loving freedom, and untried;
No sport of every random gust,
Yet being to myself a guide,
Too blindly have reposed my trust:
Resolved that nothing e'er should press
Upon my present happiness,
I shoved unwelcome tasks away;
But thee I now would serve more strictly, if I may.

Through no disturbance of my soul,
Or strong compunction in me wrought,
I supplicate for thy controul;
But in the quietness of thought:
Me this unchartered freedom tires;
I feel the weight of chance desires:
My hopes no more must change their name,
I long for a repose which ever is the same.

Yet not the less would I throughout
Still act according to the voice
Of my own wish; and feel past doubt
That my submissiveness was choice:
Not seeking in the school of pride
For 'precepts over dignified',
Denial and restraint I prize
No farther than they breed a second Will more wise.

Stern Lawgiver! yet thou dost wear
The Godhead's most benignant grace;   50
Nor know we any thing so fair
As is the smile upon thy face;
Flowers laugh before thee on their beds;
And Fragrance in thy footing treads;
Thou dost preserve the Stars from wrong;
And the most ancient Heavens through Thee are fresh and
    strong.

To humbler functions, awful Power!
I call thee: I myself commend
Unto thy guidance from this hour;
Oh! let my weakness have an end!   60
Give unto me, made lowly wise,
The spirit of self-sacrifice;
The confidence of reason give;
And in the light of truth thy Bondman let me live!

Ode

Paulò majora canamus

There was a time when meadow, grove, and stream,
The earth, and every common sight,
            To me did seem
            Apparelled in celestial light,

The glory and the freshness of a dream.
It is not now as it has been of yore; –
        Turn wheresoe'er I may,
        By night or day,
The things which I have seen I now can see no more.

        The Rainbow comes and goes,
        And lovely is the Rose,
        The Moon doth with delight
Look round her when the heavens are bare;
        Waters on a starry night
        Are beautiful and fair;
        The sunshine is a glorious birth;
        But yet I know, where'er I go,
That there hath passed away a glory from the earth.

Now, while the Birds thus sing a joyous song,
        And while the young Lambs bound
        As to the tabor's sound,
To me alone there came a thought of grief:
A timely utterance gave that thought relief,
        And I again am strong.
The Cataracts blow their trumpets from the steep,
No more shall grief of mine the season wrong;
I hear the Echoes through the mountains throng,
The Winds come to me from the fields of sleep,
        And all the earth is gay,
        Land and sea
        Give themselves up to jollity,
        And with the heart of May
Doth every Beast keep holiday,
        Thou Child of Joy,
Shout round me, let me hear thy shouts, thou happy Shepherd Boy

Ye blessed Creatures, I have heard the call
        Ye to each other make; I see
The heavens laugh with you in your jubilee;
        My heart is at your festival,

My head hath its coronal,   40
The fullness of your bliss, I feel – I feel it all.
    Oh evil day! if I were sullen
    While the Earth herself is adorning,
        This sweet May-morning,
    And the Children are pulling,
        On every side,
    In a thousand vallies far and wide,
    Fresh flowers; while the sun shines warm,
And the Babe leaps up on his mother's arm: –
    I hear, I hear, with joy I hear!   50
    – But there's a Tree, of many one,
A single Field which I have looked upon,
Both of them speak of something that is gone:
        The Pansy at my feet
        Doth the same tale repeat:
Whither is fled the visionary gleam?
Where is it now, the glory and the dream?

Our birth is but a sleep and a forgetting:
The Soul that rises with us, our life's Star,
    Hath had elsewhere its setting,   60
        And cometh from afar:
  Not in entire forgetfulness,
  And not in utter nakedness,
But trailing clouds of glory do we come
        From God, who is our home:
Heaven lies about us in our infancy!
Shades of the prison-house begin to close
        Upon the growing Boy,
But He beholds the light, and whence it flows,
        He sees it in his joy;   70
The Youth, who daily farther from the East
    Must travel, still is Nature's Priest,
        And by the vision splendid
        Is on his way attended;
At length the Man perceives it die away,
And fade into the light of common day.
. .

Earth fills her lap with pleasures of her own;
Yearnings she hath in her own natural kind,
And, even with something of a Mother's mind,
80   And no unworthy aim,
      The homely Nurse doth all she can
To make her Foster-child, her Inmate Man,
         Forget the glories he hath known,
And that imperial palace whence he came.

Behold the Child among his new-born blisses,
A four year's Darling of a pigmy size!
See, where mid work of his own hand he lies,
Fretted by sallies of his Mother's kisses,
With light upon him from his Father's eyes!
90 See, at his feet, some little plan or chart,
Some fragment from his dream of human life,
Shaped by himself with newly-learned art;
        A wedding or a festival,
        A mourning or a funeral;
           And this hath now his heart,
        And unto this he frames his song:
          Then will he fit his tongue
To dialogues of business, love, or strife;
        But it will not be long
100   Ere this be thrown aside,
        And with new joy and pride
The little Actor cons another part,
Filling from time to time his 'humorous stage'
With all the Persons, down to palsied Age,
That Life brings with her in her Equipage;
        As if his whole vocation
        Were endless imitation.

Thou, whose exterior semblance doth belie
        Thy Soul's immensity;
110 Thou best Philosopher, who yet dost keep
Thy heritage, thou Eye among the blind,
That, deaf and silent, read'st the eternal deep,

Haunted for ever by the eternal mind, –
　　　　Mighty Prophet! Seer blest!
　　　　On whom those truths do rest,
Which we are toiling all our lives to find;
Thou, over whom thy Immortality
Broods like the Day, a Master o'er a Slave,
A Presence which is not to be put by;
　　　　　　To whom the grave　　　　　　120
Is but a lonely bed without the sense or sight
　　　　Of day or the warm light,
A place of thought where we in waiting lie;
Thou little Child, yet glorious in the might
Of untamed pleasures, on thy Being's height,
Why with such earnest pains dost thou provoke
The Years to bring the inevitable yoke,
Thus blindly with thy blessedness at strife?
Full soon thy Soul shall have her earthly freight,
And custom lie upon thee with a weight,　　　130
Heavy as frost, and deep almost as life!

　　　　O joy! that in our embers
　　　　Is something that doth live,
　　　　That nature yet remembers
　　　　What was so fugitive!
The thought of our past years in me doth breed
Perpetual benedictions: not indeed
For that which is most worthy to be blest;
Delight and liberty, the simple creed
Of Childhood, whether fluttering or at rest,　　　140
With new-born hope for ever in his breast: –
　　　　Not for these I raise
　　　　The song of thanks and praise;
　　But for those obstinate questionings
　　Of sense and outward things,
　　Fallings from us, vanishings;
　　Blank misgivings of a Creature
Moving about in worlds not realized,
High instincts, before which our mortal Nature

150   Did tremble like a guilty Thing surprized:
         But for those first affections,
         Those shadowy recollections,
            Which, be they what they may,
Are yet the fountain light of all our day,
Are yet a master light of all our seeing;
         Uphold us, cherish us, and make
Our noisy years seem moments in the being
Of the eternal Silence: truths that wake,
           To perish never;
160 Which neither listlessness, nor mad endeavour,
           Nor Man nor Boy,
Nor all that is at enmity with joy,
Can utterly abolish or destroy!
      Hence, in a season of calm weather,
        Though inland far we be,
Our Souls have sight of that immortal sea
         Which brought us hither,
         Can in a moment travel thither,
And see the Children sport upon the shore,
170 And hear the mighty waters rolling evermore.

Then, sing ye Birds, sing, sing a joyous song!
        And let the young Lambs bound
        As to the tabor's sound!
    We in thought will join your throng,
        Ye that pipe and ye that play,
        Ye that through your hearts to day
        Feel the gladness of the May!
What though the radiance which was once so bright
Be now for ever taken from my sight,
180   Though nothing can bring back the hour
Of splendour in the grass, of glory in the flower;
        We will grieve not, rather find
        Strength in what remains behind,
        In the primal sympathy
        Which having been must ever be,

> In the soothing thoughts that spring
> Out of human suffering,
> In the faith that looks through death,
In years that bring the philosophic mind.

And oh ye Fountains, Meadows, Hills, and Groves, 190
Think not of any severing of our loves!
Yet in my heart of hearts I feel your might;
I only have relinquished one delight
To live beneath your more habitual sway.
I love the Brooks which down their channels fret,
Even more than when I tripped lightly as they;
The innocent brightness of a new-born Day
> Is lovely yet;
The Clouds that gather round the setting sun
Do take a sober colouring from an eye 200
That hath kept watch o'er man's mortality;
Another race hath been, and other palms are won.
Thanks to the human heart by which we live,
Thanks to its tenderness, its joys, and fears,
To me the meanest flower that blows can give
Thoughts that do often lie too deep for tears.

'Who fancied what a pretty sight'

> Who fancied what a pretty sight
> This Rock would be if edged around
> With living Snowdrops? circlet bright!
> How glorious to this Orchard ground!
> Who loved the little Rock, and set
> Upon its Head this Coronet?

Was it the humour of a Child?
Or rather of some love-sick Maid,
Whose brows, the day that she was styled
The Shepherd Queen were thus arrayed?
Of Man mature, or Matron sage?
Or old Man toying with his age?
I asked – 'twas whispered, The device
To each or all might well belong.
It is the Spirit of Paradise
That prompts such work, a Spirit strong,
That gives to all the self-same bent
Where life is wise and innocent.

10

'*I wandered lonely as a Cloud*'

I wandered lonely as a Cloud
That floats on high o'er Vales and Hills,
When all at once I saw a crowd
A host of dancing Daffodils;
Along the Lake, beneath the trees,
Ten thousand dancing in the breeze.

The waves beside them danced, but they
Outdid the sparkling waves in glee: –
A Poet could not but be gay
In such a laughing company:
I gazed – and gazed – but little thought
What wealth the shew to me had brought:

10

For oft when on my couch I lie
In vacant or in pensive mood,
They flash upon that inward eye
Which is the bliss of solitude,
And then my heart with pleasure fills,
And dances with the Daffodils.

From *The Prelude* (1805)

'THAT GREAT FEDERAL DAY'
(FROM BOOK 6)

'[T]was a time when Europe was rejoiced,
France standing on the top of golden hours,
And human nature seeming born again.
Bound, as I said, to the Alps, it was our lot
To land at Calais on the very eve
Of that great federal day; and there we saw,
In a mean city, and among a few,
How bright a face is worn when joy of one
Is joy of tens of millions. Southward thence
We took our way, direct through hamlets, towns,   10
Gaudy with reliques of that festival,
Flowers left to wither on triumphal arcs,
And window-garlands. On the public roads,
And, once, three days successively, through paths
By which our toilsome journey was abridged,
Among sequestered villages we walked
And found benevolence and blessedness
Spread like a fragrance everywhere, like spring
That leaves no corner of the land untouched:
Where elms for many and many a league in files,   20
With their thin umbrage, on the stately roads
Of that great kingdom, rustled o'er our heads,
For ever near us as we paced along:
'Twas sweet at such a time, with such delights
On every side, in prime of youthful strength,
To feed a Poet's tender melancholy
And fond conceit of sadness, to the noise
And gentle undulations which they made.
Unhoused, beneath the evening star we saw
Dances of liberty, and, in late hours   30
Of darkness, dances in the open air.
Along the vine-clad hills of Burgundy,

Upon the bosom of the gentle Saone
We glided forward with the flowing stream.
Swift Rhone! thou wert the wings on which we cut
Between thy lofty rocks. Enchanting show
Those woods and farms and orchards did present,
And single cottages and lurking towns,
Reach after reach, procession without end
40 Of deep and stately vales! A lonely pair
Of Englishmen we were, and sailed along
Clustered together with a merry crowd
Of those emancipated, with a host
Of travellers, chiefly delegates returning
From the great spousals newly solemnized
At their chief city, in the sight of Heaven.
Like bees they swarmed, gaudy and gay as bees;
Some vapoured in the unruliness of joy,
And flourished with their swords as if to fight
50 The saucy air. In this blithe company
We landed – took with them our evening meal,
Guests welcome almost as the angels were
To Abraham of old. The supper done,
With flowing cups elate and happy thoughts
We rose at signal given, and formed a ring
And, hand in hand, danced round and round the board;
All hearts were open, every tongue was loud
With amity and glee; we bore a name
Honoured in France, the name of Englishmen,
60 And hospitably did they give us hail,
As their forerunners in a glorious course;
And round and round the board they danced again.
With this same throng our voyage we pursued
At early dawn. The monastery bells
Made a sweet jingling in our youthful ears;
The rapid river flowing without noise,
And every spire we saw among the rocks
Spake with a sense of peace, at intervals

Touching the heart amid the boisterous crew
With which we were environed. Having parted   70
From this glad rout, the Convent of Chartreuse
Received us two days afterwards, and there
We rested in an awful solitude;
Thence onward to the Country of the Swiss.

'CROSSING THE ALPS'
(FROM BOOK 6)

     Upturning with a band
Of travellers, from the Vallais we had clomb
Along the road that leads to Italy;
A length of hours, making of these our guides
Did we advance, and having reached an inn
Among the mountains, we together ate
Our noon's repast, from which the travellers rose,
Leaving us at the board. Ere long we followed,
Descending by the beaten road that led
Right to a rivulet's edge, and there broke off.   10
The only track now visible was one
Upon the further side, right opposite,
And up a lofty mountain. This we took
After a little scruple, and short pause,
And climbed with eagerness, though not at length
Without surprise, and some anxiety
On finding that we did not overtake
Our comrades gone before. By fortunate chance,
While every moment now encreased our doubts,
A peasant met us, and from him we learned   20
That to the place which had perplexed us first
We must descend, and there should find the road,
Which in the stony channel of the stream,
Lay a few steps, and then along its banks;
And further, that thenceforward all our course
Was downwards, with the current of that stream.
Hard of belief, we questioned him again,

And all the answers which the man returned
To our inquiries, in their sense and substance,
Translated by the feeling which we had,
Ended in this, that we had crossed the Alps.

    Imagination! lifting up itself
Before the eye and progress of my song
Like an unfathered vapour – here that Power,
In all the might of its endowments, came
Athwart me: I was lost as in a cloud,
Halted without a struggle to break through;
And now recovering, to my soul I say –
'I recognize thy glory': in such strength
Of usurpation, in such visitings
Of awful promise, when the light of sense
Goes out in flashes that have shown to us
The invisible world, doth greatness make abode,
There harbours, whether we be young or old.
Our destiny, our nature, and our home
Is with infinitude, and only there;
With hope it is, hope that can never die,
Effort, and expectation, and desire,
And something evermore about to be.
The mind beneath such banners militant
Thinks not of spoils or trophies, nor of aught
That may attest its prowess, blest in thoughts
That are their own perfection and reward,
Strong in itself, and in the access of joy
Which hides it like the overflowing Nile.

    The dull and heavy slackening that ensued
Upon those tidings by the peasant given
Was soon dislodged. Downwards we hurried fast,
And entered with the road which we had missed
Into a narrow chasm. The brook and road
Were fellow-travellers in this gloomy pass,
And with them did we journey several hours
At a slow step. The immeasurable height

Of woods decaying, never to be decayed,
The stationary blasts of waterfalls,
And everywhere along the hollow rent
Winds thwarting winds, bewildered and forlorn,
The torrents shooting from the clear blue sky,
The rocks that muttered close upon our ears,
Black drizzling crags that spake by the wayside   70
As if a voice were in them, the sick sight
And giddy prospect of the raving stream,
The unfettered clouds and region of the Heavens,
Tumult and peace, the darkness and the light –
Were all like workings of one mind, the features
Of the same face, blossoms upon one tree;
Characters of the great Apocalypse,
The types and symbols of Eternity,
Of first, and last, and midst, and without end.

    That night our lodging was an Alpine house,   80
An inn, or hospital, as they are named,
Standing in that same valley by itself,
And close upon the confluence of two streams;
A dreary mansion, large beyond all need,
With high and spacious rooms, deafened and stunned
By noise of waters, making innocent sleep
Lie melancholy among weary bones.

    Uprisen betimes, our journey we renewed,
Led by the stream, ere noon-day magnified
Into a lordly river, broad and deep,   90
Dimpling along in silent majesty,
With mountains for its neighbours, and in view
Of distant mountains and their snowy tops,
And thus proceeding to Locarno's Lake,
Fit resting-place for such a visitant.
Locarno! spreading out in width like Heaven,
And Como! thou, a treasure by the earth
Kept to itself, a darling bosomed up
In Abyssinian privacy, I spake

100   Of thee, thy chestnut woods, and garden plots
    Of Indian corn tended by dark-eyed maids;
    Thy lofty steeps, and pathways roofed with vines,
    Winding from house to house, from town to town,
    Sole link that binds them to each other; walks,
    League after league, and cloistral avenues,
    Where silence is if music be not there:
    While yet a youth undisciplined in verse,
    Through fond ambition of my heart, I told
    Your praises; nor can I approach you now

110   Ungreeted by a more melodious Song,
    Where tones of learned Art and Nature mixed
    May frame enduring language. Like a breeze
    Or sunbeam over your domain I passed
    In motion without pause; but ye have left
    Your beauty with me, an impassioned sight
    Of colours and of forms, whose power is sweet
    And gracious, almost might I dare to say,
    As virtue is, or goodness; sweet as love,
    Or the remembrance of a noble deed,

120   Or gentlest visitations of pure thought
    When God, the giver of all joy, is thanked
    Religiously, in silent blessedness;
    Sweet as this last herself, for such it is.

      Through those delightful pathways we advanced,
    Two days, and still in presence of the Lake,
    Which winding up among the Alps, now changed
    Slowly its lovely countenance, and put on
    A sterner character. The second night,
    In eagerness, and by report misled

130   Of those Italian clocks that speak the time
    In fashion different from ours, we rose
    By moonshine, doubting not that day was near,
    And that meanwhile, coasting the water's edge
    As hitherto, and with as plain a track
    To be our guide, we might behold the scene
    In its most deep repose. We left the town

Of Gravedona with this hope; but soon
Were lost, bewildered among woods immense,
Where, having wandered for a while, we stopped
And on a rock sate down, to wait for day.   140
An open place it was, and overlooked,
From high, the sullen water underneath,
On which a dull red image of the moon
Lay bedded, changing oftentimes its form
Like an uneasy snake. Long time we sate,
For scarcely more than one hour of the night,
Such was our error, had been done, when we
Renewed our journey. On the rock we lay
And wished to sleep but could not, for the stings
Of insects, which, with noise like that of noon,   150
Filled all the woods. The cry of unknown birds;
The mountains more by darkness visible
And their own size, than any outward light;
The breathless wilderness of clouds; the clock
That told, with unintelligible voice,
The widely parted hours; the noise of streams,
And sometimes rustling motions nigh at hand,
Which did not leave us free from personal fear;
And, lastly, the withdrawing moon, that set
Before us, while she still was high in heaven; –   160
These were our food; and such a summer night
Did to that pair of golden days succeed,
With now and then a doze and snatch of sleep,
On Como's banks, the same delicious Lake.

'THE BLIND BEGGAR, AND BARTHOLOMEW FAIR'
(FROM BOOK 7)

O Friend! one feeling was there which belonged
To this great city, by exclusive right;
How often, in the overflowing streets,
Have I gone forwards with the crowd, and said
Unto myself, 'The face of every one
That passes by me is a mystery!'

Thus have I looked, nor ceased to look, oppressed
By thoughts of what and whither, when and how,
Until the shapes before my eyes became
A second-sight procession, such as glides
Over still mountains, or appears in dreams;
And all the ballast of familiar life,
The present, and the past; hope, fear; all stays,
All laws of acting, thinking, speaking man
Went from me, neither knowing me, nor known.
And once, far-travelled in such mood, beyond
The reach of common indications, lost
Amid the moving pageant, 'twas my chance
Abruptly to be smitten with the view
Of a blind Beggar, who, with upright face,
Stood, propped against a wall, upon his chest
Wearing a written paper, to explain
The story of the man, and who he was.
My mind did at this spectacle turn round
As with the might of waters, and it seemed
To me that in this label was a type,
Or emblem, of the utmost that we know,
Both of ourselves and of the universe;
And, on the shape of the unmoving man,
His fixed face and sightless eyes, I looked,
As if admonished from another world.

　　Though reared upon the base of outward things,
These, chiefly, are such structures as the mind
Builds for itself; scenes different there are,
Full-formed, which take, with small internal help,
Possession of the faculties, – the peace
Of night, for instance, the solemnity
Of nature's intermediate hours of rest,
When the great tide of human life stands still;
The business of the day to come, unborn,
Of that gone by, locked up, as in the grave;
The calmness, beauty, of the spectacle,
Sky, stillness, moonshine, empty streets, and sounds

Unfrequent as in deserts; at late hours
Of winter evenings, when unwholesome rains
Are falling hard, with people yet astir,
The feeble salutation from the voice
Of some unhappy woman, now and then
Heard as we pass, when no one looks about,
Nothing is listened to. But these, I fear,   50
Are falsely catalogued; things that are, are not,
Even as we give them welcome, or assist,
Are prompt, or are remiss. What say you, then,
To times, when half the city shall break out
Full of one passion, vengeance, rage, or fear?
To executions, to a street on fire,
Mobs, riots, or rejoicings? From those sights
Take one, – an annual festival, the Fair
Holden where martyrs suffered in past time,
And named of St Bartholomew; there, see   60
A work that's finished to our hands, that lays,
If any spectacle on earth can do,
The whole creative powers of man asleep! –
For once, the Muse's help will we implore,
And she shall lodge us, wafted on her wings,
Above the press and danger of the crowd,
Upon some showman's platform. What a hell
For eyes and ears! what anarchy and din
Barbarian and infernal, – 'tis a dream,
Monstrous in colour, motion, shape, sight, sound!   70
Below, the open space, through every nook
Of the wide area, twinkles, is alive
With heads; the midway region, and above,
Is thronged with staring pictures and huge scrolls,
Dumb proclamations of the Prodigies;
And chattering monkeys dangling from their poles,
And children whirling in their roundabouts;
With those that stretch the neck and strain the eyes,
And crack the voice in rivalship, the crowd
Inviting; with buffoons against buffoons   80
Grimacing, writhing, screaming, – him who grinds

The hurdy-gurdy, at the fiddle weaves,
Rattles the salt-box, thumps the kettle-drum,
And him who at the trumpet puffs his cheeks,
The silver-collared Negro with his timbrel,
Equestrians, tumblers, women, girls, and boys,
Blue-breeched, pink-vested, and with towering plumes. –
All moveables of wonder, from all parts,
Are here – Albinos, painted Indians, Dwarfs,
90   The Horse of knowledge, and the learned Pig,
The Stone-eater, the man that swallows fire,
Giants, Ventriloquists, the Invisible Girl,
The Bust that speaks and moves its goggling eyes,
The Wax-work, Clock-work, all the marvellous craft
Of modern Merlins, Wild Beasts, Puppet-shows,
All out-o'-the-way, far-fetched, perverted things,
All freaks of nature, all Promethean thoughts
Of man, his dulness, madness, and their feats
All jumbled up together to make up
100   This Parliament of Monsters. Tents and Booths
Meanwhile, as if the whole were one vast mill,
Are vomiting, receiving, on all sides,
Men, Women, three-years' Children, Babes in arms.

    Oh, blank confusion! and a type not false
Of what the mighty City is itself
To all except a straggler here and there,
To the whole swarm of its inhabitants;
An undistinguishable world to men,
The slaves unrespited of low pursuits,
110   Living amid the same perpetual flow
Of trivial objects, melted and reduced
To one identity, by differences
That have no law, no meaning, and no end –
Oppression, under which even highest minds
Must labour, whence the strongest are not free.
But though the picture weary out the eye,
By nature an unmanageable sight,
It is not wholly so to him who looks

In steadiness, who hath among least things
An under-sense of greatest; sees the parts   120
As parts, but with a feeling of the whole.
This, of all acquisitions first, awaits
On sundry and most widely different modes
Of education, nor with least delight
On that through which I passed. Attention comes,
And comprehensiveness and memory,
From early converse with the works of God
Among all regions; chiefly where appear
Most obviously simplicity and power.
By influence habitual to the mind   130
The mountain's outline and its steady form
Gives a pure grandeur, and its presence shapes
The measure and the prospect of the soul
To majesty. Such virtue have the forms
Perennial of the ancient hills; nor less
The changeful language of their countenances
Gives movement to the thoughts, and multitude,
With order and relation. This, if still,
As hitherto, with freedom I may speak,
And the same perfect openness of mind,   140
Not violating any just restraint,
As I would hope, of real modesty, –
This did I feel, in that vast receptacle.
The Spirit of Nature was upon me here;
The soul of Beauty and enduring Life
Was present as a habit, and diffused,
Through meagre lines and colours, and the press
Of self-destroying, transitory things,
Composure, and ennobling Harmony.

'THE SEPTEMBER MASSACRES'
(FROM BOOK 10)

This was the time in which, inflamed with hope,
To Paris I returned. Again I ranged,
More eagerly than I had done before,
Through the wide city, and in progress passed
The prison where the unhappy monarch lay,
Associate with his children and his wife
In bondage; and the palace, lately stormed
With roar of cannon and a numerous host.
I crossed (a black and empty area then)
10   The square of the Carrousel, few weeks back
Heaped up with dead and dying, upon these
And other sights looking, as doth a man
Upon a volume whose contents he knows
Are memorable, but from him locked up,
Being written in a tongue he cannot read,
So that he questions the mute leaves with pain,
And half upbraids their silence. But that night
When on my bed I lay, I was most moved
And felt most deeply in what world I was.
20   My room was high and lonely, near the roof
Of a large mansion or hotel, a spot
That would have pleased me in more quiet times,
Nor was it wholly without pleasure then.
With unextinguished taper I kept watch,
Reading at intervals; the fear gone by
Pressed on me almost like a fear to come.
I thought of those September massacres,
Divided from me by a little month,
And felt and touched them, a substantial dread:
30   The rest was conjured up from tragic fictions,
And mournful calendars of true history,
Remembrances and dim admonishments.
The horse is taught his manage, and the wind
Of heaven wheels round and treads in his own steps;
Year follows year, the tide returns again,

Day follows day, all things have second birth;
The earthquake is not satisfied at once;
And in such way I wrought upon myself,
Until I seemed to hear a voice that cried,
To the whole city, 'Sleep no more.' To this   40
Add comments of a calmer mind, from which
I could not gather full security,
But at the best it seemed a place of fear
Unfit for the repose of night,
Defenceless as a wood where tigers roam.

    Betimes next morning to the Palace-walk
Of Orleans I repaired and entering there
Was greeted, among divers other notes,
By voices of the hawkers in the crowd
Bawling, 'Denunciation of the crimes   50
Of Maximilian Robespierre'; the speech
Which in their hands they carried was the same
Which had been recently pronounced, the day
When Robespierre, well knowing for what mark
Some words of indirect reproof had been
Intended, rose in hardihood, and dared
The man who had an ill surmise of him
To bring his charge in openness; whereat,
When a dead pause ensued, and no one stirred,
In silence of all present, from his seat   60
Louvet walked singly through the avenue,
And took his station in the Tribune, saying,
'I, Robespierre, accuse thee!' 'Tis well known
What was the issue of that charge, and how
Louvet was left alone without support
Of his irresolute friends; but these are things
Of which I speak, only as they were storm
Or sunshine to my individual mind,
No further. Let me then relate that now –
In some sort seeing with my proper eyes   70
That Liberty, and Life, and Death would soon
To the remotest corners of the land

Lie in the arbitrement of those who ruled
The capital City; what was struggled for,
And by what combatants victory must be won;
The indecision on their part whose aim
Seemed best, and the straightforward path of those
Who in attack or in defence alike
Were strong through their impiety – greatly I
80   Was agitated; yea, I could almost
Have prayed that throughout earth upon all souls,
By patient exercise of reason made
Worthy of liberty, upon every soul
Matured to live in plainness and in truth,
The gift of tongues might fall, and men arrive
From the four quarters of the winds to do
For France, what without help she could not do,
A work of honour; think not that to this
I added, work of safety: from such thought
90   And the least fear about the end of things
I was as far as angels are from guilt.

'THE DEATH OF ROBESPIERRE'
(FROM BOOK 10)

O Friend! few happier moments have been mine
Through my whole life than that when first I heard
That this foul Tribe of Moloch was o'erthrown,
And their chief regent levelled with the dust.
The day was one which haply may deserve
A separate chronicle. Having gone abroad
From a small village where I tarried then,
To the same far-secluded privacy
I was returning. Over the smooth sands
10   Of Leven's ample estuary lay
My journey, and beneath a genial sun,
With distant prospect among gleams of sky
And clouds, and intermingled mountain tops,

In one inseparable glory clad,
Creatures of one ethereal substance met
In consistory, like a diadem
Or crown of burning seraphs as they sit
In the empyrean. Underneath this show
Lay, as I knew, the nest of pastoral vales
Among whose happy fields I had grown up   20
From childhood. On the fulgent spectacle,
Which neither changed nor stirred nor passed away,
I gazed, and with a fancy more alive
On this account, that I had chanced to find
That morning, ranging through the churchyard graves
Of Cartmel's rural town, the place in which
An honoured teacher of my youth was laid.
While we were schoolboys he had died among us,
And was borne hither, as I knew, to rest
With his own family. A plain stone, inscribed   30
With name, date, office, pointed out the spot,
To which a slip of verses was subjoined,
(By his desire, as afterwards I learnt)
A fragment from the elegy of Gray.
A week, or little less, before his death
He had said to me, 'My head will soon lie low';
And when I saw the turf that covered him,
After the lapse of full eight years, those words,
With sound of voice and countenance of the Man,
Came back upon me, so that some few tears   40
Fell from me in my own despite. And now,
Thus travelling smoothly o'er the level sands,
I thought with pleasure of the verses graven
Upon his tombstone, saying to myself:
He loved the Poets, and, if now alive,
Would have loved me, as one not destitute
Of promise, nor belying the kind hope
Which he had formed, when I, at his command,
Began to spin, at first, my toilsome songs.

50   Without me and within, as I advanced,
   All that I saw, or felt, or communed with
   Was gentleness and peace. Upon a small
   And rocky island near, a fragment stood
   (Itself like a sea rock) of what had been
   A Romish chapel, where in ancient times
   Masses were said at the hour which suited those
   Who crossed the sands with ebb of morning tide.
   Not far from this still ruin all the plain
   Was spotted with a variegated crowd
60   Of coaches, wains, and travellers, horse and foot,
   Wading beneath the conduct of their guide
   In loose procession through the shallow stream
   Of inland water; the great sea meanwhile
   Was at safe distance, far retired. I paused,
   Unwilling to proceed, the scene appeared
   So gay and cheerful, when a traveller
   Chancing to pass, I carelessly inquired
   If any news were stirring; he replied
   In the familiar language of the day
70   That, *Robespierre was dead* – nor was a doubt,
   On further question, left within my mind
   But that the tidings were substantial truth;
   That he and his supporters all were fallen.

   Great was my glee of spirit, great my joy
   In vengeance, and eternal Justice, thus
   Made manifest. 'Come now, ye golden times,'
   Said I, forth-breathing on those open sands
   A hymn of triumph: 'as the morning comes
   Out of the bosom of the night, come ye:
80   Thus far our trust is verified; behold!
   They who with clumsy desperation brought
   Rivers of Blood, and preached that nothing else
   Could cleanse the Augean stable, by the might
   Of their own helper have been swept away;
   Their madness is declared and visible;
   Elsewhere will safety now be sought, and earth

March firmly towards righteousness and peace.' –
Then schemes I framed more calmly, when and how
The madding factions might be tranquillized,
And, though through hardships manifold and long,   90
The mighty renovation would proceed.
Thus interrupted by uneasy bursts
Of exultation, I pursued my way
Along that very shore which I had skimmed
In former times, when – spurring from the Vale
Of Nightshade, and St Mary's mouldering fane,
And the stone abbot, after circuit made
In wantonness of heart, a joyous crew
Of schoolboys hastening to their distant home
Along the margin of the moonlight sea –   100
We beat with thundering hoofs the level sand.

'THE CLIMBING OF SNOWDON'
(FROM BOOK 13)

In one of these excursions, travelling then
Through Wales on foot, and with a youthful friend,
I left Bethgelert's huts at couching-time,
And westward took my way, to see the sun
Rise from the top of Snowdon. Having reached
The cottage at the mountain's foot, we there
Roused up the shepherd who by ancient right
Of office is the stranger's usual guide;
And after short refreshment sallied forth.

It was a summer's night, a close warm night,   10
Wan, dull and glaring, with a dripping mist
Low-hung and thick that covered all the sky,
Half threatening storm and rain; but on we went
Unchecked, being full of heart and having faith
In our tried pilot. Little could we see
Hemmed round on every side with fog and damp,
And, after ordinary traveller's chat
With our conductor, silently we sank

231

Each into commerce with his private thoughts:
Thus did we breast the ascent, and by myself
Was nothing either seen or heard the while
Which took me from my musings, save that once
The shepherd's cur did to his own great joy
Unearth a hedgehog in the mountain crags
Round which he made a barking turbulent.
This small adventure, for even such it seemed
In that wild place and at the dead of night,
Being over and forgotten, on we wound
In silence as before. With forehead bent
Earthward, as if in opposition set
Against an enemy, I panted up
With eager pace, and no less eager thoughts.
Thus might we wear perhaps an hour away,
Ascending at loose distance each from each,
And I, as chanced, the foremost of the band;
When at my feet the ground appeared to brighten,
And with a step or two seemed brighter still;
Nor had I time to ask the cause of this,
For instantly a light upon the turf
Fell like a flash: I looked about, and lo!
The Moon stood naked in the heavens, at height
Immense above my head, and on the shore
I found myself of a huge sea of mist,
Which, meek and silent, rested at my feet.
A hundred hills their dusky backs upheaved
All over this still ocean; and beyond,
Far, far beyond, the vapours shot themselves,
In headlands, tongues, and promontory shapes,
Into the sea, the real sea, that seemed
To dwindle, and give up its majesty,
Usurped upon as far as sight could reach.
Meanwhile, the Moon looked down upon this show
In single glory, and we stood, the mist
Touching our very feet; and from the shore
At distance not the third part of a mile
Was a blue chasm; a fracture in the vapour,

A deep and gloomy breathing-place through which
Mounted the roar of waters, torrents, streams
Innumerable, roaring with one voice!
The universal spectacle throughout   60
Was shaped for admiration and delight,
Grand in itself alone, but in that breach
Through which the homeless voice of waters rose,
That dark deep thoroughfare, had Nature lodged
The soul, the imagination of the whole.

   A meditation rose in me that night
Upon the lonely mountain when the scene
Had passed away, and it appeared to me
The perfect image of a mighty mind,
Of one that feeds upon infinity,   70
That is exalted by an underpresence,
The sense of God, or whatsoe'er is dim
Or vast in its own being, above all
One function of such mind had Nature there
Exhibited by putting forth, and that
With circumstance most awful and sublime,
That domination which she oftentimes
Exerts upon the outward face of things,
So moulds them, and endues, abstracts, combines,
Or by abrupt and unhabitual influence   80
Doth make one object so impress itself
Upon all others, and pervade them so
That even the grossest minds must see and hear
And cannot choose but feel. The power, which these
Acknowledge when thus moved, which Nature thus
Thrusts forth upon the senses, is the express
Resemblance, in the fullness of its strength
Made visible, a genuine counterpart
And brother of the glorious faculty
Which higher minds bear with them as their own.   90
That is the very spirit in which they deal
With all the objects of the universe:
They from their native selves can send abroad

Like transformation; for themselves create
A like existence, and, whene'er it is
Created for them, catch it by an instinct:
Them the enduring and the transient both
Serve to exalt; they build up greatest things
From least suggestions; ever on the watch,
100   Willing to work and to be wrought upon,
They need not extraordinary calls
To rouse them; in a world of life they live,
By sensible impressions not enthralled,
But quickened, roused, and made thereby more fit
To hold communion with the invisible world.
Such minds are truly from the Deity,
For they are Powers; and hence the highest bliss
That can be known is theirs – the consciousness
Of Whom they are, habitually infused
110   Through every image and through every thought,
And all impressions; hence religion, faith,
And endless occupation for the Soul,
Whether discursive or intuitive:
Hence sovereignty within and peace at will,
Emotion which best foresight need not fear,
Most worthy then of trust when most intense.
Hence cheerfulness in every act of life,
Hence truth in moral judgments and delight
That fails not in the external universe.

Three Elegies for John Wordsworth

TO THE DAISY

Sweet Flower! belike one day to have
A place upon thy Poet's grave,
I welcome thee once more;
But He, who was, on land, at sea,
My Brother, too, in loving thee,
Although he loved more silently,
Sleeps by his native shore.

Ah! hopeful, hopeful was the day
When to that Ship he went his way,
To govern and to guide: 10
His wish was gained; a little time
Would bring him back in manhood's prime,
And free for life, these hills to climb
With all his wants supplied.

And hopeful, hopeful was the day
When that stout Ship at anchor lay
Beside the shores of Wight:
The May had then made all things green;
And goodly, also, to be seen
Was that proud Ship, of Ships the Queen,   20
His hope and his delight.

Yet then, when called ashore (I know
The truth of this, he told me so)
In more than happy mood
To your abodes, Sweet Daisy Flowers!
He oft would steal at leisure hours;
And loved you glittering in the bowers,
A starry multitude.

But hark the Word! the Ship is gone;
Returns from her long course: anon
Sets sail: in season due
Once more on English earth they stand:
But, when a third time from the land
They parted, sorrow was at hand
For him and for his Crew.

Six weeks beneath the moving Sea
He lay in slumber quietly,
Unforced by Wind or wave
To quit the Ship for which he died,
(All claims of duty satisfied)
And there they found him at her side,
And bore him to the grave.

Vain service! yet not vainly done
For this, if other end were none,
That he, who had been cast
Upon a way of life unmeet
For such a gentle Soul and sweet,
Should find an undisturbed retreat
Near what he loved at last:

That neighbourhood of Wood and Field
To him a resting-place should yield,
A meek Man and a brave!
The Birds shall sing, and Ocean make
A mournful murmur for *his* sake:
And Thou sweet Flower! shalt sleep and wake
Upon his senseless Grave.

'I ONLY LOOKED FOR PAIN AND GRIEF'

I only looked for pain and grief
And trembled as I drew more near:
But God's unbounded love is here,
And I have found relief.

The precious Spot is all my own,
Save only that this Plant unknown,
A little one and lowly sweet,
Not surely now without Heaven's grace,
First seen, and seen too in this place,
Is flowering at my feet.   10

The Shepherd Boy hath disappeared;
The Buzzard too hath soared away;
And undisturbed I now may pay
My debt to what I feared.
Sad register! but this is sure:
Peace built on suffering will endure.
But such the peace that will be ours,
Though many suns, alas! must shine
Ere tears shall cease from me and mine
To fall in bitter showers.   20

The Sheep-boy whistled loud, and lo!
Thereafter, having felt the shock,
The Buzzard mounted from the rock
Deliberate and slow:
Lord of the air, he took his flight;
Oh could he on that woeful night
Have lent his wing, my Brother dear!
For one poor moment's space to Thee
And all who struggle with the Sea
When safety is so near.   30

Thus in the weakness of my heart
I said (but let that pang be still)
When rising from the rock at will,
I saw the Bird depart.
And let me calmly bless the Power
That meets me in this unknown Flower,

Affecting type of Him I mourn!
With calmness suffer and believe,
And grieve, and know that I must grieve,
40   Not cheerless, though forlorn.

Here did we stop, and here looked round
While each into himself descends
For that last thought of parting Friends
That is not to be found.
Our Grasmere vale was out of sight,
Our home and his, his heart's delight,
His quiet heart's delicious home.
But time before him melts away,
And he hath feeling of a day
50   Of blessedness to come.

Here did we part, and halted here
With One he loved, I saw him bound
Downwards along the rocky ground
As if with eager cheer.
A lovely sight as on he went,
For he was bold and innocent,
Had lived a life of self-command.
Heaven, did it seem to me and her,
Had laid on such a Mariner
60   A consecrating hand.

And therefore also do we weep,
To find that such a faith was dust,
With sorrow, but for higher trust,
How miserably deep!
All vanished, in a single word,
A breath, a sound, and scarcely heard.
Sea, Ship, drowned, shipwreck – so it came,
The meek, the brave, the good was gone;
He who had been our living John
70   Was nothing but a name.

That was indeed a parting! oh,
Glad am I, glad that it is past;
For there were some on whom it cast
Unutterable woe.
But they as well as I have gains,
The worthiest and the best; to pains
Like these, there comes a mild release;
Even here I feel it, even this Plant
So peaceful is ministrant
Of comfort and of peace.   80

He would have loved thy modest grace,
Meek flower! to Him I would have said,
'It grows upon its native bed
Beside our Parting-place;
Close to the ground like dew it lies
With multitude of purple eyes
Spangling a cushion green like moss;
But we will see it, joyful tide!
Some day to see it in its pride
The mountain we will cross.'   90

Well, well, if ever verse of mine
Have power to make his merits known,
Then let a monumental Stone
Stand here – a sacred Shrine;
And to the few who come this way,
Traveller or Shepherd, let it say,
Long as these mighty rocks endure,
Oh do not Thou too fondly brood,
Although deserving of all good,
On any earthly hope, however pure!   100

'DISTRESSFUL GIFT! THIS BOOK RECEIVES'

Distressful gift! this Book receives
Upon its melancholy leaves,
This poor ill-fated Book:
I wrote, and when I reached the end
Started to think that thou, my Friend,
Upon the words which I had penned
Must never, never look.

Alas, alas, it is a Tale
Of Thee thyself; fond heart and frail!
The sadly-tuneful line
The written words that seem to throng
The dismal page, the sound, the song,
The murmur all to thee belong,
Too surely they are thine.

And so I write what neither Thou
Must look upon, nor others now,
Their tears would flow too fast;
Some solace thus I strive to gain,
Making a kind of secret chain,
If so I may, betwixt us twain
In memory of the past.

Oft have I handled, often eyed,
This volume with delight and pride,
The written page and white;
Oft have I turned them o'er and o'er,
One after one and score by score,
All filled or to be filled with store
Of verse for his delight.

He framed the Book which now I see,
This very Book upon my knee,   30
He framed with dear intent;
To travel with him night and day,
And in his private hearing say
Refreshing things, whatever way
His weary Vessel went.

But now – upon the written leaf
I look indeed with pain and grief,
I do, but gracious God,
Oh grant that I may never find
Worse matter or a heavier mind,   40
For those which yet remain behind
Grant this, and let me be resigned
Beneath thy chast'ning rod.

Stepping Westward

While my Fellow-traveller and I were walking by the
side of Loch Ketterine, one fine evening after sun-set,
in our road to a Hut where in the course of our Tour we
had been hospitably entertained some weeks before, we
met, in one of the loneliest parts of that solitary region,
two well-dressed Women, one of whom said to us, by
way of greeting, 'What you are stepping westward?'

'*What you are stepping westward?*' – '*Yea.*'
– 'Twould be a wildish destiny,
If we, who thus together roam
In a strange Land, and far from home,
Were in this place the guests of Chance:
Yet who would stop, or fear to advance,
Though home or shelter he had none,
With such a Sky to lead him on?

The dewy ground was dark and cold;
Behind, all gloomy to behold;
And stepping westward seemed to be
A kind of *heavenly* destiny;
I liked the greeting; 'twas a sound
Of something without place or bound;
And seemed to give me spiritual right
To travel through that region bright.

The voice was soft, and she who spake
Was walking by her native Lake:
The salutation had to me
The very sound of courtesy:
Its power was felt; and while my eye
Was fixed upon the glowing sky,
The echo of the voice enwrought
A human sweetness with the thought
Of travelling through the world that lay
Before me in my endless way.

The Solitary Reaper

Behold her, single in the field,
Yon solitary Highland Lass!
Reaping and singing by herself;
Stop here, or gently pass!
Alone she cuts, and binds the grain,
And sings a melancholy strain;
O listen! for the Vale profound
Is overflowing with the sound.

No Nightingale did ever chaunt
So sweetly to reposing bands
Of Travellers in some shady haunt,
Among Arabian Sands:

No sweeter voice was ever heard
In spring-time from the Cuckoo-bird,
Breaking the silence of the seas
Among the farthest Hebrides.

Will no one tell me what she sings?
Perhaps the plaintive numbers flow
For old, unhappy, far-off things,
And battles long ago: 20
Or is it some more humble lay,
Familiar matter of today?
Some natural sorrow, loss, or pain,
That has been, and may be again!

Whate'er the theme, the Maiden sang
As if her song could have no ending;
I saw her singing at her work,
And o'er the sickle bending;
I listened till I had my fill:
And, as I mounted up the hill,   30
The music in my heart I bore,
Long after it was heard no more.

Elegiac Stanzas,

Suggested by a Picture of Peele Castle, in a Storm, Painted by Sir George Beaumont

I was thy Neighbour once, thou rugged Pile!
Four summer weeks I dwelt in sight of thee:
I saw thee every day; and all the while
Thy Form was sleeping on a glassy sea.

So pure the sky, so quiet was the air!
So like, so very like, was day to day!
Whene'er I looked, thy Image still was there;
It trembled, but it never passed away.

How perfect was the calm! it seemed no sleep;
No mood, which season takes away, or brings:
I could have fancied that the mighty Deep
Was even the gentlest of all gentle Things.

Ah! THEN, if mine had been the Painter's hand,
To express what then I saw; and add the gleam,
The light that never was, on sea or land,
The consecration, and the Poet's dream;

I would have planted thee, thou hoary Pile!
Amid a world how different from this!
Beside a sea that could not cease to smile;
On tranquil land, beneath a sky of bliss:

Thou shouldst have seemed a treasure-house, a mine
Of peaceful years; a chronicle of heaven: –
Of all the sunbeams that did ever shine
The very sweetest had to thee been given.

A Picture had it been of lasting ease,
Elysian quiet, without toil or strife;
No motion but the moving tide, a breeze,
Or merely silent Nature's breathing life.

Such, in the fond delusion of my heart,
Such Picture would I at that time have made:
And seen the soul of truth in every part;
A faith, a trust, that could not be betrayed.

So once it would have been, – 'tis so no more;
I have submitted to a new controul:
A power is gone, which nothing can restore;
A deep distress hath humanized my Soul.

Not for a moment could I now behold
A smiling sea and be what I have been:
The feeling of my loss will ne'er be old;
This, which I know, I speak with mind serene.   40

Then, Beaumont, Friend! who would have been the Friend,
If he had lived, of Him whom I deplore,
This Work of thine I blame not, but commend;
This sea in anger, and that dismal shore.

Oh 'tis a passionate Work! – yet wise and well;
Well chosen is the spirit that is here;
That Hulk which labours in the deadly swell,
This rueful sky, this pageantry of fear!

And this huge Castle, standing here sublime,
I love to see the look with which it braves,   50
Cased in the unfeeling armour of old time,
The light'ning, the fierce wind, and trampling waves.

Farewell, farewell the Heart that lives alone,
Housed in a dream, at distance from the Kind!
Such happiness, wherever it be known,
Is to be pitied; for 'tis surely blind.

But welcome fortitude, and patient cheer,
And frequent sights of what is to be borne!
Such sights, or worse, as are before me here. –
Not without hope we suffer and we mourn.   60

'Yes! full surely 'twas the Echo'

Yes! full surely 'twas the Echo,
Solitary, clear, profound,
Answering to Thee, shouting Cuckoo!
Giving to thee Sound for Sound;

Whence the Voice? from air or earth?
This the Cuckoo cannot tell;
But a startling sound had birth,
As the Bird must know full well;

Like the voice through earth and sky
By the restless Cuckoo sent;
Like her ordinary cry,
Like – but oh how different!

Hears not also mortal Life?
Hear not we, unthinking Creatures!
Slaves of Folly, Love, or Strife,
Voices of two different Natures?

Have not We too? Yes we have
Answers, and we know not whence;
Echoes from beyond the grave,
Recognized intelligence?

Such within ourselves we hear
Oft-times, ours though sent from far;
Listen, ponder, hold them dear;
For of God, of God they are!

'The rains at length have ceased'

The rains at length have ceased, the winds are stilled,
The stars shine brightly between clouds at rest,
And as a cavern is with darkness filled,
The vale is by a mighty sound possessed.

Lines,

Composed at Grasmere, during a walk, one Evening,
after a stormy day, the Author having just read in a
Newspaper that the dissolution of Mr Fox was hourly
expected.

Loud is the Vale! the Voice is up
With which she speaks when storms are gone,
A mighty Unison of streams!
Of all her Voices, One!

Loud is the Vale; – this inland Depth
In peace is roaring like the Sea;
Yon Star upon the mountain-top
Is listening quietly.

Sad was I, ev'n to pain depressed,
Importunate and heavy load!   10
The Comforter hath found me here,
Upon this lonely road;

And many thousands now are sad,
Wait the fulfilment of their fear;
For He must die who is their Stay,
Their Glory disappear.

A Power is passing from the earth
To breathless Nature's dark abyss;
But when the Mighty pass away
What is it more than this,

That Man, who is from God sent forth,
Doth yet again to God return? –
Such ebb and flow must ever be,
Then wherefore should we mourn?

Thought of a Briton on the Subjugation of Switzerland

Two Voices are there; one is of the Sea,
One of the Mountains; each a mighty Voice:
In both from age to age Thou didst rejoice,
They were thy chosen Music, Liberty!
There came a Tyrant, and with holy glee
Thou fought'st against Him; but hast vainly striven;
Thou from thy Alpine Holds at length art driven,
Where not a torrent murmurs heard by thee.
Of one deep bliss thine ear hath been bereft:
Then Cleave, O cleave to that which still is left!
For, high-souled Maid, what sorrow would it be
That mountain Floods should thunder as before,
And Ocean bellow from his rocky shore,
And neither awful Voice be heard by thee!

A Complaint

There is a change – and I am poor;
Your Love hath been, nor long ago,
A Fountain at my fond Heart's door,
Whose only business was to flow;
And flow it did; not taking heed
Of its own bounty, or my need.

What happy moments did I count!
Blessed was I then all bliss above!
Now, for this consecrated Fount
Of murmuring, sparkling, living love,   10
What have I? shall I dare to tell?
A comfortless, and hidden WELL.

A Well of love – it may be deep –
I trust it is, and never dry:
What matter? if the Waters sleep
In silence and obscurity.
– Such change, and at the very door
Of my fond Heart, hath made me poor.

November, 1806

Another year! – another deadly blow!
Another mighty Empire overthrown!
And we are left, or shall be left, alone;
The last that dares to struggle with the Foe.
'Tis well! from this day forward we shall know
That in ourselves our safety must be sought;
That by our own right hands it must be wrought,
That we must stand unpropped, or be laid low.
O Dastard whom such foretaste doth not cheer!

10 We shall exult, if They who rule the land
Be Men who hold its many blessings dear,
Wise, upright, valiant; not a venal Band,
Who are to judge of danger which they fear,
And honour which they do not understand.

Gipsies

Yet are they here? – the same unbroken knot
Of human Beings, in the self-same spot!
    Men, Women, Children, yea the frame
    Of the whole Spectacle the same!
Only their fire seems bolder, yielding light:
Now deep and red, the colouring of night;
    That on their Gipsy-faces falls,
    Their bed of straw and blanket-walls.
– Twelve hours, twelve bounteous hours, are gone while I
10 Have been a Traveller under open sky,
    Much witnessing of change and cheer,
    Yet as I left I find them here!

The weary Sun betook himself to rest.
– Then issued Vesper from the fulgent West,
    Outshining like a visible God
    The glorious path in which he trod.
And now, ascending, after one dark hour,
And one night's diminution of her power,
    Behold the mighty Moon! this way
20   She looks as if at them – but they
Regard not her: – oh better wrong and strife
Better vain deeds or evil than such life!
    The silent Heavens have goings on;
    The stars have tasks – but these have none.

'Eve's lingering clouds extend in solid bars'

Eve's lingering clouds extend in solid bars
Through the grey west; and lo! these waters, steeled
By breezeless air to smoothest polish, yield
A vivid repetition of the stars;
Jove – Venus – and the ruddy crest of Mars,
Amid his fellows, beauteously revealed
At happy distance from earth's groaning field,
Where ruthless mortals wage incessant wars.
Is it a mirror? – or the nether sphere
Opening its vast abyss, while fancy feeds   10
On the rich show! – But list! a voice is near;
Great Pan himself low-whispering through the reeds,
'Be thankful thou; for, if unholy deeds
Ravage the world, tranquillity is here!'

St Paul's

Pressed with conflicting thoughts of love and fear
I parted from thee, Friend, and took my way
Through the great City, pacing with an eye
Downcast, ear sleeping, and feet masterless
That were sufficient guide unto themselves,
And step by step went pensively. Now, mark!
Not how my trouble was entirely hushed,
(That might not be) but how, by sudden gift,
Gift of Imagination's holy power,
My Soul in her uneasiness received   10
An anchor of stability. – It chanced
That while I thus was pacing, I raised up
My heavy eyes and instantly beheld,
Saw at a glance in that familiar spot
A visionary scene – a length of street

Laid open in its morning quietness,
Deep, hollow, unobstructed, vacant, smooth,
And white with winter's purest white, as fair,
As fresh and spotless as he ever sheds
On field or mountain. Moving Form was none
Save here and there a shadowy Passenger
Slow, shadowy, silent, dusky, and beyond
And high above this winding length of street,
This moveless and unpeopled avenue,
Pure, silent, solemn, beautiful, was seen
The huge majestic Temple of St Paul
In awful sequestration, through a veil,
Through its own sacred veil of falling snow.

Upon the Sight of a Beautiful Picture

Praised be the Art whose subtle power could stay
Yon Cloud, and fix it in that glorious shape;
Nor would permit the thin smoke to escape,
Nor those bright sunbeams to forsake the day;
Which stopped that Band of Travellers on their way
Ere they were lost within the shady wood;
And shewed the Bark upon the glassy flood
For ever anchored in her sheltering Bay.
Soul-soothing Art! which Morning, Noon-tide, Even
Do serve with all their changeful pageantry!
Thou, with ambition modest yet sublime,
Here, for the sight of mortal man, hast given
To one brief moment caught from fleeting time
The appropriate calm of blest eternity.

Characteristics of a Child Three Years Old

Loving she is, and tractable, though wild;
And Innocence hath privilege in her
To dignify arch looks and laughing eyes;
And feats of cunning; and the pretty round
Of trespasses, affected to provoke
Mock-chastisement and partnership in play.
And, as a faggot sparkles on the hearth,
Not less if unattended and alone
Than when both young and old sit gathered round
And take delight in its activity,   10
Even so this happy Creature of herself
Is all sufficient: solitude to her
Is blithe society, who fills the air
With gladness and involuntary songs.
Light are her sallies as the tripping Fawn's
Forth-startled from the fern where she lay couched;
Unthought-of, unexpected as the stir
Of the soft breeze ruffling the meadow flowers;
Or from before it chasing wantonly
The many-coloured images impressed   20
Upon the bosom of a placid lake.

'Surprized by joy'

Surprized by joy – impatient as the Wind
I wished to share the transport – Oh! with whom
But Thee, long buried in the silent Tomb,
That spot which no vicissitude can find?
Love, faithful love recalled thee to my mind –
But how could I forget thee? – Through what power,
Even for the least division of an hour,
Have I been so beguiled as to be blind
To my most grievous loss? – That thought's return

253

10 Was the worst pang that sorrow ever bore,
Save one, one only, when I stood forlorn,
Knowing my heart's best treasure was no more;
That neither present time, nor years unborn
Could to my sight that heavenly face restore.

Yew-Trees

There is a Yew-tree, pride of Lorton Vale,
Which to this day stands single, in the midst
Of its own darkness, as it stood of yore,
Not loth to furnish weapons for the Bands
Of Umfraville or Percy ere they marched
To Scotland's Heaths; or Those that crossed the Sea
And drew their sounding bows at Azincour,
Perhaps at earlier Crecy, or Poictiers.
Of vast circumference and gloom profound
10 This solitary Tree! – a living thing
Produced too slowly ever to decay;
Of form and aspect too magnificent
To be destroyed. But worthier still of note
Are those fraternal Four of Borrowdale,
Joined in one solemn and capacious grove;
Huge trunks! – and each particular trunk a growth
Of intertwisted fibres serpentine
Up-coiling, and inveterately convolved, –
Nor uninformed with Phantasy, and looks
20 That threaten the prophane; – a pillared shade,
Upon whose grassless floor of red-brown hue,
By sheddings from the pining umbrage tinged
Perennially – beneath whose sable roof
Of boughs, as if for festal purpose, decked
With unrejoicing berries, ghostly Shapes
May meet at noontide – Fear and trembling Hope,
Silence and Foresight – Death the Skeleton

And Time the Shadow, – there to celebrate,
As in a natural temple scattered o'er
With altars undisturbed of mossy stone,   30
United worship; or in mute repose
To lie, and listen to the mountain flood
Murmuring from Glaramara's inmost caves.

Yarrow Visited,

September, 1814

And is this – Yarrow? – *This* the Stream
Of which my fancy cherished,
So faithfully, a waking dream?
An image that hath perished!
O that some Minstrel's harp were near,
To utter notes of gladness,
And chase this silence from the air,
That fills my heart with sadness!

Yet why? – a silvery current flows
With uncontrolled meanderings;   10
Nor have these eyes by greener hills
Been soothed, in all my wanderings.
And, through her depths, Saint Mary's Lake
Is visibly delighted;
For not a feature of those hills
Is in the mirror slighted.

A blue sky bends o'er Yarrow vale,
Save where that pearly whiteness
Is round the rising sun diffused,
A tender, hazy brightness;   20

Mild dawn of promise! that excludes
All profitless dejection;
Though not unwilling here to admit
A pensive recollection.

Where was it that the famous Flower
Of Yarrow Vale lay bleeding?
His bed perchance was yon smooth mound
On which the herd is feeding:
And haply from this crystal pool,
Now peaceful as the morning,
The Water-wraith ascended thrice –
And gave his doleful warning.

Delicious is the Lay that sings
The haunts of happy Lovers,
The path that leads them to the grove,
The leafy grove that covers:
And Pity sanctifies the verse
That paints, by strength of sorrow,
The unconquerable strength of love;
Bear witness, rueful Yarrow!

But thou, that didst appear so fair
To fond imagination,
Dost rival in the light of day
Her delicate creation:
Meek loveliness is round thee spread,
A softness still and holy;
The grace of forest charms decayed,
And pastoral melancholy.

That Region left, the Vale unfolds
Rich groves of lofty stature,
With Yarrow winding through the pomp
Of cultivated nature;

And, rising from those lofty groves,
Behold a Ruin hoary!
The shattered front of Newark's Towers,
Renowned in Border story.

Fair scenes for childhood's opening bloom,
For sportive youth to stray in;
For manhood to enjoy his strength;
And age to wear away in!   60
Yon Cottage seems a bower of bliss;
It promises protection
To studious ease, and generous cares,
And every chaste affection!

How sweet, on this autumnal day,
The wild wood's fruits to gather,
And on my True-love's forehead plant
A crest of blooming heather!
And what if I enwreathed my own!
'Twere no offence to reason;   70
The sober Hills thus deck their brows
To meet the wintry season.

I see – but not by sight alone,
Loved Yarrow, have I won thee;
A ray of Fancy still survives –
Her sunshine plays upon thee!
Thy ever-youthful waters keep
A course of lively pleasure;
And gladsome notes my lips can breathe,
Accordant to the measure.   80

The vapours linger round the Heights,
They melt – and soon must vanish;
One hour is theirs, nor more is mine –
Sad thought, which I would banish,

But that I know, where'er I go,
Thy genuine image, Yarrow,
Will dwell with me – to heighten joy,
And cheer my mind in sorrow.

November 1, 1815

How clear, how keen, how marvellously bright
The effluence from yon distant mountain's head,
Which, strewn with snow as smooth as Heaven can shed,
Shines like another Sun – on mortal sight
Uprisen, as if to check approaching night,
And all her twinkling stars. Who now would tread,
If so he might, yon mountain's glittering head –
Terrestrial – but a surface, by the flight
Of sad mortality's earth-sullying wing,
Unswept, unstained? Nor shall the aerial Powers
Dissolve that beauty – destined to endure
White, radiant, spotless, exquisitely pure,
Through all vicissitudes – till genial spring
Have filled the laughing vales with welcome flowers.

September 1815

While not a leaf seems faded, – while the fields,
With ripening harvests prodigally fair,
In brightest sunshine bask, – this nipping air,
Sent from some distant clime where Winter wields
His icy scymetar, a foretaste yields
Of bitter change – and bids the Flowers beware;
And whispers to the silent Birds, 'prepare
Against the threatening Foe your trustiest shields.'
For me, who under kindlier laws belong

To Nature's tuneful quire, this rustling dry   10
Through the green leaves, and yon crystalline sky,
Announce a season potent to renew,
Mid frost and snow, the instinctive joys of song, –
And nobler cares than listless summer knew.

Ode.

The Pass of Kirkstone

I.

Within the mind strong fancies work,
A deep delight the bosom thrills,
Oft as I pass along the fork
Of these fraternal hills:
Where, save the rugged road, we find
No appanage of human kind;
Nor hint of man, if stone or rock
Seem not his handy-work to mock
By something cognizably shaped;
Mockery – or model – roughly hewn,   10
And left as if by earthquake strewn,
Or from the Flood escaped: –
Altars for Druid service fit;
(But where no fire was ever lit
Unless the glow-worm to the skies
Thence offer nightly sacrifice;)
Wrinkled Egyptian monument;
Green moss-grown tower; or hoary tent;
Tents of a camp that never shall be raised;
On which four thousand years have gazed!   20

II.

Ye plowshares sparkling on the slopes!
Ye snow-white lambs that trip
Imprisoned mid the formal props
Of restless ownership!
Ye trees that may to-morrow fall,
To feed the insatiate Prodigal!
Lawns, houses, chattels, groves, and fields,
All that the fertile valley shields;
Wages of folly – baits of crime, –
Of life's uneasy game the stake, –
Playthings that keep the eyes awake
Of drowsy, dotard Time; –
O care! O guilt! – O vales and plains,
Here, mid his own unvexed domains,
A Genius dwells, that can subdue
At once all memory of You, –
Most potent when mists veil the sky,
Mists that distort and magnify;
While the coarse rushes, to the sweeping breeze,
Sigh forth their ancient melodies!

III.

List to those shriller notes! – *that* march
Perchance was on the blast,
When through this Height's inverted arch
Rome's earliest legion passed!
– They saw, adventurously impelled,
And older eyes than theirs beheld,
This block – and yon whose Church-like frame
Gives to the savage Pass its name.
Aspiring Road! that lov'st to hide
Thy daring in a vapoury bourn,
Not seldom may the hour return
When thou shalt be my Guide;

And I (as often we find cause,
When life is at a weary pause,
And we have panted up the hill
Of duty with reluctant will)
Be thankful, even though tired and faint,
For the rich bounties of Constraint;
Whence oft invigorating transports flow
That Choice lacked courage to bestow!   60

IV.

My soul was grateful for delight
That wore a threatening brow;
A veil is lifted – can she slight
The scene that opens now?
Though habitation none appear,
The greenness tells, man must be there;
The shelter – that the perspective
Is of the clime in which we live;
Where Toil pursues his daily round;
Where Pity sheds sweet tears, and Love,   70
In woodbine bower or birchen grove,
Inflicts his tender wound.
– Who comes not hither ne'er shall know
How beautiful the world below;
Nor can he guess how lightly leaps
The brook adown the rocky steeps.
Farewell thou desolate Domain!
Hope, pointing to the cultured Plain,
Carols like a shepherd boy;
And who is she? – can that be Joy?   80
Who, with a sun-beam for her guide,
Smoothly skims the meadows wide;
While Faith, from yonder opening cloud,
To hill and vale proclaims aloud,
'Whate'er the weak may dread the wicked dare,
Thy lot, O man, is good, thy portion fair!'

Ode,

Composed upon an Evening of Extraordinary Splendor and Beauty

I.

Had this effulgence disappeared
With flying haste, I might have sent
Among the speechless clouds a look
Of blank astonishment;
But 'tis endued with power to stay,
And sanctify one closing day,
That frail Mortality may see,
What is? – ah no, but what *can* be!
Time was when field and watery cove
With modulated echoes rang,
While choirs of fervent Angels sang
Their vespers in the grove;
Or, ranged like stars along some sovereign height,
Warbled, for heaven above and earth below,
Strains suitable to both. – Such holy rite,
Methinks, if audibly repeated now
From hill or valley, could not move
Sublimer transport, purer love,
Than doth this silent spectacle – the gleam –
The shadow – and the peace supreme!

II.

No sound is uttered, – but a deep
And solemn harmony pervades
The hollow vale from steep to steep,
And penetrates the glades.
Far-distant images draw nigh,
Called forth by wond'rous potency
Of beamy radiance, that imbues
Whate'er it strikes, with gem-like hues!

In vision exquisitely clear,
Herds range along the mountain side;   30
And glistening antlers are descried;
And gilded flocks appear.
Thine is the tranquil hour, purpureal Eve!
But long as god-like wish, or hope divine,
Informs my spirit, ne'er can I believe
That this magnificence is wholly thine!
– From worlds not quickened by the sun
A portion of the gift is won;
An intermingling of Heaven's pomp is spread
On ground which British shepherds tread!   40

III.

And, if there be whom broken ties
Afflict, or injuries assail,
Yon hazy ridges to their eyes,
Present a glorious scale,
Climbing suffused with sunny air,
To stop – no record hath told where!
And tempting fancy to ascend,
And with immortal spirits blend!
– Wings at my shoulder seem to play;
But, rooted here, I stand and gaze   50
On those bright steps that heaven-ward raise
Their practicable way.
Come forth, ye drooping old men, look abroad
And see to what fair countries ye are bound!
And if some Traveller, weary of his road,
Hath slept since noon-tide on the grassy ground,
Ye Genii! to his covert speed;
And wake him with such gentle heed
As may attune his soul to meet the dow'r
Bestowed on this transcendent hour!   60

IV.

Such hues from their celestial Urn
Were wont to stream before my eye,
Where'er it wandered in the morn
Of blissful infancy.
This glimpse of glory, why renewed?
Nay, rather speak with gratitude;
For, if a vestige of those gleams
Survived, 'twas only in my dreams.
Dread Power! whom peace and calmness serve
70   No less than Nature's threatening voice,
If aught unworthy be my choice,
From THEE if I would swerve,
O, let thy grace remind me of the light,
Full early lost and fruitlessly deplored;
Which, at this moment, on my waking sight
Appears to shine, by miracle restored!
My soul, though yet confined to earth,
Rejoices in a second birth;
  – 'Tis past, the visionary splendour fades,
80   And Night approaches with her shades.

The River Duddon

CONCLUSION

I thought of Thee, my partner and my guide,
As being past away. – Vain sympathies!
For, *backward*, Duddon! as I cast my eyes,
I see what was, and is, and will abide;
Still glides the Stream, and shall for ever glide;
The Form remains, the Function never dies;
While *we*, the brave, the mighty, and the wise,
We Men, who in our morn of youth defied
The elements, must vanish; – be it so!

Enough, if something from our hands have power   10
To live, and act, and serve the future hour;
And if, as tow'rd the silent tomb we go,
Thro' love, thro' hope, and faith's transcendent dower,
We feel that we are greater than we know.

Gold and Silver Fishes,

in a Vase

The soaring Lark is blest as proud
    When at Heaven's gate she sings;
The roving Bee proclaims aloud
    Her flight by vocal wings;
While Ye, in lasting durance pent,
    Your silent lives employ
For something 'more than dull content
    Though haply less than joy.'

Yet might your glassy prison seem
    A place where joy is known,   10
Where golden flash and silver gleam
    Have meanings of their own;
While, high and low, and all about,
    Your motions, glittering Elves!
Ye weave – no danger from without,
    And peace among yourselves.

Type of a sunny human breast
    Is your transparent Cell;
Where Fear is but a transient Guest,
    No sullen Humours dwell;   20
Where, sensitive of every ray
    That smites this tiny sea,
Your scaly panoplies repay
    The loan with usury.

How beautiful! Yet none knows why
   This ever-graceful change,
Renewed – renewed incessantly –
   Within your quiet range.
Is it that ye with conscious skill
   For mutual pleasure glide;
And sometimes, not without your will,
   Are dwarfed, or magnified?

Fays – Genii of gigantic size –
   And now, in twilight dim,
Clustering like constellated Eyes
   In wings of Cherubim,
When they abate their fiery glare:
   Whate'er your forms express,
Whate'er ye seem, whate'er ye are,
   All leads to gentleness.

Cold though your nature be, 'tis pure;
   Your birthright is a fence
From all that haughtier kinds endure
   Through tyranny of sense.
Ah! not alone by colours bright
   Are Ye to Heaven allied,
When, like essential Forms of light,
   Ye mingle, or divide.

For day-dreams soft as e'er beguiled
   Day-thoughts while limbs repose;
For moonlight fascinations mild
   Your gift, ere shutters close;
Accept, mute Captives! thanks and praise;
   And may this tribute prove
That gentle admirations raise
   Delight resembling love.

Yarrow Revisited

The following Stanzas are a memorial of a day passed
with Sir Walter Scott, and other Friends visiting the
Banks of the Yarrow under his guidance, immediately
before his departure from Abbotsford, for Naples.

   The title *Yarrow Revisited* will stand in no need of
explanation, for Readers acquainted with the Author's
previous poems suggested by that celebrated Stream.

The gallant Youth, who may have gained,
   Or seeks, a 'Winsome Marrow',
Was but an Infant in the lap
   When first I looked on Yarrow;
Once more, by Newark's Castle-gate
   Long left without a Warder,
I stood, looked, listened, and with Thee,
   Great Minstrel of the Border!

Grave thoughts ruled wide on that sweet day,
   Their dignity installing
In gentle bosoms, while sere leaves
   Were on the bough, or falling;
But breezes played, and sunshine gleamed –
   The forest to embolden;
Reddened the fiery hues, and shot
   Transparence through the golden.

For busy thoughts the Stream flowed on
   In foamy agitation;
And slept in many a crystal pool
   For quiet contemplation:
No public and no private care
   The freeborn mind enthralling,
We made a day of happy hours,
   Our happy days recalling.

10

20

Brisk Youth appeared, the Morn of youth,
　　With freaks of graceful folly, –
Life's temperate Noon, her sober Eve,
　　Her Night not melancholy,
Past, present, future, all appeared
　　In harmony united,
Like guests that meet, and some from far,
　　By cordial love invited.

And if, as Yarrow, through the woods
　　And down the meadow ranging,
Did meet us with unaltered face,
　　Though we were changed and changing;
If, *then*, some natural shadows spread
　　Our inward prospect over,
The soul's deep valley was not slow
　　Its brightness to recover.

Eternal blessings on the Muse,
　　And her divine employment!
The blameless Muse, who trains her Sons
　　For hope and calm enjoyment;
Albeit sickness lingering yet
　　Has o'er their pillow brooded;
And Care waylay their steps – a Sprite
　　Not easily eluded.

For thee, O SCOTT! compelled to change
　　Green Eildon-hill and Cheviot
For warm Vesuvio's vine-clad slopes;
　　And leave thy Tweed and Teviot
For mild Sorento's breezy waves;
　　May classic Fancy, linking
With native Fancy her fresh aid,
　　Preserve thy heart from sinking!

O! while they minister to thee,
    Each vying with the other,
May Health return to mellow Age,
    With Strength, her venturous brother;   60
And Tiber, and each brook and rill
    Renowned in song and story,
With unimagined beauty shine,
    Nor lose one ray of glory!

For Thou, upon a hundred streams,
    By tales of love and sorrow,
Of faithful love, undaunted truth,
    Hast shed the power of Yarrow;
And streams unknown, hills yet unseen,
    Where'er thy path invite thee,   70
At parent Nature's grateful call,
    With gladness must requite Thee.

A gracious welcome shall be thine,
    Such looks of love and honour
As thy own Yarrow gave to me
    When first I gazed upon her;
Beheld what I had feared to see,
    Unwilling to surrender
Dreams treasured up from early days,
    The holy and the tender.   80

And what, for this frail world, were all
    That mortals do or suffer,
Did no responsive harp, no pen,
    Memorial tribute offer?
Yea, what were mighty Nature's self?
    Her features, could they win us,
Unhelped by the poetic voice
    That hourly speaks within us?

Nor deem that localised Romance
    Plays false with our affections;
Unsanctifies our tears – made sport
    For fanciful dejections:
Ah, no! the visions of the past
    Sustain the heart in feeling
Life as she is – our changeful Life,
    With friends and kindred dealing.

Bear witness, Ye, whose thoughts that day
    In Yarrow's groves were centered;
Who through the silent portal arch
    Of mouldering Newark entered,
And clomb the winding stair that once
    Too timidly was mounted
By the 'last Minstrel', (not the last)
    Ere he his Tale recounted!

Flow on for ever, Yarrow Stream!
    Fulfil thy pensive duty,
Well pleased that future Bards should chant
    For simple hearts thy beauty,
To dream-light dear while yet unseen,
    Dear to the common sunshine,
And dearer still, as now I feel,
    To memory's shadowy moonshine!

On the Departure of Sir Walter Scott from Abbotsford, for Naples

A trouble, not of clouds, or weeping rain,
Nor of the setting sun's pathetic light
Engendered, hangs o'er Eildon's triple height:
Spirits of Power, assembled there, complain
For kindred Power departing from their sight;

While Tweed, best pleased in chanting a blithe strain,
Saddens his voice again, and yet again.
Lift up your hearts, ye Mourners! for the might
Of the whole world's good wishes with him goes;
Blessings and prayers in nobler retinue   10
Than sceptred King or laurelled Conqueror knows,
Follow this wondrous Potentate. Be true,
Ye winds of ocean, and the midland sea,
Wafting your Charge to soft Parthenope!

Airey-Force Valley

————Not a breath of air
Ruffles the bosom of this leafy glen.
From the brook's margin, wide around, the trees
Are stedfast as the rocks; the brook itself,
Old as the hills that feed it from afar,
Doth rather deepen than disturb the calm
Where all things else are still and motionless.
And yet, even now, a little breeze, perchance
Escaped from boisterous winds that rage without,
Has entered, by the sturdy oaks unfelt,   10
But to its gentle touch how sensitive
Is the light ash! that, pendent from the brow
Of yon dim cave, in seeming silence makes
A soft eye-music of slow-waving boughs,
Powerful almost as vocal harmony
To stay the wanderer's steps and soothe his thoughts.

Extempore Effusion upon the Death of James Hogg

When first, descending from the moorlands,
I saw the Stream of Yarrow glide
Along a bare and open valley,
The Ettrick Shepherd was my guide.

When last along its banks I wandered,
Through groves that had begun to shed
Their golden leaves upon the pathways,
My steps the Border-minstrel led.

The mighty Minstrel breathes no longer,
'Mid mouldering ruins low he lies;
And death upon the braes of Yarrow,
Has closed the Shepherd-poet's eyes:

Nor has the rolling year twice measured,
From sign to sign, its stedfast course,
Since every mortal power of Coleridge
Was frozen at its marvellous source;

The rapt One, of the godlike forehead,
The heaven-eyed creature sleeps in earth:
And Lamb, the frolic and the gentle,
Has vanished from his lonely hearth.

Like clouds that rake the mountain-summits,
Or waves that own no curbing hand,
How fast has brother followed brother,
From sunshine to the sunless land!

Yet I, whose lids from infant slumber
Were earlier raised, remain to hear
A timid voice, that asks in whispers,
'Who next will drop and disappear?'

272

Our haughty life is crowned with darkness,
Like London with its own black wreath,
On which with thee, O Crabbe! forth-looking,
I gazed from Hampstead's breezy heath.

As if but yesterday departed,
Thou too art gone before; but why,
O'er ripe fruit, seasonably gathered,
Should frail survivors heave a sigh?

Mourn rather for that holy Spirit,
Sweet as the spring, as ocean deep;
For Her who, ere her summer faded,
Has sunk into a breathless sleep.

No more of old romantic sorrows,
For slaughtered Youth or love-lorn Maid!
With sharper grief is Yarrow smitten,
And Ettrick mourns with her their Poet dead.

From *The Prelude* (1850)

'GENIUS OF BURKE!'
(FROM BOOK 7)

Genius of Burke! forgive the pen seduced
By specious wonders, and too slow to tell
Of what the ingenuous, what bewildered men,
Beginning to mistrust their boastful guides,
And wise men, willing to grow wiser, caught,
Rapt auditors! from thy most eloquent tongue –
Now mute, for ever mute in the cold grave.
I see him, – old, but vigorous in age, –
Stand like an oak whose stag-horn branches start
Out of its leafy brow, the more to awe
The younger brethren of the grove. But some –

While he forewarns, denounces, launches forth,
Against all systems built on abstract rights,
Keen ridicule; the majesty proclaims
Of Institutes and Laws, hallowed by time;
Declares the vital power of social ties
Endeared by Custom; and with high disdain,
Exploding upstart Theory, insists
Upon the allegiance to which men are born –
20 Some – say at once a froward multitude –
Murmur (for truth is hated, where not loved)
As the winds fret within the Æolian cave,
Galled by their monarch's chain. The times were big
With ominous change, which, night by night, provoked
Keen struggles, and black clouds of passion raised;
But memorable moments intervened,
When Wisdom, like the Goddess from Jove's brain,
Broke forth in armour of resplendent words,
Startling the Synod. Could a youth, and one
30 In ancient story versed, whose breast had heaved
Under the weight of classic eloquence,
Sit, see, and hear, unthankful, uninspired?

Notes

Abbreviations cited in these notes are as follows:

DW   Dorothy Wordsworth
DWJ *Journals of Dorothy Wordsworth*, ed. Mary Moorman
       (Oxford, 1971)
IF   Wordsworth's notes on his poems, dictated to Isabella Fen-
       wick in 1843
STC Samuel Taylor Coleridge
W   William Wordsworth

The Baker's Cart

Composed late 1796–March 1797. Not published by W. **3.** *wain* A
wagon. **21.** *access* Onset.

Old Man Travelling

Composed late 1796–June 1797. Published *Lyrical Ballads*, 1798.
Recalled by W as 'an overflow from "The Old Cumberland Beggar"'
(IF).

Lines Left upon a Seat in a Yew-Tree

Composed February–July 1797. Published *Lyrical Ballads*, 1798. A
few lines may date from Wordsworth's schooldays at Hawkshead, *c*.
1787. As a schoolboy W had been 'delighted' by the view from the
tree (IF). W's 'lost man' has been identified as Rev. William Braith-
waite of Satterhow, Far Sawrey.

The Ruined Cottage

Composed April 1797–March 1798. Published, after further develop-
ment and revision, as Book One of *The Excursion* (1814). The text
reproduced here is drawn from MS B of 'The Ruined Cottage',
which dates from *c*. 5 March 1798. This is the earliest surviving text
of 'The Ruined Cottage' that is complete, and it is close to the
version of the poem read by Wordsworth at his first meetings with
Coleridge and Charles Lamb in June–July 1797. For detailed analysis
of this poem's evolution, see *'The Ruined Cottage' and 'The Pedlar'*,

ed. James Butler (Ithaca: Cornell University Press, 1979) and Jonathan Wordsworth, *The Music of Humanity* (London: Nelson, 1969). **Epigraph:** from Robert Burns's 'Epistle to J. L*****k [Lapraik], an Old Scotch Bard' in *Poems, chiefly in the Scottish Dialect* (1786). **16.** *impending* Overhanging. **47.** *race* Family. **68.** *curious* Inquisitive. **102.** *agency* Action. **144–5.** Cf. Ecclesiastes 12: 6: 'the pitcher . . . broken at the fountain'. **161.** *tricked* Decorated. **196.** Cf. Job 7: 10: 'He shall return no more to his house, neither shall his place know him any more.' **196.** *abridged* Deprived. **206.** *artisans* Workmen. **208.** *parish charity* Relief administered by parish authorities under the Poor Law. Cf. l.405, and 'The Last of the Flock' l.44. **210–11.** Cf. 'Old Man Travelling' ll.1–2. **217.** *uncouth* Strange. **224.** *passenger* Traveller. **228.** *braiding* Weaving. **251.** *untoward* Perverse. **280.** *wantonness* Irresponsibility. **282.** *dalliance* Trifling, idle amusement. **291.** *moving accidents* Cf. *Othello* I.iii.134: 'moving accidents by flood and field'. **294.** *palpable* Perceptible. **306–9.** W recalled: 'For several passages describing the employment and demeanour of Margaret during her affliction, I was indebted to observations made in Dorsetshire, and afterwards at Alfoxden, in Somersetshire, where I resided in 1797 and 1798' (IF). **309.** *wist* Knew. **323.** The gold left by Robert is his bounty money, received on enlistment as a soldier. **388–94.** Cf. DWJ 4 February 1798: 'The moss rubbed from the pailings by the sheep, that leave locks of wool, and the red marks with which they are spotted, upon the wood.' **402.** *board* Table. **418.** *Her voice was low* Cf. *King Lear* V.iii.270–71: 'Her voice was ever soft, / Gentle and low'. **494.** *greensward* Grassy turf. **500.** *Mendicant* Beggar. **517.** *reckless* Careless, desperate. **518.** *this reft house* The cottage, like Margaret, is bereft in Robert's absence; both Margaret and her house are physically *reft* (broken) by the harsh winter weather. **528.** In early March 1798 the poem ended at this line. Shortly afterwards, W added two further paragraphs in which Margaret's tragedy is reconciled through meditation on 'the calm oblivious tendencies / Of nature': 'She sleeps in the calm earth, and peace is here.' For this version of the poem, see the texts in Butler and J. Wordsworth cited above.

A Night-Piece

Composed *c*. 25 January 1798. Published *Poems*, 1815. W: 'Composed on the road between Nether Stowey and Alfoxden, extempore. I distinctly remember the very moment when I was struck, as described, "He looks up at the clouds"' (IF). DWJ, 25 January 1798, describes this moment: 'Went to Poole's after tea. The sky spread over with one continuous cloud, whitened by the light of the moon, which, though her dim shape was seen, did not throw forth so strong a light as to chequer the earth with shadows. At once the clouds seemed to cleave asunder, and left her in the centre of a black-blue vault. She sailed along, followed by multitudes of stars, small, and bright, and sharp. Their brightness seemed concentrated, (half-moon).'

The Discharged Soldier

Composed January–March 1798. A revised version of the poem forms the conclusion to Book 4 of *The Prelude*. As a young man W had met a discharged soldier in the road at Far Sawrey, three miles from Hawkshead. **7–11.** Cf. DWJ, 31 January 1798: 'The road to the village of Holford glittered like another stream.' **20.** *dark blue vault* Cf. 'A Night-Piece' l. 11, and DWJ, 25 January 1798. **38.** *an uncouth shape* Cf. Death at the gates of Hell, *Paradise Lost*, II.666–9. **48–50.** The soldier resembles Malegar in *The Faerie Queene* II.xi.22: 'His bodie leane and meagre as a rake'. **51.** *ghastly* Ghostly. **80–2, 130–35.** Cf. DWJ, 27 January 1798: 'The manufacturer's dog makes a strange, uncouth howl, which it continues many minutes after there is no noise near it but that of the brook. It howls at the murmur of the village stream.'

The Old Cumberland Beggar

Composed January–March 1798. Published *Lyrical Ballads*, 1800. The poem grew out of W's verse 'Description of a Beggar', written at a time when 'political economists were . . . beginning their war upon mendicity in all its forms, and by implication, if not directly, on alms giving also' (IF). W was preoccupied with the condition of the poor as an issue in the 1790s, and throughout his life. See especially his letter to Fox, 14 January 1801. **76.** *noxious* Harmful. **127.** *Decalogue* The Ten Commandments. **151.** *scrip* Satchel. **168.** *chartered* Privileged, at liberty. Cf. *As You Like It* II.vii.47–8: 'I must have liberty / Withal, as large a charter as the wind'. **172.** *House, misnamed of industry* The workhouse, in which paupers were maintained in spinning, weaving and other employment.

Goody Blake and Harry Gill

Composed *c*. 7–13 March 1798. Published *Lyrical Ballads*, 1798. W's ballad draws upon the following passage from Erasmus Darwin's *Zoonomia, or the Laws of Organic Life* (1794–6), borrowed by W from

Joseph Cottle by 13 March 1798: 'A young farmer in Warwickshire, finding his hedges broke, and the sticks carried away during a frosty season, determined to watch for the thief. He lay many cold hours under a hay-stack, and at length an old woman, like a witch in a play, approached, and began to pull up the hedge; he waited till she had tied up her bottle of sticks, and was carrying them off, that he might convict her of the theft, and then springing from his concealment, he seized his prey with violent threats. After some altercation . . . she kneeled upon her bottle of sticks, and raising her arms to heaven beneath the bright moon then at the full, spoke to the farmer already shivering with cold, "Heaven grant, that thou never mayest know again the blessing to be warm." He complained of cold all the next day, and wore an upper coat, and in a few days another, and in a fortnight took to his bed, always saying nothing made him warm . . . and from this one insane idea he kept his bed above twenty years for fear of the cold air, till at length he died.' In the Preface to *Lyrical Ballads*, 1800, W comments: 'I wished to draw attention to the truth that the power of the human imagination is sufficient to produce such changes even in our physical nature as might almost appear miraculous.' **6.** *flannel* Woollen. **33.** *pottage* Thick soup, or oatmeal porridge. **39.** *canty* Cheerful, brisk, lively.

Lines Written at a Small Distance from My House
Composed *c*. 10 March 1798. Published *Lyrical Ballads*, 1798. See DWJ, 10 March 1798: 'We all passed the morning in sauntering about the park and gardens, the children playing about, the old man at the top of the hill gathering furze; interesting groups of human creatures, the young frisking and dancing in the sun, the elder quietly drinking in the life and soul of the sun and air.' 'Composed in front of Alfoxden House,' W recalled: 'My little boy-messenger on this occasion was the son of Basil Montagu. The larch mentioned in the first stanza was standing when I revisited the place in May, 1841, more than forty years after' (IF). Basil Montagu's son (called Basil, not Edward) had been in the care of W and Dorothy since September 1795; he also figures in 'Anecdote for Fathers'.

The Thorn
Composed *c*. 19 March 1798. Published *Lyrical Ballads*, 1798. See DWJ, 19 March 1798: 'William wrote some lines describing a stunted thorn.' W: 'Arose out of my observing on the ridge of Quantock Hill, on a stormy day, a thorn, which I had often past in calm and bright

weather without noticing it. I said to myself, cannot I by some invention do as much to make this Thorn permanently an impressive object as the storm has made it to my eyes at this moment? I began the poem accordingly, and composed it with great rapidity' (IF). W comments in the Advertisement to *Lyrical Ballads*, 1798, that this poem 'is not supposed to be spoken in the author's own person: the character of the loquacious narrator will sufficiently shew itself in the course of the story.' In *Lyrical Ballads*, 1800, W included a more extensive note on the poem to explain the 'credulous' and 'superstitious' character of his narrator. For STC's important criticism of the narrator's role in the poem see Chapter 17 of *Biographia Literaria*.

'*A whirl-blast from behind the hill*'

Composed 18 March 1798. Published *Lyrical Ballads*, 1800. See DWJ, 18 March 1798: 'The Coleridges left us. A cold, windy morning. Walked with them half way. On our return, sheltered under the hollies, during a hail-shower. The withered leaves danced with the hailstones. William wrote a description of the storm.'

The Idiot Boy

Composed late March 1798. Published *Lyrical Ballads*, 1798. 'The last stanza, "The cocks did crow, and the sun did shine so cold", was the foundation of the whole. The words were reported to me by my dear friend Thomas Poole . . . [T]his long poem was composed in the groves of Alfoxden, almost extempore; not a word, I believe, being corrected, though one stanza was omitted. I mention this in gratitude to those happy moments, for, in truth, I never wrote anything with so much glee' (IF). In the Preface to *Lyrical Ballads*, 1800, W explains that one of his purposes in the poem is to trace in Betty Foy's maternal feelings 'the fluxes and refluxes of the mind when agitated by the great and simple affections of our nature'. See also W's letter to John Wilson, 7 June 1802, in which he discusses this poem at length. **14.** *girt* Belt to secure the saddle on a horse. **52.** *he must post without delay* Johnny must hurry on his journey. **104.** *guide-post* Sign-post. **139.** *porringer* A small bowl. **191.** *rue* Regret. **247.** *distemper* Turmoil, anguish. **250.** *cattle* Animals. **299–301.** The owls call to each other like bashful lovers; the quavering of the echoes suggests the distance between them rather than 'hob nob' familiarity. **347–8.** *I to the muses have been bound, | These fourteen years, by strong indentures* W's first composition, a poem on 'The Summer Vacation', was written as an exercise after his return to Hawkshead School in September 1784. The 'indentures' of his long apprenticeship as a poet can be dated from this time. **349.** *Oh gentle muses!* W's humorous invocation to the muses is in keeping with the mock-heroic idiom of his ballad. **365.** *romances* Extravagant tales of knighthood and chivalry. **390.** *quaffs* Drinks deeply.

Lines Written in Early Spring

Composed *c.* 12 April 1798. Published *Lyrical Ballads*, 1798. See DWJ, 12 April 1798: 'The Spring advances rapidly, multitudes of primroses, dog-violets, periwinkles, stitchwort.' W: 'Actually composed while I was sitting by the side of the brook that runs down the *Comb*, in which stands the village of Alford, through the grounds of Alfoxden. It was a chosen resort of mine' (IF).

Anecdote for Fathers

Composed March–May 1798. Published *Lyrical Ballads*, 1798. 'This was suggested in front of Alfoxden,' W recalled: 'The boy was a son of my friend Basil Montagu . . . The name of Kilve is from a village in the Bristol Channel, about a mile from Alfoxden; and the name of Liswyn Farm was taken from a beautiful spot on the Wye' (IF). Liswyn Farm (near Hay-on-Wye) was the home of John Thelwall, the political reformer and poet who had been tried for high treason in 1794. In a letter of 7 March 1796 W says that young Basil 'lies like a little devil'. **52.** *vane* A weathercock.

We are Seven

Composed March–May 1798. Published *Lyrical Ballads*, 1798. W met the little girl near Goodrich Castle, on his first visit to the Wye Valley in July 1793. 'I composed it while walking in the grove of Alfoxden,' W recalled: 'I composed the last stanza first, having begun with the last line. When it was all but finished, I came in and recited it to Mr Coleridge and my sister, and said, "A prefatory stanza must be added, and I should sit down to our little tea-meal with greater pleasure if my task was finished." I mentioned in substance what I wished to be expressed, and Coleridge immediately threw off the stanza' (IF). **47.** *porringer* A small bowl.

Simon Lee, the Old Huntsman

Composed March–May 1798. Published *Lyrical Ballads*, 1798. W: 'This old man had been huntsman to the Squires of Alfoxden . . .

The old man's cottage stood upon the Common, a little way from the entrance to Alfoxden Park ... I have, after an interval of forty-five years, the image of the old man as fresh before my eyes as if I had seen him yesterday. The expression when the hounds were out "I dearly love their voice," was word for word from his own lips' (IF). **14.** *running huntsman* Simon Lee would have followed the hounds on foot. **38.** *husbandry or tillage* Farming or cultivating the land. **44.** *stone-blind* Blind as a stone, completely blind.

The Last of the Flock

Composed March–May 1798. Published *Lyrical Ballads*, 1798. W: 'The incident occurred in the village of Holford, close by Alfoxden' (IF), but note W's letter to John Kenyon, 24 September 1836: 'I never in my whole life saw a man weep *alone* in the roads; but a friend of mine *did* see this poor man weeping *alone*, with the Lamb, the last of his flock, in his arms.' **44.** *I of the parish asked relief* The shepherd applied for support administered by the parish authorities under the Poor Law. **93.** *a weather* A castrated ram.

Expostulation and Reply

Composed *c.* 23 May 1798. Published *Lyrical Ballads*, 1798. In the Advertisement to *Lyrical Ballads*, 1798, W writes that this poem and 'The Tables Turned' 'arose out of conversation with a friend who was somewhat unreasonably attached to modern books of moral philosophy'. The 'friend' was William Hazlitt, who first met W at Nether Stowey in late May 1798: see Hazlitt's essay 'My First Acquaintance with Poets'. **13.** *Esthwaite lake* Near Hawkshead in the Lake District. **21.** *I deem* I declare; I am of the opinion.

The Tables Turned

Composed *c.* 23 May 1798. Published *Lyrical Ballads*, 1798. **4.** *double* bent double.

Lines Written a Few Miles above Tintern Abbey

Composed 11–13 July 1798. Published *Lyrical Ballads*, 1798. 'No poem of mine was composed under circumstances more pleasant for me to remember than this. I began it upon leaving Tintern, after crossing the Wye, and concluded it just as I was entering Bristol in the evening, after a ramble of four or five days with my sister. Not a line of it was altered, and not any part of it written down till I reached Bristol' (IF). A climactic achievement at the end of W's

Alfoxden year, 'Tintern Abbey' concluded *Lyrical Ballads* as published in 1798. **1.** *Five years have passed* W first visited Tintern in summer 1793. See note to 'We are Seven'. **4.** In 1798 W noted: 'The river is not affected by the tides a few miles above Tintern.' **17.** *sportive* Growing unchecked. **21.** *vagrant dwellers* Beggars, homeless people. **21.** *houseless woods* Cf. *King Lear* III.iv.30 'houseless heads and unfed sides'. **43.** *affections* Tender feelings. **44.** *corporeal* Bodily. **57.** *sylvan* Wooded. **89.** *Abundant recompence* Ample compensation. **107.** In 1798, W noted: 'This line has a close resemblance to an admirable line of Young, the exact expression of which I cannot recollect.' W's note refers to Edward Young's *Night Thoughts* (1742–5) vi.427: 'And half create the wonderous World, they see'. **114.** *genial* Vital. Cf. Milton, *Samson Agonistes* 594–5: 'So much I feel my genial spirits droop, / My hopes all flat'. **129.** *evil tongues* W alludes to the 'evil tongues' of *Paradise Lost*, VII.26, where Milton writes about his dangerous predicament as a republican after the Restoration of Charles II. **141.** *mansion* Abiding-place, abode.

'There was a Boy'
Composed October–December 1798. Published *Lyrical Ballads*, 1800. Subsequently incorporated, with revisions, in *The Prelude* Book 5. **14.** *long halloos* Cf. *Twelfth Night* I.v.261: 'Halloo your name to the reverberate hills'.

'If Nature, for a favorite Child'
Composed October 1798–February 1799. Published *Lyrical Ballads*, 1800. Retitled 'Matthew' from 1836–7. 'This and other poems connected with Matthew would not gain by a literal detail of facts. Like the wanderer in the "Excursion", this schoolmaster was made up of several, both of his class and men of other occupations' (IF).

The Fountain
Composed October 1798–February 1799. Published *Lyrical Ballads*, 1800. See note to 'If Nature' above.

The Two April Mornings
Composed October 1798–February 1799. Published *Lyrical Ballads*, 1800. See note to 'If Nature' above. **60.** *wilding* Crab-apple.

'A slumber did my spirit seal'
Composed October 1798–January 1799. Published *Lyrical Ballads*, 1800.

Song ('She dwelt among th'untrodden ways')

Composed October–December 1798. Published *Lyrical Ballads*, 1800.

'Strange fits of passion I have known'

Composed October–December 1798. Published *Lyrical Ballads*, 1800. **10.** *lea* Grassland. **18.** *boon* Blessing.

Lucy Gray

Composed October 1798–February 1799. Published *Lyrical Ballads*, 1800. W said the poem was 'founded in a circumstance told me by my sister, of a little girl, who, not far from Halifax, in Yorkshire, was bewildered in a snow-storm' (IF).

A Poet's Epitaph

Composed October 1798–February 1799. Published *Lyrical Ballads*, 1800. **1.** *van* Vanguard.

Nutting

Composed October–December 1798. Published *Lyrical Ballads*, 1800. 'Written in Germany: intended as part of a poem on my own life [*The Prelude*], but struck out as not being wanted there' (IF). **3.** *our cottage-door* In 1800 W noted: 'The house at which I was boarded during the time I was at School'. He boarded with Ann Tyson, the 'frugal Dame' mentioned in l.9 of this poem. **7.** *weeds* Clothes. **10.** *Motley accoutrements* A multicoloured outfit. **11.** *brakes* Thickets of bramble. **40.** *Stocks* Logs of wood.

Written in Germany

Composed *c.* 25 December 1798. Published *Lyrical Ballads*, 1800. See DW's letter, 3 February 1799: 'The cold of Christmas day has not been equalled even in this climate during the last century.'

'Three years she grew'

Composed February 1799. Published *Lyrical Ballads*, 1800.

The Two-Part Prelude

Composed October 1798–December 1799. Not published by W. Part I, which treats the formative experiences of the poet's early childhood, dates from W's residence in Goslar, Germany, October 1798–January 1799; Part II, which comprises W's adolescent years, was composed

September–December 1799 at Sockburn, Co. Durham, the home of W's future wife Mary Hutchinson. In 1804 W resumed work on his poem, and expanded it to form the thirteen-book *Prelude* completed in May 1805. For a discussion of *The Prelude* as a preliminary to *The Recluse*, and for the publication of *The Prelude* in 1850, see the Introduction to this volume.

First Part. 8. *'sweet birthplace'* W quotes from STC's 'Frost at Midnight', l.28, which refers to his 'sweet birth-place' at Ottery St Mary, Devon. **24.** *Skiddaw* To the east of Cockermouth, Skiddaw rises over the town of Keswick and Bassenthwaite Lake. **34.** *springes* Snares. Cf. *Hamlet* I.iii.115: 'springes to catch woodcocks'. **35.** *fell* Savage, ruthless, but also a Lake District mountain. **44.** *toils* Labours, but also snares or traps. **45.** *when the deed was done* Cf. *Macbeth* II.ii.14: 'I have done the deed. Didst thou not hear a noise?' **61.** *amain* With full force, violently. **78.** *haply* Perhaps. **86.** *hoary* White (in the moonlight). **90.** Cf. *Paradise Lost* XII.2. **109.** *instinct* Imbued. **135.** *vulgar* Ordinary, commonplace. **149.** *intercourse* Communion. **158.** *Confederate* United. **173.** *shadow* Reflection. **186–9.** Cf. *The Tempest* V.i.33: 'Ye elves of hills, brooks, standing lakes, and groves'. **194.** *Impressed* Stamped, imprinted. *characters* Marks, signs. **198.** *work* Act, move. **210.** *cyphers* Noughts. **215.** *lu* The card game, loo. **219.** *husbanded* Saved, preserved. **233.** *Bothnic main* The Baltic Sea. **234.** *rehearse* Describe. **249.** *Venial* Forgivable. **261–5.** Hawkshead village, where W attended the Grammar School 1779–1787, is near Esthwaite Lake in the southern Lake District, between Windermere and Coniston Water. **276.** *Sounded* Investigated the water. **279.** *ghastly* Ghostly. *advert* Refer. **290.** *fructifying virtue* A creative power, the imagination. **351.** *he died* W's father John Wordsworth died on 30 December 1783. **385.** *intellectual* Ideal, spiritual. **430.** *lineaments* Features or characteristics. **442.** *affections* Feelings. **447.** *my friend* STC, to whom *The Prelude* was addressed.

Second Part. 44. *huckster* A stall-keeper. **52.** *grateful* Pleasing. **55.** *plain of Windermere* The surface of the lake. **59.** *umbrageous* Shady. **81.** *Sabine* Frugal. **107–11.** Furness Abbey, near Barrow-in-Furness, on the southern coast of the Lake District. **146.** *gavel-end* Gable. **286.** *that most apprehensive habitude* A relationship in which the child learns. **335.** *palpable access* Evident addition or increase. **380.** *little lake* Esthwaite Lake. **382.** *friend* W's school friend John Fleming. **411.** *plastic* Formative, creative.

The Brothers

Composed December 1799 – early 1800. Published *Lyrical Ballads*, 1800. In 1800 W noted: 'This Poem was intended to be the concluding poem of a series of pastorals, the scene of which was laid among the mountains of Cumberland and Westmoreland.' The origin of 'The Brothers' was the story of the death of James Bowman, heard by W and STC at Ennerdale during their tour of the Lake District, November 1799. STC's notebook (entry 540) records that Bowman 'broke his neck . . . by falling off a Crag – supposed to have layed down & slept – but walked in his sleep, & so came to this crag, & fell off – This was at Proud Knot on the mountain called Pillar up Ennerdale – his Pike staff stuck midway & stayed there till it rotted away.' W explained his intentions in writing 'The Brothers' in his letter to Charles James Fox, 14 January 1801: see the note to 'Michael' below. **16.** *Ennerdale* In the western fells of the Lake District, at the feet of Great Gable and Pillar mountain. **44.** *shrouds* Ropes. **56–62.** In 1800 W noted: 'This description of the Calenture is sketched from an imperfect recollection of an admirable one in prose, by Mr Gilbert, Author of the Hurricane.' The calenture was a delirium, experienced by sailors in the tropics. **100.** *complacency* Pleasure. **138.** In 1800 W noted: 'The impressive circumstance here described, actually took place some years ago in this country, upon an eminence called Kidstow Pike, one of the highest of the mountains that surround Haweswater. The summit of the pike was stricken by lightning; and every trace of one of the fountains disappeared, while the other continued to flow as before.' **157.** *web spun* Cloth woven. **168.** *type* Symbol. **179.** In 1800 W noted: 'There is not any thing more worthy of remark in the manners of the inhabitants of these mountains, than the tranquillity, I might say indifference, with which they think and talk upon the subject of death. Some of the country church-yards, as here described, do not contain a single tombstone, and most of them have a very small number.' **200.** *hale* Vigorous, healthy. **265.** *mealy* Powdery, pale. **267.** *sabbath breach* Breaking God's Fourth Commandment, to do no work on Sunday. **288.** *trafficked* Traded. **305.** *the great Gavel* Great Gable. In 1800 W noted: 'so called I imagine, from its resemblance to the Gable end of a house . . . one of the highest of the Cumberland mountains. It stands at the head of the several vales of Ennerdale, Wastdale, and Borrowdale.' *Leeza's Banks* In 1800 W noted: 'a River which flows into the lake of Ennerdale; on issuing from the Lake, it changes its name, and is called the End, Eyne, or Enna. It falls into the sea a little below Egremont.' **313.** *Barbary*

Coast The north coast of Africa. **360.** *rock* Pillar Rock is a large twin-pinnacled crag on the side of Pillar mountain.

Poems on the Naming of Places

Composed December 1799–October 1800. Published *Lyrical Ballads*, 1800. In 1800 W introduced the poems: 'By Persons resident in the country and attached to rural objects, many places will be found unnamed or of unknown names, where little Incidents will have occurred, or feelings been experienced, which will have given to such places a private and peculiar interest. From a wish to give some sort of record to such Incidents or renew the gratification of such Feelings, Names have been given to Places by the Author and some of his Friends, and the following Poems written in consequence.' All five poems published in 1800 under this heading are reproduced here:

I. 'It was an April Morning'. 'This poem was suggested on the banks of the brook that runs through Easedale' (IF). **39.** *EMMA* DW.

II. To Joanna. Joanna Hutchinson was the sister of Mary, whom W married 4 October 1802. **27-30.** In 1800 W noted: 'In Cumberland and Westmoreland are several Inscriptions upon the native rock which from the wasting of Time and the rudeness of the Workmanship had been mistaken for Runic. They are without doubt Roman.' **31.** *the Rotha* In 1800 W noted: 'The Rotha, mentioned in this poem, is the River which flowing through the Lakes of Grasmere and Rydole falls in to Wyndermere.' He added that the mountains named in the poem 'either immediately surround the vale of Grasmere, or belong to the same Cluster'.

III. 'There is an Eminence'. 'It is not accurate that the eminence here alluded to could be seen from our orchard seat. It arises above the road by the side of Grasmere Lake, towards Keswick, and its name is Stone Arthur' (IF).

IV. 'A narrow girdle of rough stones and crags'. 'The friends spoken of were Coleridge and my sister' (IF).

V. To M.H. Mary Hutchinson, whom W married 4 October 1802. 'The pool alluded to is in Rydal Upper Park' (IF).

''Tis said, that some have died for love'

Composed by August 1800. Published *Lyrical Ballads*, 1800.

Michael

Composed October–December 1800. Published *Lyrical Ballads*, 1800. 'The character and circumstances of Luke were taken from a family to whom had belonged, many years before, the home we lived in at Town-

End, along with some fields and woodlands on the eastern shore of Grasmere' (IF). See W's letter to Charles James Fox about the condition of the poor, 14 January 1801, in which he enclosed *Lyrical Ballads* (1800) and noticed 'The Brothers' and 'Michael' as poems written to show 'that men who do not wear fine cloaths can feel deeply'. **11.** *kites* Birds of prey. **19.** *ungarnished* Not embellished, plain. **35.** *rude* Artless, plain. **73.** *grateful* Pleasing. **102.** *mess of pottage* Oatmeal porridge. **156.** *inquietude* Disturbance. **177.** *covert* Shelter. **179.** *The* CLIPPING TREE In 1800 W noted: 'Clipping is the word used in the North of England for shearing.' **196.** *stem* Stop. **201.** *hire* Reward. **225.** *discharge the forfeiture* Pay the loan he had guaranteed. **234.** *patrimonial* Inherited from his father. **268–80.** In 1800 W noted: 'The story alluded to here is well known in the country. The chapel is called Ings Chapel; and is on the right hand side of the road leading from Kendal to Ambleside.' **309.** *jocund* Joyful, cheering. **334.** In 1800 W noted: 'A sheep-fold in these mountains is an unroofed building of stone walls, with different divisions. It is generally placed by the side of a brook, for the convenience of washing the sheep.' **380.** *mold* Earth of the grave. **384.** *burthened* Mortgaged.

The Affliction of Margaret ——— of ———

Composed 1800–1802. Published *Poems, in Two Volumes*, 1807. 'This was taken from the case of a poor widow who lived in the town of Penrith' (IF).

'I travelled among unknown Men'

Composed *c.* 29 April 1801. Published *Poems, in Two Volumes*, 1807. In a letter to Mary Hutchinson, 29 April 1801, W transcribed the poem with the comment that it was to be read after 'She dwelt among th' untrodden ways'.

To a Sky-Lark

Composed March–July 1802. Published *Poems, in Two Volumes*, 1807. **20.** *loth* Unwilling, reluctant.

The Sailor's Mother

Composed 11–12 March 1802. Published *Poems, in Two Volumes*, 1807. 'I met this woman near the Wishing-Gate, on the high-road that then led from Grasmere to Ambleside. Her appearance was exactly as here described, and such was her account, nearly to the letter' (IF). See also DWJ, 11 March 1802: 'William worked at the poem of the Singing Bird.' See Chapter 18 of *Biographia Literaria* for

STC's comment that stanzas 4–6 'furnish the only fair instance that I have been able to discover in all Mr Wordsworth's writings, of an *actual* adoption, or true imitation, of the *real* and *very* language of *low and rustic life*, freed from provincialisms'. **6.** *mien* Bearing, manner. *gait* Walk.

Alice Fell

Composed 12–13 March 1802. Published *Poems, in Two Volumes*, 1807. The poem was based on the experience of Robert Grahame, solicitor of Glasgow, noted in DWJ, 16 February 1802: 'He was riding in a post chaise and he heard a strange cry that he could not understand, the sound continued and he called to the chaise driver to stop. It was a little girl that was crying as if her heart would burst. She had got up behind the chaise and her cloak had been caught by the wheel and was jammed in and it hung there. She was crying after it. Poor thing. Mr Graham took her into the chaise and the cloak was released from the wheel but the child's misery did not cease for her cloak was torn to rags; it had been a miserable cloak before, but she had no other and it was the greatest sorrow that could befal her. Her name was Alice Fell.' For STC's criticism that this incident was inappropriate for poetic treatment, see Chapters 4 and 18 of *Biographia Literaria*. **29.** *nave* The hub of a wheel.

To a Butterfly ('Stay near me')

Composed 14 March 1802. Published *Poems, in Two Volumes*, 1807. DWJ, 14 March 1802: 'While we were at Breakfast . . . [W], with his Basin of Broth before him untouched and a little plate of Bread and butter . . . wrote the Poem to a Butterfly! He ate not a morsel, nor put on his stockings but sate with his shirt neck unbuttoned, and his waistcoat open while he did it. The thought first came upon him as we were talking about the pleasure we both always feel at the sight of a Butterfly. I told him that I used to chase them a little but that I was afraid of brushing the dust off their wings, and did not catch them – He told me how they used to kill all the white ones when he went to school because they were frenchmen.' See also W: 'My sister and I were parted immediately after the death of our mother' (IF).

The Sparrow's Nest

Composed March–April 1802. Published *Poems, in Two Volumes*, 1807. W: 'At the end of the garden of my Father's house at Cockermouth was a high terrace that commanded a fine view of the river

Derwent and Cockermouth Castle. This was our favourite playground. The terrace wall, a low one, was covered with closely-clipt privet and roses, which gave an almost impervious shelter to birds that built their nests there. The latter of these stanzas alludes to one of these nests' (IF).

To the Cuckoo
Composed 23–26 March 1802. Published *Poems, in Two Volumes*, 1807. See W's Preface to *Poems* (1815) for his analysis of imagination and 'impressions of sound' in this poem.

'My heart leaps up when I behold'
Composed 26 March 1802. Published *Poems, in Two Volumes*, 1807. In *Poems* (1815). ll.7–9 stand as an epigraph to 'Ode. Intimations of Immortality'.

To H.C.
Composed March–June 1802. Published *Poems, in Two Volumes*, 1807. STC's son Hartley was born 19 September 1796.

'Among all lovely things my Love had been'
Composed 12 April 1802. Published *Poems, in Two Volumes*, 1807. See DWJ, 20 April 1802 for circumstances of the poem's composition. W says (letter of 16 April 1802) that the incident in the poem occurred in 1795, when W and DW lived at Racedown Lodge, Dorset.

Written in March
Composed 16 April 1802. Published *Poems, in Two Volumes*, 1807. See DWJ, 16 April 1802: 'When we came to the foot of Brothers water I left William sitting on the Bridge ... When I returned I found William writing a poem descriptive of the sights and sounds we saw and heard.'

The Green Linnet
Composed 16 April–8 July 1802. Published *Poems, in Two Volumes*, 1807. Some aspects of language and imagery resemble DWJ, 28 May 1802. **12.** *pinion* Wing.

To the Daisy ('In youth')
Composed April–June 1802. Published *Poems, in Two Volumes*, 1807.

To a Butterfly ('I've watched you now')

Composed 20 April 1802. Published *Poems, in Two Volumes*, 1807. See DWJ 20 April 1802: 'William wrote a conclusion to the poem of the Butterfly – "I've watched you now a full half-hour" . . . When I came in he had finished the poem.'

'I have been here in the Moon-light'

Composed *c.* 22 April 1802. Not published by W.

'These chairs they have no words to utter'

Composed *c.* 22 April 1802. Not published by W. See DWJ, 22 April 1802: 'A fine mild morning. We walked into Easedale . . . I sate upon the grass till [W and STC] came from the Waterfall . . . When they returned William was repeating the poem "I have thoughts that are fed by the Sun". It had been called to his mind by the dying away of the stunning of the waterfall when he came behind a stone.' **19.** Cf. Chaucer, 'The Knight's Tale', ll. 2778–9: 'in his colde grave / Allone, withouten any compaignye.'

To the Small Celandine ('Pansies, Lilies')

Composed 30 April–1 May 1802. Published *Poems, in Two Volumes*, 1807. DWJ, 30 April 1802: 'William began to write the poem of the Celandine.' W: 'It is remarkable that this flower coming out so early in the spring as it does, and so bright and beautiful, and in such profusion, should not have been noticed earlier in English verse' (IF). **13.** *I trow* I believe.

To the Same Flower ('Pleasures newly found')

Composed 1 May 1802. Published *Poems, in Two Volumes*, 1807. DWJ, 1 May 1802: 'Wm wrote the Celandine 2nd part tonight.'

Resolution and Independence

Composed May–July 1802. Published *Poems, in Two Volumes*, 1807. 'This old man I met a few hundred yards from my cottage at Town-End, Grasmere; and the account of him is taken from his own mouth. I was in the state of feeling described in the beginning of the poem, while crossing over Barton Fell from Mr Clarkson's at the foot of Ullswater, towards Askham. The image of the hare I then observed on the ridge of the Fell' (IF). For W's meeting with the old man, see DWJ, 3 October 1800. See also W's and DW's responses to criticism of this poem in their letter to Mary and Sara Hutchinson, 14 June

1802. **39.** *genial* Vital, generative, cheerful. **43.** Thomas Chatterton (1752–70) poet and forger of poems purportedly written by a fifteenth-century priest Thomas Rowley. Committed suicide in 1770. 'Resolution and Independence' uses the Spenserian stanza of Chatterton's 'An Excelente Balade of Charitie'. **45–6.** Robert Burns (1759–96), Scottish poet, an important early influence on Wordsworth. **54.** *untoward* Perverse. **64–70.** W analysed these lines in the Preface to *Poems* (1815) as an instance of 'the modifying powers of the Imagination'. **87.** *conned* Studied.

Stanzas Written in my Pocket-Copy of Thomson's Castle of Indolence

Composed 9–11 May 1802. Published *Poems*, 1815. 'Composed in the Orchard, Grasmere, Town-End. Coleridge living with us much at the time, his son Hartley has said that his father's character and history are here preserved in a livelier way than in anything that has been written about him' (IF). See also DWJ: 9 May 1802, 'After tea [W] wrote 2 stanzas in the manner of Thomson's Castle of Indolence'; 11 May 1802, 'William finished the stanzas about C. and himself.' Using James Thomson's Spenserian poem *The Castle of Indolence* (1748) as a stylistic model, W's poem portrays first himself and, second, STC. The two portraits are however not distinct, and blur the poets' personalities. **15.** *driving* Striding purposefully, hurrying onward. **18.** *crew* Company. **36.** *Wight* Man. **43.** *Phantasy* Imagination. **46.** *forefend* Forbid. **54.** *certes* Certainly. **55.** *Expedients* Devices.

'I grieved for Buonaparte'

Composed 21 May 1802. Published *The Morning Post*, 16 September 1802; *Poems, in Two Volumes*, 1807. See DWJ, 21 May 1802: 'Wm wrote two sonnets on Buonaparte after I had read Milton's sonnets to him.'

'I am not One who much or oft delight'

Composed May 1802–March 1804. Published *Poems, in Two Volumes*, 1807. Titled 'Personal Talk' from 1820. **6.** *withering on the stalk* Cf. *A Midsummer Night's Dream* I.i.77, 'withering on the virgin thorn'; and *Comus*, ll. 742–3, 'If you let slip time, like a neglected rose / It withers on the stalk'. **26.** Cf. William Collins, 'The Passions. An Ode for Music', l.60: 'Notes by distance made more sweet'. **41–2.** W alludes to *Othello* and Book One of *The Faerie Queene*.

'The world is too much with us'

Composed May 1802–March 1804. Published *Poems, in Two Volumes*, 1807. **13.** Cf. *Paradise Lost*, III.603–4: 'call up unbound / In various shapes old Proteus from the sea'.

'The Sun has long been set'

Composed 8 June 1802. Published *Poems, in Two Volumes*, 1807. DWJ, 8 June 1802: 'After tea William went out and walked and wrote that poem, "The sun has long been set" ... he walked on our own path and wrote the lines – he called me into the orchard and there repeated them to me.' **10–11.** *'parading'* ... *'masquerading'* W alludes to Burns's 'The Twa Dogs, a Tale': 'At Operas an' Plays parading, / Mortgaging, gambling, masquerading'. **13–15.** Cf. *The Merchant of Venice* V.i.1–2: 'The moon shines bright. In such a night as this, / When the sweet wind did gently kiss the trees ...'

Calais, August, 1802

Composed August 1802. Published *The Morning Post*, 13 January 1803; *Poems, in Two Volumes*, 1807. Napoleon became Life Consul, May 1802; the Peace of Amiens (March 1802–May 1803) encouraged numerous visitors from Britain to Paris.

To a Friend, Composed near Calais

Composed 7 August 1802. Published *Poems, in Two Volumes*, 1807. W's friend was Robert Jones (1769–1835) with whom he had landed at Calais, 13 July 1790 (the day before the *Fête de la Fédération*), at the start of their walking tour to the Alps.

'It is a beauteous Evening, calm and free'

Composed August 1802. Published *Poems, in Two Volumes*, 1807. 'This was composed on the beach near Calais' (IF). For W and DW at Calais, see DWJ, August 1802. **9.** *Dear Child* W's French daughter Caroline.

Composed by the Sea-Side, near Calais

Composed August 1802. Published *Poems, in Two Volumes*, 1807. See DWJ, August 1802: 'The Evening star sank down and the colours of the west faded away.'

To Toussaint L'Ouverture

Composed August 1802. Published *The Morning Post*, 2 February

1803; *Poems, in Two Volumes*, 1807. François Dominique Toussaint (surnamed L'Ouverture), governor of St Domingo (Haiti), resisted Napoleon's re-enforcement of slavery on the island and was imprisoned at Paris, June 1802. He died in prison, April 1803. **14.** *Man's unconquerable mind* Cf. Thomas Gray, 'The Progress of Poesy', l.65: 'The unconquerable Mind and Freedom's holy flame'.

Calais, August 15th, 1802

Composed 15 August 1802. Published *The Morning Post*, 26 February 1803; *Poems, in Two Volumes*, 1807. **1.** *Festivals* The *Fête de la Fédération*, witnessed by W on his first visit to France, 14 July 1790. See note to 'To a Friend' above. **13.** *sound* Ascertain.

September 1st, 1802

Composed 29 August–1 September 1802. Published *The Morning Post*, 11 February 1803; *Poems, in Two Volumes*, 1807. **14.** *Ordinance* Decree.

Composed upon Westminster Bridge

Composed 31 July–3 September 1802. Published *Poems, in Two Volumes*, 1807. W and DW left London for Calais early on 31 July and returned on 3 September 1802. For this journey, and the poet's visit to Annette Vallon and their daughter Caroline, see DWJ, August 1802.

'Great Men have been among us'

Composed May–December 1802. Published *Poems in Two Volumes*, 1807. W names five English republicans of the seventeenth century: Algernon Sydney (1622–83); Andrew Marvell (1621–78); James Harrington (1611–77); Sir Henry Vane (1613–62); John Milton (1608–74).

London, 1802

Composed September 1802. Published *Poems, in Two Volumes*, 1807. As a poet and as a republican, Milton was a heroic figure for W. **5.** *dower* Endowment.

'Nuns fret not at their Convent's narrow room'

Composed late 1802. Published *Poems, in Two Volumes*, 1807.

Yarrow Unvisited

Composed October 1803–March 1804. Published *Poems, in Two Volumes*, 1807. In her *Recollections of a Tour made in Scotland*, 18 September 1803, DW records: 'At Clovenford, being so near to the Yarrow, we could not but think of the possibility of going thither, but came to the conclusion of reserving the pleasure for some future time, in consequence of which, after our return, Wm wrote the poem.' See *Journals of Dorothy Wordsworth*, ed. E. de Selincourt (2 vols., London: Macmillan, 1952). **Headnote:** W notices 'The Braes of Yarrow' by William Hamilton of Bangour; ll.6 and 35 of the poem allude to this ballad. **6.** *Marrow* Companion. **8.** *Braes* Banks. **20.** *Lintwhites* Linnets. **33.** *Holms* Low-lying ground by a river. **37.** *Strath* Wide valley. **41.** *Beeves* Oxen.

'She was a Phantom of delight'

Composed October 1803–March 1804. Published *Poems, in Two Volumes*, 1807. **22.** *machine* The human body.

The Small Celandine (*'There is a Flower'*)

Composed *c.* March 1804. Published *Poems, in Two Volumes*, 1807. See W's note to 'To the Small Celandine' ('Pansies, Lilies') above.

Ode to Duty

Composed early 1804–January 1807. Published *Poems, in Two Volumes*, 1807. 'This Ode, written in 1805, is on the model of Gray's "Ode to Adversity", which is copied from Horace's "Ode to Fortune"' (IF).

Ode (*'Intimations of Immortality'*)

Composed March 1802–March 1804. Published *Poems, in Two Volumes*, 1807. (Titled 'Ode. Intimations of Immortality' in *Poems*, 1815). W: 'This was composed during my residence at Town-End, Grasmere. Two years at least passed between the writing of the four first stanzas and the remaining part' (IF). See also W's letter to Catherine Clarkson, January 1815: 'This poem rests entirely upon two recollections of childhood, one that of a splendour in the objects of sense which is passed away, and the other an indisposition to bend to the law of death as applying to our own particular case.' The poem should be compared with W's first *Essay upon Epitaphs* (1810), especially W's sense of 'an intimation or assurance within us, that some part of our nature is imperishable'. Stanzas 1–4 were probably written *c.* 27 March 1802, with further composition on 17 June 1802 (see DWJ). The poem was completed by 6 March 1804. STC responded to W's early work on the 'Ode', 1802, in 'A Letter to Sara Hutchinson' and 'Dejection: an Ode'; this dialogue was continued by W in 'Resolution and Independence'. **Epigraph:** 'Come let us sing a somewhat loftier strain', Virgil, *Eclogues*, IV, i. From 1815 W substituted ll.7–9 of 'My heart leaps up' as an epigraph. **21.** *tabor* A small drum. **40.** *coronal* Garland, crown. **58ff.** W: 'I took hold of the notion of pre-existence as having sufficient foundation in humanity for authorizing me to make for my purpose the best use of it I could as a Poet' (IF). **103.** *'humorous stage'* Alludes to the dedicatory poem to Samuel Daniel's *Musophilus*, ll. 1–3: 'I doe not here upon this hum'rous Stage, / Bring my transformed Verse, apparelled / With others passions'. **105.** *Equipage* Retinue, following. **110–19.** For STC's criticism of these lines as 'mental bombast', see Chapter 22 of *Biographia Literaria*. **120–23.** For STC these lines suggested 'the frightful notion of lying *awake* in the grave' (*Biographia Literaria*, Ch. 22), but for W and DW the notion was attractive; see DWJ, 29 April 1802: '[W] thought that it would be as sweet thus to lie so in the grave, to hear the *peaceful* sounds of the earth and just to know that our dear friends were near.' **150.** *a guilty Thing surprized* Cf. *Hamlet* I.i.148–9: 'it started like a guilty thing / Upon a fearful summons.' **205.** Cf. Thomas Gray, 'Ode on the Pleasure Arising from Vicissitude', l.45: 'The meanest flowret of the vale'.

'Who fancied what a pretty sight'
Composed late March 1804–April 1807. Published *Poems, in Two Volumes*, 1807. **13.** *device* Invention.

'I wandered lonely as a Cloud'
Composed late March 1804–April 1807. Published *Poems, in Two Volumes*, 1807. W: 'The two best lines in it [ll.15–16] are by Mary. The daffodils grew and still grow on the margin of Ulswater, and probably may be seen to this day as beautiful in the month of March nodding their golden heads beside the dancing and foaming waves' (IF). See also DWJ, 15 April 1802: 'I never saw daffodils so beautiful they grew among the mossy stones about and about them, some rested their heads upon these stones as on a pillow for weariness and the rest tossed and reeled and danced and seemed

as if they verily laughed with the wind that blew upon them over the lake, they looked so gay ever glancing ever changing.'

From *The Prelude* (1805)

See the Introduction, and notes to 'The Two-Part Prelude', for details of composition and publication.

'**That Great Federal Day**' (from Book 6). W and his college friend Robert Jones walked through France, July 1790, on their way to the Alps. This was W's first experience of the French Revolution. **2.** *on the top of golden hours* Cf. Shakespeare, Sonnet 16: 'Now stand you on the top of happy hours'. **6.** *great federal day* The *Fête de la Fédération*, 14 July 1790, the first anniversary of the Revolution. **21.** *umbrage* Shadows. **45.** *great spousals* Louis XVI had sworn allegiance to the new constitution at Paris, 14 July 1790. **48.** *vapoured* Boasted. **52–3.** See Genesis 18: 1–15. **61.** W alludes to the Glorious Revolution of 1688.

'**Crossing the Alps**' (from Book 6). W recalls his crossing of the Simplon Pass into Italy, August 1790. **14.** *scruple* Doubt, uncertainty. **33.** *eye and progress* Cf. *Much Ado about Nothing*, IV.i.227: 'the eye and prospect of his soul'. **79.** Cf. *Paradise Lost* V.165: 'Him first, him last, him midst, and without end.' **88.** *betimes* Early in the morning. **94.** *Locarno's Lake* Lake Maggiore. **137.** *Gravedona* On Lake Como. **152.** *darkness visible* Cf. *Paradise Lost* I.63–4: 'No light, but rather darkness visible / Served only to discover sights of woe'.

'**The Blind Beggar, and Bartholomew Fair**' (from Book 7). This passage draws on W's various visits to and residences in London. He visited Bartholomew Fair in 1802 with Charles Lamb. **58–60.** Bartholomew Fair was held 3–7 September at Smithfield, formerly the site of executions. **96.** Cf. *Paradise Lost* II.625: 'Perverse, all monstrous, all prodigious things'. **97.** *Promethean* Inventive.

'**The September Massacres**' (from Book 10). W returned to Paris from Orléans, October 1792, just after the September Massacres. The extract describes his fears for France at that time, and recalls Louvet's denunciation of Robespierre's ambition in the National Convention on 29 October. **5.** Louis XVI and his family were imprisoned in the Temple, in north-east Paris. **7.** *palace* The Tuileries, stormed on 10 August 1792. **10.** *Carrousel* The square in front of the Tuileries, where corpses had been burned during the massacres. **28.** *a little month* Cf. *Hamlet* I.ii.147: 'A little month'. **40.** '*Sleep no more*' Cf. *Macbeth* II.ii.35–6: 'Sleep no more! / Macbeth does murder sleep'. **46.** *next morning* 30 October 1792. **73.** *arbitrement* Absolute control.

'**The Death of Robespierre**' (from Book 10). In summer 1794 W was staying with cousins in the coastal village of Rampside, near Barrow-in-Furness. The extract recalls his visit to the grave of William Taylor (W's schoolmaster at Hawkshead Grammar School, who died in 1786) and the occasion on which, while crossing Leven Sands, W heard news of Robespierre's death. **1.** *Friend!* STC. **3.** *foul Tribe of Moloch* Cf. *Paradise Lost* 1.392: 'Moloch, horrid King besmeared with blood'. **5.** *haply* Perhaps. **7.** *small village* Rampside. **10.** W's journey from Rampside to Cartmel and back involved crossing the sands of the Leven estuary at low tide. **15.** *ethereal substance* Cf. *Paradise Lost* VI.330. **16.** *In consistory* Cf. *Paradise Regained* I.42: 'A gloomy consistory'. A consistory is a council or court. **17.** *burning seraphs* Cf. Milton, 'At a Solemn Music', l.10: 'the bright seraphim in burning row'. **18.** *empyrean* The highest heaven, associated with the sphere of fire. **21.** *fulgent* Shining. **26.** *Cartmel's rural town* In the far south of the Lake District. William Taylor is buried in the churchyard of Cartmel Priory. **34.** Gray's 'Elegy Written in a Country Church-yard', ll. 125–8. **70.** Robespierre had been executed 28 July 1794. **83.** *Augean stable* One of Hercules' labours was to clean the stables of King Augeas. **84.** *their own helper* The guillotine. **95–101.** Cf. 'The Two-Part Prelude', II.118–39.

'**The Climbing of Snowdon**' (from Book 13). The extract, which forms the visionary climax of the thirteen-book *Prelude*, recalls W's ascent of Snowdon with Robert Jones in summer 1791. **11.** *glaring* Clammy. **45.** Cf. *Paradise Lost* VII.285–6: 'the Mountains huge appear / Emergent, and their broad bare backs upheave'. **113.** *discursive or intuitive* Cf. *Paradise Lost* V.488.

Three Elegies for John Wordsworth

Composed May–July 1805. The poet's brother John Wordsworth was drowned when his ship, the *Earl of Abergavenny*, was wrecked off Portland Bill 5–6 February 1805.

To the Daisy ('Sweet Flower!'). Published *Poems*, 1815. See W's note to Lady Beaumont, 7 August 1805, enclosing this poem 'written in remembrance of a beautiful Letter of my Brother John, sent to us from Portsmouth, when he had left us at Grasmere, and first taken the command of his unfortunate Ship, more than four years ago. Some of the expressions in the Poem are the very words he used in his Letter.' John Wordsworth's letter, 2–9 April 1801, is reproduced in *The Letters of John Wordsworth*, ed. C. Ketcham (Ithaca: Cornell University Press, 1969). **38.** *unforced* Not compelled, not constrained.

'I only looked for pain and grief'. Published, after revision, as 'Elegiac Verses in Memory of my Brother, John Wordsworth', *Poems, Chiefly of Early and Late Years*, 1842. For W's parting with his brother at Grisedale Tarn (between Grasmere and Patterdale) see DWJ, 29 September 1800; for W's composition of this poem at Grisedale, 8 June 1805, see DW's letter to Lady Beaumont, 11 June 1805.

'Distressful gift! this Book receives'. Not published by W.

Stepping Westward

Composed 3 June 1805. Published *Poems, in Two Volumes*, 1807. See DW's *Recollections of a Tour made in Scotland*, 11 September 1803: 'We met two neatly dressed women, without hats, who had probably been taking their Sunday evening's walk. One of them said to us in a friendly, soft tone of voice, "What! you are stepping westward?" I cannot describe how affecting this simple expression was in that remote place, with the western sky in front, *yet* glowing with the departed sun. Wm wrote the . . . poem long after, in remembrance of his feelings and mine.'

The Solitary Reaper

Composed 5 November 1805. Published *Poems, in Two Volumes*, 1807. W noted that the poem was suggested by the following passage in Thomas Wilkinson's *Tours to the British Mountains* (1824), read by the poet in manuscript: 'Passed a female who was reaping alone: she sung in Erse as she bended over her sickle; the sweetest human voice I ever heard: her strains were tenderly melancholy, and felt delicious, long after they were heard no more.' **18.** *numbers* Verses. **21.** *lay* Song.

Elegiac Stanzas, Suggested by a Picture of Peele Castle, in a Storm

Composed May–June 1806. Published *Poems, in Two Volumes*, 1807. W's brother John was drowned in the shipwreck of the *Earl of Abergavenny*, off Portland Bill, 5–6 February 1805. W probably saw Sir George Beaumont's painting 'A Storm: Peel Castle' at a private view of the Royal Academy exhibition, 2 May 1806. Peele Castle stands on an island off the south coast of the Lake District, some two miles from Rampside where in August–September 1794 W stayed with his cousins.

'Yes! full surely 'twas the Echo'

Composed *c*. 15 June 1806. Published *Poems, in Two Volumes*, 1807. 'The Echo came from Nabscar, when I was walking on the opposite side of Rydal Mere' (IF).

'The rains at length have ceased'

Composed early September 1806. Not published by W.

Lines, Composed at Grasmere

Composed early September 1806. Published *Poems, in Two Volumes*, 1807. Charles James Fox died 13 September 1806. See also W's letter to Fox, 14 January 1801, enclosing a copy of *Lyrical Ballads* (1800): 'I have observed in your public character a constant predominance of sensibility of heart.'

Thought of a Briton on the Subjugation of Switzerland

Composed October 1806–January 1807. Published *Poems, in Two Volumes*, 1807. Napoleon invaded Switzerland in 1798 and 1802. In a letter of 27 September 1808 W described this sonnet as 'the best [he] had written'.

A Complaint

Composed *c*. December 1806. Published *Poems, in Two Volumes*, 1807. 'Suggested by a change in the manners of a friend' (IF). The friend was STC, who stayed with the Wordsworths and Sir George Beaumont at Coleorton from 21 December 1806. Cf. DW's letter to Catherine Clarkson, 6 November 1806, describing her 'shock' at the change in STC's appearance on first meeting him after his return from Malta.

November, 1806

Composed October–December 1806. Published *Poems, in Two Volumes*, 1807. **2.** *mighty Empire overthrown* Prussia, at the Battle of Jena, 14 October 1806.

Gipsies

Composed *c*. 26 February 1807. Published *Poems, in Two Volumes*, 1807. W: 'Composed at Coleorton, 1807. I had observed them, as here described, near Castle Donnington on my way to and from Derby' (IF). **14.** *Vesper* The evening star. *fulgent* Shining brightly.

'Eve's lingering clouds extend in solid bars'

Composed early September 1807. Published *The Waggoner. A Poem. To which are Added, Sonnets* (1819).

St Paul's

Composed April–Autumn 1808. Not published by W. See W's letter to Sir George Beaumont, 8 April 1808: 'I left Coleridge at 7 o'clock on Sunday morning; and walked towards the City in a very thoughtful and melancholy state of mind; I had passed through Temple Bar and by St Dunstan's, noticing nothing, and entirely occupied with my own thoughts, when looking up, I saw before me the avenue of Fleet street, silent, empty, and pure white, with a sprinkling of new-fallen snow, not a cart or Carriage to obstruct the view, no noise, only a few soundless and dusky foot-passengers, here and there; you remember the elegant curve of Ludgate Hill in which this avenue would terminate, and beyond and towering above it was the huge and majestic form of St Pauls, solemnised by a thin veil of falling snow.' **21.** *Passenger* A passer by.

Upon the Sight of a Beautiful Picture

Composed June 1811. Published *Poems*, 1815. 'This was written when we dwelt in the Parsonage at Grasmere. The principal features of the picture are Bredon Hill and Cloud Hill, near Coleorton' (IF). W's picture was by Sir George Beaumont.

Characteristics of a Child Three Years Old

Composed probably January 1813–May 1814. Published *Poems*, 1815. 'Picture of my daughter Catharine' (IF). Catharine was born 6 September 1808, died 4 June 1812. **1.** *tractable* Docile, obedient. **3.** *arch* Mischievous.

'Surprized by joy'

Composed 1813–mid October 1814. Published *Poems*, 1815. 'This was in fact suggested by my daughter Catharine long after her death' (IF). **2.** *transport* Ecstasy.

Yew-Trees

Composed 1811–14. Published *Poems*, 1815. W and DW visited the Lorton Vale yew late September or early October 1804. See DW to Lady Beaumont, 7 and 10 October 1804: 'Went to visit a Yew tree which is the Patriarch of Yew trees, green and flourishing, in very old age – the largest tree I ever saw.' The poem may date from this visit, although no manuscript composed earlier than 1811 survives. 'I have often thought that the [yew-tree] I am describing must have been as old as the Christian era' (IF). **1.** *Lorton Vale* South of Cockermouth, presided over by the villages of High and Low Lorton. **33.** *Glaramara* Stands between the head of Borrowdale and the Langstrath valley; it is part of a main spur of the central massif of the Lake District fells.

Yarrow Visited

Composed September 1814. Published *Poems*, 1815. W first visited the Yarrow, 1 September 1814, with his wife Mary, Sara Hutchinson, and the 'Ettrick Shepherd' James Hogg. **1–4.** Cf. 'Yarrow Unvisited'. **56.** *Border story* Sir Walter Scott's *The Lay of the Last Minstrel*.

November 1, 1815

Composed *c.* 1 December 1815. Published 28 January 1816 in the *Examiner*, and in W's *Thanksgiving Ode* volume (1816). 'Suggested on the banks of the Brathay by the sight of Langdale Pikes. It is delightful to remember those moments of far-distant days, which probably would have been forgotten if the impression had not been transferred to verse' (IF).

September 1815

Composed *c.* 2 December 1815. Published 11 February 1816 in the *Examiner*, and in W's *Thanksgiving Ode* volume (1816).

Ode. The Pass of Kirkstone

Composed June 1817. Published in the *River Duddon* volume (1820). 'Thoughts and feelings of many walks in all weathers by day and night over this Pass alone, and with beloved friends' (IF). Kirkstone Pass is on the road between Ullswater and the villages of Troutbeck and Ambleside. **6.** *No appanage of human kind* No indication of human presence. **9.** *cognizably* Recognizably.

Ode, Composed upon an Evening of Extraordinary Splendor and Beauty

Composed June–December 1817. Published in the *River Duddon* volume (1820). 'Felt, and in a great measure composed, upon the little mound in front of our abode at Rydal' (IF). **43–52.** W notes: 'The multiplication of mountain-ridges, described, at the commencement of the third stanza of this Ode, as a kind of Jacob's Ladder, leading to Heaven, is produced either by watery vapours or sunny haze, – in the present instance by the latter cause.'

The River Duddon. Conclusion
Composed 1818–20. Published in the *River Duddon* volume (1820). This is the final poem in W's 'The River Duddon' series of sonnets.

Gold and Silver Fishes
Composed 1829. Published in *Yarrow Revisited, and Other Poems* (1835). 1–2 Cf. *Cymbeline* II.iii.19: 'Hark, hark, the lark at heaven's gate sings'. 7. *'more than dull content'* See Anne Finch, Countess of Winchilsea, 'A Nocturnal Reverie', l.39: 'a sedate content the spirit feels'.

Yarrow Revisited
Composed Autumn 1831. Published *Yarrow Revisited, and Other Poems* (1835). 'In the autumn of 1831, my daughter and I set off from Rydal to visit Sir Walter Scott, before his departure for Italy ... How sadly changed did I find him from the man I had seen so healthy, gay, and hopeful a few years before ... Sir Walter Scott accompanied us, and most of the party, to Newark Castle, on the *Yarrow*. When we alighted from the carriages, he walked pretty stoutly, and had great pleasure in revisiting these his favourite haunts. Of that excursion, the verses, "Yarrow Revisited" are a memorial' (IF). 2. *'Winsome Marrow'* See 'Yarrow Unvisited' l.6 and note. 8. *Great Minstrel* Sir Walter Scott. 51–3. Cf. 'On the Departure of Sir Walter Scott from Abbotsford, for Naples'. 100–103. Newark Castle is the scene of Scott's *The Lay of the Last Minstrel*.

On the Departure of Sir Walter Scott from Abbotsford, for Naples
Composed late 1831. Published 1833 in *The Literary Souvenir*, and *Yarrow Revisited, and Other Poems* (1835). Scott left Abbotsford for Italy, 23 September 1831, hoping to recover his health in the warm climate. W visited Scott just before his departure (see note to 'Yarrow Revisited', above), and recalled their excursion to Newark Castle as the occasion of this sonnet: 'On our return in the afternoon, we had to cross the Tweed, directly opposite Abbotsford ... A rich, but sad light, of rather a purple than a golden hue, was spread over the Eildon Hills at that moment; and, thinking it probable that it might

be the last time Sir Walter would cross the stream, I was not a little moved, and expressed some of my feelings in the sonnet' (IF). **14.** *Parthenope* Naples.

Airey-Force Valley
Composed September 1835. Published in *Poems, Chiefly of Early and Late Years* (1842).

Extempore Effusion upon the Death of James Hogg
Composed late November 1835. Published in the *Athenaeum*, 12 December 1835, and *Poetical Works* (1836–7). 'These verses were written extempore immediately after reading a notice of the Ettrick Shepherd's death ... The persons lamented in these Verses were all either of my friends or acquaintance' (IF). **4.** W first visited the Yarrow, September 1814, in James Hogg's company; see 'Yarrow Visited' and note above. Hogg died 21 November 1835. **8.** *the Border-minstrel* Sir Walter Scott (died 21 September 1832) and W revisited Yarrow 20 September 1831; see 'Yarrow Revisited' and note above. **15–16.** STC died 25 July 1834. **19.** Charles Lamb died 27 December 1834. **31.** George Crabbe died 3 February 1832. **39.** Felicia Hemans died 16 May 1835.

From *The Prelude* (1850)
'**Genius of Burke**' (from Book 7). Composed *c.* 1832. Published 1850.

Index of Titles

Index of First Lines

READ MORE IN PENGUIN

In every corner of the world, on every subject under the sun, Penguin represents quality and variety – the very best in publishing today.

For complete information about books available from Penguin – including Puffins, Penguin Classics and Arkana – and how to order them, write to us at the appropriate address below. Please note that for copyright reasons the selection of books varies from country to country.

In the United Kingdom: Please write to *Dept. EP, Penguin Books Ltd, Bath Road, Harmondsworth, West Drayton, Middlesex UB7 0DA*

In the United States: Please write to *Consumer Sales, Penguin USA, P.O. Box 999, Dept. 17109, Bergenfield, New Jersey 07621-0120.* VISA and MasterCard holders call 1-800-253-6476 to order Penguin titles

In Canada: Please write to *Penguin Books Canada Ltd, 10 Alcorn Avenue, Suite 300, Toronto, Ontario M4V 3B2*

In Australia: Please write to *Penguin Books Australia Ltd, P.O. Box 257, Ringwood, Victoria 3134*

In New Zealand: Please write to *Penguin Books (NZ) Ltd, Private Bag 102902, North Shore Mail Centre, Auckland 10*

In India: Please write to *Penguin Books India Pvt Ltd, 706 Eros Apartments, 56 Nehru Place, New Delhi 110 019*

In the Netherlands: Please write to *Penguin Books Netherlands bv, Postbus 3507, NL-1001 AH Amsterdam*

In Germany: Please write to *Penguin Books Deutschland GmbH, Metzlerstrasse 26, 60594 Frankfurt am Main*

In Spain: Please write to *Penguin Books S. A., Bravo Murillo 19, 1° B, 28015 Madrid*

In Italy: Please write to *Penguin Italia s.r.l., Via Felice Casati 20, I–20124 Milano*

In France: Please write to *Penguin France S. A., 17 rue Lejeune, F–31000 Toulouse*

In Japan: Please write to *Penguin Books Japan, Ishikiribashi Building, 2–5–4, Suido, Bunkyo-ku, Tokyo 112*

In Greece: Please write to *Penguin Hellas Ltd, Dimocritou 3, GR–106 71 Athens*

In South Africa: Please write to *Longman Penguin Southern Africa (Pty) Ltd, Private Bag X08, Bertsham 2013*

A SELECTION OF POETRY

James Fenton   Out of Danger

A collection wonderfully open to experience – of foreign places, differences, feelings and languages.

U. A. Fanthorpe   Selected Poems

She is an erudite poet, rich in experience and haunted by the classical past ... fully at home in the world of the turbulent NHS, the decaying academies, and all the draughty corners of the abandoned Welfare State' – *Observer*

Yehuda Amichai   Selected Poems
Translated by Chana Bloch and Stephen Mitchell

'A truly major poet ... there's a depth, breadth and weighty momentum in these subtle and delicate poems of his' – Ted Hughes

Czesław Miłosz   Collected Poems 1931–1987
Winner of the 1980 Nobel Prize for Literature

'One of the greatest poets of our time, perhaps the greatest' – Joseph Brodsky

Joseph Brodsky   To Urania
Winner of the 1987 Nobel Prize for Literature

Exiled from the Soviet Union in 1972, Joseph Brodsky has been universally acclaimed as the most talented Russian poet of his generation.

Paul Celan   Selected Poems
Winner of the first European Translation Prize, 1990

'The English reader can now enter the hermetic universe of a German–Jewish poet who made out of the anguish of his people, things of terror and beauty' – *The Times Literary Supplement*

Geoffrey Hill   Collected Poems

'Sternly formal, wry, grand, sensually direct: the contraries of a major poet' – *Observer*, Books of the Year

READ MORE IN PENGUIN

POETRY LIBRARY

Arnold	Selected by Kenneth Allott
Blake	Selected by W. H. Stevenson
Browning	Selected by Daniel Karlin
Burns	Selected by Angus Calder and William Donnelly
Byron	Selected by A. S. B. Glover
Clare	Selected by Geoffrey Summerfield
Coleridge	Selected by Richard Holmes
Donne	Selected by John Hayward
Dryden	Selected by Douglas Grant
Hardy	Selected by David Wright
Herbert	Selected by W. H. Auden
Jonson	Selected by George Parfitt
Keats	Selected by John Barnard
Kipling	Selected by James Cochrane
Lawrence	Selected by Keith Sagar
Milton	Selected by Laurence D. Lerner
Pope	Selected by Douglas Grant
Rubáiyát of Omar Khayyám	Translated by Edward FitzGerald
Shelley	Selected by Isabel Quigley
Tennyson	Selected by W. E. Williams
Wordsworth	Selected by Nicholas Roe
Yeats	Selected by Timothy Webb